MICHAEL JAMESON'S

LEO 1

THE ENEMY WITHIN

Leo 1: The Enemy Within

Published by Piscataqua Press
An imprint of RiverRun Bookstore, Inc
142 Fleet St | Portsmouth NH | 03801

www.piscataquapress.com

ISBN: 978-1-939739-78-0

Printed in the United States of America

THE ENEMY WITHIN

••• 1

"Is there anything else that should be brought to our attention before you start your shift, 9-7-8?" asked Dr. Fletcher.

"No, sir," answered 978.

"What about your marital status?"

"The divorce was finalized two days ago."

"Then I, Dr. Aaron Fletcher, Director of the Care Control Division, Eastern Region, grants Mark Allen Royce, guard number 978 permission to report for duty. The official starting time will be at 12AM on March 25th, 2062 in the Peterson Prison's Psychiatric Unit located on the North Shore. Is there anyone here who has an objection?"

978 looked up at all the suits present at the hearing. The total number of them added up to eight, including Dr. Fletcher. The response was just complete silence, which meant the vote was unanimous. 978 had gotten permission to return to work tonight, thanks to the approval of the entire Council of the Care Control Division. It didn't matter. The entire process was torture for the poor guard. If a meeting is required it isn't supposed to last more than thirty minutes. This is almost always the case for any guard who is expected to return for duty. With 978 obviously no one foresaw any real problems. Otherwise the suits wouldn't have met with him this late at night. He honestly didn't know what to make of them. There was absolutely no expression on their faces. Even if one of them made eye contact, the look was simply blank. A stone-cold stare might have been intimidating, but at least that would have been something. Dr. Fletcher was the only one to show any hint of emotion, which 978 knew was caused

by a distraction.

It was difficult not to notice the earpiece that Dr. Fletcher wore. Still, it wasn't strange to find a lot of people who worked in the prison system to have one. What 978 found unusual in this situation was being able to hear a voice that Dr. Fletcher was listening to. Maybe that was why he was the only one at the meeting who displayed any expression at all. The guard had been acquainted with him for the past several months, long before this ordeal happened. It was troubling that listening to someone on your earpiece was the only thing to arouse any feelings at all. Most people probably prefer to get a late night meeting over and done with. But 978 felt disturbed by this because it seemed like Dr. Fletcher was taking orders from whoever was talking to him on the earpiece. There was no way to determine what this person was saying. The sound was not up high enough to decipher so much as a single word. 978 noticed throughout the entire duration of the meeting that Dr. Fletcher would only make a statement after hearing the voice in his right ear.

For some reason, 978 contemplated Dr. Fletcher's overall physical appearance. He was at least six feet tall with a very strong build. He may have been heavy-set, but not necessarily from being overweight. His hands were especially large, convincing 978 that this guy could easily grip something like a glass beer bottle and break it into pieces. Obviously he would have no problem winning in a bar fight, but 978 thought the doctor was too smart to allow himself to get in that kind of trouble. However, seeing him listening to that earpiece throughout the entire meeting left the guard feeling a strange vibe. Last, the dark hair and the thick beard. Dr. Fletcher hadn't expressed any sense of humor but 978 could imagine a bubblier side to the guy's personality, perhaps whenever he burst out laughing. There wasn't any chance of seeing that right now, the most important thing to everyone present at this gathering was the final decision to allow the guard to report back for duty. It was hard to imagine that anyone in the room would even consider cracking a smile. Of course 978 also had to consider the fact that there was no desire from within to express any positive feelings, either. All that mattered was getting out of this hearing and reporting for duty.

"Sign your name and number," ordered Fletcher, right after placing the release form in front of 978.

He would sign his name, Mark Allen Royce, and his number, 978. It was a process that only took maybe five seconds to complete, but it felt like an eternity. As he looked up at Dr. Fletcher and handed back the release form, the suits wasted no time getting up from their chairs and preparing to leave. It was the most energy that these guys would display throughout the entire hearing. That wasn't saying much if you also considered the fact that it was very unlikely any of them broke a sweat. At least that decreased the chance of smelling any nasty body odors in there. But it was somewhat surprising not to be the case with the big, bright fluorescent lights shining down on everyone. But 978 knew better than to question good fortune.

After 978 quickly shook Dr. Fletcher's hand and got ready to exit the conference room, he realized he should have assessed the entire situation a lot more. He found it strange that only two of the suits had taken folders out of their briefcases. He had always assumed that each individual would be taking notes to keep accurate records for single sections of the Care Control Division they represented. The only real explanation that came to mind was perhaps since they were supposed to reach a unanimous decision at this hearing all of them had to write down the exact same thing, and simply copy each other's notes before leaving. Now he started to worry that he was beginning to obsess over formalities again. He didn't understand why, especially since the way the suits conduct their hearings wasn't his problem. He decided it was best to walk out of there and start preparing for his shift.

As 978 headed down the corridor, he checked and saw how much time had passed since the hearing started. He couldn't believe it. The entire length of the meeting with Dr. Fletcher and the suits only lasted twelve minutes, which was amazing since everyone always had to be prepared for it to take at least half-an-hour. That didn't matter. 978 honestly thought he would be eligible for retirement once he got out of there. Then again, that wouldn't be so bad if that was actually the case. Granted, the situation with retirement would be another issue altogether. It was something he didn't want to think about, because that day would be coming sooner than it was originally supposed to. He got more frustrated with every thought entering his head. He just couldn't continue accurately determining the pros and cons of various aspects of the job, it all felt like a mass of contradictions rocking back and forth in his brain. He was still very fragile emotionally, but there was nothing that could be done about it. It was time to move forward and fulfill his duties.

978 started thinking about the release form he had just signed. He liked the fact that he could acknowledge himself by his real name, as well as hearing it straight from Dr. Fletcher's mouth. The only time you were supposed to hear your real name was from your own mouth when you checked in at the start of your shift. At the end of the shift you could only say your number, supposedly for protection purposes. This seemed strange, especially since the top priority a guard has is to protect the prison and the inmates. But that didn't matter. Formalities always came first. 978 learned that very quickly when he started this job nine years ago. Guards and prisoners only communicate with each other by using their assigned numbers. And if these formalities were not followed, there was immediate disciplinary action.

After working there for almost a decade, 978 couldn't understand why the suits wouldn't consider changing a couple of things. Not that anybody would listen to him. He couldn't imagine any warden or Dr. Fletcher contemplate the idea of having a suggestion box outside their office door. And he also knew no one would take him seriously at this point, especially after being forced into taking a mandatory two week leave of absence due to health issues cited by Fletcher's all-new Care Control Division. The panic attack he suffered from on duty was said to be caused by job stress and family issues. 978 always thought that certain aspects of working in any prison could cause this problem, so what was the big deal? Why the divorce was factored in didn't make any sense. He'd been separated from Michelle for the past two years.

He still loved her, and had visitation rights with their son Paul on the weekends. Paul's seventh birthday wasn't until July, but he'd already started thinking about what to get the little guy. At least there were two people in his life he could refer to by their real names. Of course he couldn't forget Samantha, Michelle's daughter from a previous relationship. At this point 978 thought the guards should at least be allowed to call the prisoners by their first name, not that it will ever happen. You would think the prisoners would need an emotional connection to a place designed for rehabilitation. Tell that to the so-called Care Control Division, who could stand to learn a thing or two about compassion.

978 started to thinking about the suits at the hearing he had just walked out of moments ago. There was no hint of concern among any of them. Of course he still considered the fact that it was very late at night and those guys probably wanted to get out of there as soon as possible. In some ways, he may have been more prepared than they were since he came in ready to work the night shift. He was simply going through the motions, probably from being used to working the off-hours. It didn't seem to matter that he started sleeping through the night during the leave of absence. It was a nice change but he had no desire to apply for a nine-to-five job

anytime soon, and all he gained from it was being more awake for the final court hearing that would finalize his divorce from Michelle. The suits attending Dr. Fletcher's so-called night court weren't even going through the motions. They might as well have just stared off into space. 978 reached the point where he was done thinking about all of this. It was time to get back into the swing of things.

2 •••

978 already had the boots on required for the guard uniform. Not that it really mattered. Once he was inside the men's bathroom they would be taken off again just so he could put on the rest of the outfit required for work. He thought it was smart to dress formally for the hearing, so he wore slacks, a white shirt, and a tie. This was the only thing he could think of to convince Dr. Fletcher and the suits that he really wanted his job back. The real truth was that he simply wanted to make it look like he had his head together. Other than that he knew there would be no problem whatsoever. It would have been so much easier just to show up in his guard uniform. Upon entering the men's bathroom the first thing he did was lock the door. After that he took off the boots and changed out of his formal clothing then put on the guard uniform. It just dawned on him that he wore the same tie at his best friend's wedding, which he happened to be the best man at. That particular event was something he would always consider to be one of the best memories of his adult life. It may have been quite a few years back, but he preferred to think about that over the mandatory hearing he'd just gotten out of.

Normally, 978 did not like dressing up for anything. The wedding was a different story, and the guard uniform was worn specifically for work only, so that wasn't so bad. He couldn't believe that he actually wanted to make a decent impression while meeting with the Council of the Care Control Division. The only person present that he'd ever spoken to was Dr. Fletcher. All those other guys that 978 collectively called the suits were nothing but a bunch of bureaucratic boneheads, or at least that was how he felt about them. He would be absolutely amazed if he found out one of them actually completed an entire tour of the Peterson Prison. They probably weren't required to since Doc Fletcher had spent enough time there to fill them in on all the details, so all they really needed to do was take notes. He now concluded he had a little respect for Fletcher, who was now becoming well-known for taking serious interest in prison reform. He also had to remember that this was the only person from this point on he would have to deal with. He knew that those suits were present at the hearing for just one simple reason: formalities.

978 needed to remind himself there was always going to be some red tape if you work in the prison systems. It didn't matter if changes were actually made to improve the job, formalities would come first. The problem was that it felt like there were standard procedures for every aspect of his life. This included work, family, or the routines he forced himself into over the years. It was tough for him to appreciate the two weeks he was gone, especially since he would be going back to the same old thing. At the end of his shift, he would head straight home and sleep from 9am to 2pm. Not much ever got in the way of this. Even when Michelle wasn't working for the first few years after Paul was born. She was the quintessential stay-at-home mother, yet somehow he was always able to get the shut-eye he needed. Granted, he never objected to looking after his son whenever she wanted to go shopping, socialize, or whatever. He would even pick up Samantha from after-school activities. As the old saying goes, you just do what you have to.

978 didn't have a problem with checking in early tonight.

He had arrived an hour before his start time for the hearing, anyway. It would have been nice to be paid overtime for doing so. Wishful thinking, it would never ever happen. If the suits found out someone had actually thought about suggesting something so outrageous it would probably be made very clear to that person they should feel lucky to still have their job. Still, 978 liked that idea. Maybe it would stir up some kind of a reaction from those bureaucratic boneheads. He certainly didn't sense any stimulation throughout the entire hearing, which would've been a nice change. Regardless, he was all geared up and ready to go. Eight hours of working the night shift were on the horizon.

Before exiting the bathroom, 978 briefly glimpsed at his reflection in the mirror. He honestly did not care about looking good for anyone that he might interact with during his shift, so he could not think of a reason to even bother. After throwing his backpack over his shoulder, he pulled the handle to open the door but was unsuccessful. He forgot to unlock it. No big deal. He turned the bolt to the right and that took care of the problem, allowing him to easily pull it open then headed down the corridor toward the office area. He was curious to find out how many people would be working at the front desk area.

It only took 978 about two minutes to reach the front office. There was one person working at the front desk, which was usually the case during the night shift. He thought there may have been more because of the hearing being conducted at such a late hour. Then again, these hearings were private. And whoever he saw working at the front desk seemed like poor substitutes for any kind of security. He thought they were really nothing more than over-glorified data-entry clerks, whose main job was to keep records of the time any guard reported for duty. He was tempted to request for a transfer if a position was open, and didn't care if there was a cut in pay and a demotion. There would be some people, especially certain prisoners he knew he'd never miss.

978 quickly remembered who was working at the front desk. Her name was Linda. She was young, probably in her mid-twenties, about five-foot-two with a thin build. Her curly, shoulder-length blond hair helped contribute to her good looks. At least he thought so, anyway. But he wouldn't tell her that. Not anytime soon. Any conversation between them was always brief, and extremely rare. However, he had always sensed something about her that was a little more personable. It would be nice if everyone who worked in the front office was like that, but he knew that would never happen. Requesting so much as a slight change within the system would fall on deaf ears. It all boiled down to the same thing: formalities.

When 978 stood in front of Linda he took his identification card out of his pocket and presented it to her. All guards were required to carry it on them at all times. Linda's job was to make sure that was the case along with the exact time the guard arrived for duty, and all of this information would be typed into the prison's central computer. Not that it was necessary. They were surrounded by several cameras that recorded their every move, so why bother having somebody who is expected to perform the same tasks as technology's watchful eyes? Whatever, it wasn't worth dwelling upon it too much. 978 knew the answer to his question. It was simply another formality, even if his superiors didn't use that specific word. He tried to convince himself that he didn't mind seeing someone like Linda before the start of his shift, one less thing to complain about.

"Welcome back, 9," said Linda, who glanced up at 978 slightly before entering the time he arrived in the computer.

"Hi," said 978, in response to Linda's greeting, surprised that he even did that.

"You're all set."

"Thanks."

Just referring to him as 9 sounded a bit more casual. It stood out in his mind because she was the only one who would do that. He didn't know if she spoke that way to other guards who reported for duty, but it still had plenty of appeal. At least she never referred to him as K-9, which actually would have made sense since there were a number of prisoners and guards who felt they were being treated like dogs. In his case, however, that would have been better. Being a dog lover helped convince him that the worst kennel on the planet would be a far nicer place to work at. Now he felt the urge to check the classified sections of the local newspapers to see if there was any work available in that field. He also knew at some point during the night when it got dead quiet he might start fantasizing about opening up his own kennel. It all came down to whatever he could think of to pass the time. Maybe if the prison got overcrowded he could convince Dr. Fletcher to allow some of the prisoners finish doing time at his new kennel, and all he'd need to do was make sure there were large supplies of kibble in stock so they wouldn't go hungry.

978 never had a problem with checking in early. He'd continually told himself on a number of occasions that it would have been nice to get paid for that, or at the very least get a little recognition for it, but felt it was better than being a last minute kind of guy. Right now he could take his sweet time. After Linda conducted the identification inspection, he marched passed her and slowly made his way through the office area. As expected, there wasn't another soul to be seen. But he always wondered why the entire place was brightly lit throughout the night. During the day shift every desk would be occupied. And it was probably more hectic than a 9-1-1 emergency services center, at least 978 thought so. But he also knew his perspective might not be accurate. He only saw the activities taking place on his way out in the morning.

978 arrived at the main entrance. It was time to conduct the safety check with the weapons. He did it as thoroughly as

always, and could relax because of the additional time. The helmet check was easier. All he had to do was state his number into a mini-microphone then hear it back through the ear transmitters. Last he had to test the visor to make sure it worked properly. This was done with the helmet on and stating "shields up" then "shields down". The safety specialists trusted you to do this on your own, which he'd been told at the job orientation after being officially hired. Were you trusted otherwise? No. And it didn't matter because the visor or "shields" could only be used if a state of emergency was declared. The suits wanted to make sure every single guards' facial features were exposed constantly, that way all improper emotions could be detected on camera. Expectations were very high regarding job performance at the Peterson Prison, even more so in the Psychiatric Unit, body language included.

It was time to check in. 978 pressed the green-lit button located on the panel directly above the intercom right by the main entrance. He had to wait a couple of seconds before getting a response.

"State your name, number, and shift," said a cold, robotic voice over the intercom.

"Mark Allen Royce, 978, night shift," responded 978.

"Mark Allen Royce, 978, night shift, 12am to 8am on March 25th, 2062, the time is 11:43pm. The date is March 24th, 2062. Your arrival is early. Thank you."

978 couldn't believe it. The only time he would get to hear thanks came from this machine. Then again, he had thought to himself that it would have been nice to get some kind of recognition for coming in early. In the end, he got it from a machine. At least his name was said three times tonight. The last time he spoke it himself, which he had to do every night when he reported for duty. It still didn't make him feel very fortunate. And the old saying goes everything happens in threes. Whatever occurred could easily go one way or the other. In his case it wasn't good. A mandatory leave of

absence, a divorce, what next? He had to erase that thought quickly. It didn't matter how bad things got, it could always be worse.

978's position in the prison system did have some very historical significance. He was the last of one thousand guards to be employed in law enforcement. This was specifically in the northern section of the Eastern Region in the state of Massachusetts. Once he completed his fifteen years of service, he would automatically receive a pension. Whether he liked it or not, he was becoming obsolete and technology would be taking over almost entirely. It was because of something he only knew as LEO1, supposedly the solution to everybody's prayers. Well, not really. It was worthwhile to the Care Control Division and the rest of the folks in charge of the Peterson Prison. It would be cost effective, for sure. Besides, what good is a salary or health benefits to a computer? Only a small group of people will be selected to work at the facility. All of whom would be more qualified than him. Half the job's requirement was being able to operate the LEO1 computers, the other half performing routine guard duties. The latter being a lot less, and at some point robot guards would be brought in.

For 978, it was all the same.

Formalities.

Not much else was known about what the future would be like in prison. Maybe these robot guards would have some human physical features, making it easier for the prisoners. Then again, nobody was allowed to know about any future developments. Everything might continue to look normal. Of course 978 knew that was merely wishful thinking. The tormented souls will become more confused than ever, especially in his unit.

The number 978 itself also had some historical significance going back several decades. It was originally a telephone area code used in the state of Massachusetts up until 2035. It's not surprising he would know this, especially since he had just turned ten years old when this system would stop being used nationwide. Nowadays there were only regional codes divided into three sections. Whenever you had to call a residence or business, you would simply press the numbers 1, 2, or 3 first. This verified what section of the state you wished to call. It was easy enough, especially considering the small size of Massachusetts. Naturally, the state possessing the largest number of regional codes was Texas, obviously due to its size and population.

Texas made 978 think of possible employment opportunities. Of course that would depend on the number of job openings and a desire to relocate. The brutal heat automatically decreased any motivation to pack up and leave. Then again, it didn't take much to get tired of the New England weather. Snow may look beautiful and picturesque, but if you didn't ski there wasn't much else to enjoy. That was how 978 saw it, anyway. Black ice was something he wanted to block out of his mind completely, along with temperatures that went below zero.

He was surprised at how warm it was on the way in to work tonight. Even though the first day of spring had officially arrived a few days ago, it was definitely far from the end of mixed and extreme weather conditions for the next several weeks. But he still appreciated the fact that he could drive in with the windows rolled down.

978 continued to think about the kind of employment that might be available in Texas. All the jobs he would be qualified for would have something to do with law enforcement. One option was doing border patrol, which was pretty easy if you could actually land the position. There wasn't as a strong demand for that stuff compared to years ago. Negotiations between the United States and Mexico were much more peaceful nowadays, especially when it had to with legal matters. And the number of Mexicans able to speak English

fluently had increased rapidly. It still helped if an American working down there spoke some Spanish, or a little bit of Portuguese, but you were not required to be an expert. 978 hadn't applied his bi-lingual skills for quite some time, but that was alright. Spanish he could never forget completely, thanks to his late aunt who taught him much of the language at a very young age. The best part was when he took Spanish classes in high school he didn't have to apply himself. Especially since he had learned so much of it as a child he could still get half-decent grades. Looking back in hindsight, he could have done better and appreciated the gift his aunt had given him. Just because he had an advantage over the other kids didn't mean he had all the answers or a true understanding of what his capabilities were. Maybe he could have tutored some classmates. He had friends who struggled to get passing grades. It never fazed him in any way whatsoever.

It suddenly occurred to 978 that he was qualified for a position as a translator for the American Embassy. There were offices located both in Texas and Mexico. It wouldn't hurt to send out his resume. Perhaps he could start out doing part-time stuff, as a consultant or a data-entry clerk. In most cases he would be bored to death staring at a computer screen, but if he specifically translated all the necessary work from Spanish to English or vice versa, it would not take long for his bi-lingual skills to kick in again and feel like second nature. Of course he also knew that if you landed a position at the American Embassy there was a long and arduous training process. Without a doubt this particular job would be far more important than working at a prison facility. 978 also knew that he only had six more years to go before he would be forced into an early retirement, so he figured it best not to explore any other options until he started collecting his pension. Unfortunately, being stuck working in Peterson Prison's Psychiatric Unit for another six years felt like a life sentence.

978 started to develop a guilty conscience, all the time that he and Michelle were together he never made any effort to teach Spanish to Paul. He hadn't even thought about it. The kid wasn't out of the first grade yet. If he had done the same thing for his son that his aunt did for him he would have seen phenomenal results. Young Paul would have been the first translator the American Embassy recruited out of elementary school. That was a crazy idea he needed to get out of his head, because Paul was a smart kid already. He knew never to push things like that, much less be a parent who thrives on the success of your child.

978's aunt had taken a very natural approach to teaching him the language. She was always around to help his mother out after he was born, so it never felt like something that was forced on him. Now he felt sadly reminded of the fact that, for the most part, she was the only person who he engaged in regular conversations with in Spanish. But as a small child it felt like it was their own little secret, like they were spies or something. He had learned of her passing only two days after completing his freshman year in college, she had been battling cancer for less than six months.

No one saw it coming.

Especially him.

The following week brought the funeral and final grades for the spring semester, indicating he had made the dean's list. Neither of which provided any source of comfort. Her being the only person he occasionally spoke Spanish to felt special, and now that, along with his heart, had been taken away. The emptiness inside didn't start to fill up again until Michelle entered his life.

Thinking about all of this stuff reminded 978 that next month was the anniversary of dad's death, which occurred long before his aunt's did. It was a difficult loss at a young age, but not as bad compared to his aunt. By the time he had entered college he probably thought that everything would be smooth sailing from that point forward. When you're nineteen years old, what do you know? Not much. However, he liked thinking about the guy's passion for old Harley-Davidson motorcycles. There were the countless nights when they would both talk endlessly about riding across the country together when he was old enough.

That day would never come.

The gate began to open slowly and 978 walked through. Within seconds it closed behind him. This was nothing new, especially since it was the same routine every night. Maybe he wasn't paying attention because of being gone for the past two weeks and that meeting going on forever. Things were going way smoother than expected, and he wanted to concentrate on the job. He marched through the overpass, which measured a distance of exactly fifty feet from the office to the checkpoint of the prison itself. He walked on the right side to take a look through the glass. The overpass was located on the second floor, so it wasn't very high up. He wanted to catch a glimpse of the grass on the ground, thanks to the area being brightly lit. Amazingly, he spotted a raccoon. He could only remember one other time where he spotted wildlife on the property. A squirrel roamed through the same spot about six months ago, but that was it. Neither of these sightings provided any real fulfillment, which was too bad. It was the last view of nature he would see for the rest of the night.

The next thought that came to mind was that this entrance was the only way out, at least as far as the prisoners knew. Not that it would do them much good, because without having the proper clearance and voice analysis escape was impossible. Prisoners locked in cells next to the second and final exit and entrance gate could hear the guards coming in at the start of their shift. There were the four prisoners who barely ever slept because they believed that they could see the light. Their cells had small openings at eye level which allowed them to see out into the corridor. The brief glimpses of the bright lights from the overpass convinced them it was a sign from God and truly believed they were coming closer to enlightenment.

After reaching the other side of the overpass, the next gate would automatically open. Within seconds, you were inside of the prison. 978 found that amusing. It felt like those bureaucratic boneheads actually trusted the guards enough to enter the prison without going through the ritual of confirming your identity twice. Then again, the confirmation of a guard's identification was required at the end of each shift. Regardless, it would not surprise him if the suits were dreaming about creating sleeping quarters for the guards. That way they could live there and be on call for twenty-four hours a day, essentially turning them into slaves. If this particular scenario ever came to be, the prisoners would be better off than the guards.

As soon as the gate closed, 978 turned right and marched down the first corridor. Guard 401 was heading in his direction. He was very much aware of the fact that 401 was originally an old Rhode Island telephone area code, but he spent too much time thinking about stuff like that. 401 was his old friend Charles Willard Grant, someone he had known since his sophomore year in high school. Will convinced him to get into law enforcement. This worked out well for 978 due to the fact that he now had a bachelor's degree in psychology and could directly apply for a position in the psychiatric unit. Will, or 401 while on duty, was a military police officer in the army for four years. This was an automatic qualification for a guard job following an honorable discharge. It always felt good to see 401 at the start of the shift. He could easily think back to the times when they played one-on-one basketball in the gym after school. He could also fondly remember borrowing mom's car on the weekends to travel to collector's shops to find old comic books and movies. The times when they would actually score with girls he wouldn't trade for anything. Most of them were metal head or hippy wannabes, but that was okay. Some of them smoked too much pot or were considered easy, but he and Will always treated them well. But there was no point in dwelling on the past, especially since they couldn't talk about it while on duty.

"What's up, chief?" asked 401, starting the most casual interaction they would have all night.

"Not much, really," answered 978.

"You back for good?"

"Yeah, I think so, as long as I haven't jeopardized my retirement."

That was 978's best attempt to show a sense of humor. It didn't really matter since he hadn't so much as cracked a smile. At least he was trying to put up a good front. Hopefully, that would keep 401 from worrying. He knew his friend had his back, probably because of their long-time friendship. Even Michelle was unaware of his mandatory leave of absence, which worked out well once the divorce was finalized. The timing couldn't have been better, it gave him extra time to relax and prepare for the hearing with Dr. Fletcher and the Care Control Division. The worst was behind him, he had hoped.

Now something else came to mind. 978 realized that he didn't speak to Will the entire time he was gone. It hadn't occurred to him to call or leave a message online. Then again, he'd left his computer off since the day in court, so he really had no idea if anyone had made an attempt to contact him. Still, those closest to him knew he preferred them to dial direct. Someone like Will was probably more aware of that than anybody, and it surprised him that his friend didn't say more during this interaction. But he had to remind himself that as a fellow guard who would only go by 401 while on the job, always stayed focused on the job and didn't like to engage in extended conversations. This obviously had to do with the discipline and training received while in the army. An excellent example was displayed as a result of that, inspiring all the guards how to endure working in a prison. But they had known each other for a long time, causing him to anticipate his friend to be a little more inquisitive. He was curious what 401 would say next.

"D5 is in the white room for the next 72 hours," said 401.

"Lutz?" asked 978.

"Uh-huh."

D5 is one guy who had everything going against him. 978's predicament was nothing compared to this inmate. Gordon Lutz, better known as Lutz the Putz to his fellow inmates, had been locked up for almost a year. He was only in his early twenties and serving a five-year sentence. Lutz was convicted of assaulting his mother with a baseball bat. In most cases a judge would have handed down a seven-year sentence in a regular state prison with no parole. Luckily, Lutz had a strong advantage. He had no prior criminal record and had been receiving psychiatric treatment since his early teens. The only person to come and visit him was his father, who came up from Atlanta every three or four months. At least there was a genuine effort. That wasn't the case with a lot of the other inmates, and after finding out more about his background 978 had a lot more empathy.

Lutz, or D5, just wasn't dealt a very good hand. His father left when he was only four years old. They remained in contact even though daddy moved to Atlanta. Not exactly a close relationship.

His mother would remarry when he was nine, but got divorced again two years later. She tried to make him feel responsible, saying it was hard enough for her being a single mother and that his behavior made things worse. That didn't make sense. She barely let him speak to anyone visiting her at the house. It also didn't help that she called him an idiot on a daily basis. By the time he was a teenager she would throw pots, pans, and silverware at him just because she was in a bad mood. The only saving grace was Olivia, his girlfriend during the last two years of high school. This was great. His desire to commit suicide faded the moment they first met. A month prior to that he swallowed a bottle of sleeping pills and jumped into the deep end of a neighbor's swimming pool. Counseling and medication became the norm from that point on.

At first Olivia did everything she could to help Gordon deal with his mother. At some point, however, it felt like she became his mother. When the relationship began, she was always trying to convince him how strong he was. Eventually, it became more about how she could get the upper hand over him. Manipulation was the number one priority. Gordon constantly had to hear it from who he thought was his true love that he was an idiot when she couldn't get exactly what she wanted. Yet he felt liberated by recognizing that things weren't working out. About a week after his high school graduation, he met up with her and said they both needed to move on. The result was a shouting match which ended with her punching him in the nose. Blood would flow out of both nostrils for over an hour. He wasn't going to call the police, because that would have made him the laughing stock to both his mother and the few friends that he had. It only made sense that he earned the nickname Lutz the Putz. The women in his life were always wearing the pants, so to speak.

It was easy to understand why D5 reached his boiling point. Mother Lutz would carry on saying that only someone like her son would get himself into a bad situation with a girl and deserve it. The sad thing was the poor guy really wanted to succeed in life. Not long after graduation he landed a position as a shipper-receiver at an auto parts factory warehouse in town. The pay was half-decent and he thought that by working full-time he could successfully avoid dealing with his mother. After saving up some money he looked into buying property. An inexpensive townhouse would have been nice, a mobile home would have been sufficient as well. This could have worked in his favor, but having a mother playing the role of an antagonist instead of a support system prevented it from ever happening.

What a shame. The poor guy was so on edge he didn't even want to go home after work. At some point his mother would go on about how his life would never improve. But he was happy, or at least content. Didn't that mean anything to her? Not a chance. She could not live with the idea of her little Gordon being happy. Finally, he had had enough. The rage had built up to the point that when he went upstairs to his bathroom to get a baseball bat it didn't require much thought. Something inside caused him to operate on automatic pilot. He walked into the kitchen where his mother was and proceeded to bash her brutally. The injuries she sustained would hopefully take years to recover. At least that was how he wanted it to be. Now all he needed to do was dial the local emergency number. Gordon, soon to be D5, just left the phone on and said nothing. He dropped the bat next to his mother, who was lying on the floor in serious shock, then sat down at the kitchen table. Now it was just a matter of time until an ambulance arrived, along with the authorities. He knew it wouldn't take long for them to figure out what happened, which suited him fine. The court would request an immediate psychiatric evaluation, along with an analysis of the long history of treatment during his adolescence. Soon after that he would be tried and convicted, which meant serving no less than a five-year sentence at Peterson Prison's psychiatric unit. Inmates serving there were treated better compared to the other units. D5 should be grateful. Regardless, his mother now knew the pain she caused him, and could no longer torment him. The best part was she now shared at least one common diagnosis with her son: post-traumatic stress disorder.

However, the physical pain she now had to endure couldn't be shared with anyone.

That suited her boy just fine.

"He was smashing his head against the wall again," said 401.

"What?" asked 978, losing track of thought. "That's the second time this month."

"Yup, and to think he isn't forced to wear a helmet unless he's put into a padded cell."

"Right, remember how our parents used to joke about that when we were kids? Maybe they were onto something."

978 felt slightly relieved that his sense of humor was still intact. What he had just said came out naturally, so he wasn't simply putting up a front. Still, he expressed as much humor as a guard was allowed to show. Just by sharing a laugh on duty the Care Control Division might suspect insubordination. He thought it might help to suggest that being happy on the job should be taken into consideration.

Yeah, right.

Checking to see what time it was revealed that only a few minutes had passed since reporting for duty. The shift didn't actually begin until midnight, and a long night it would be. For 978, taking time to remember everything he knew about D5 seemed to take an eternity. But so far all he really knew was that the poor guy decided to take up head-banging again. Still, he was glad that the first person he saw at the start of his shift was an old friend.

"Which doctor is going to meet with D5?" asked 978.

"No one as far as I know," answered 401. "Right now it's just being treated like a routine incident."

"It is becoming more frequent. Maybe his condition is getting worse."

"Who cares? It's not our job to determine what's best for him."

Is that all that Will could say? Granted, on the job 978

could onlythink of Will as a number, not an actual name. But he thought that his best friend was better than that. Maybe after fifteen years the job had become nothing more than a routine and a paycheck, which easily explained why the guy started to sound like everyone else who worked in their unit, including those who possessed higher authority. Again, it all boiled down to the same thing.

Formalities.

••• 3

As 978 started his first patrol, he couldn't help noticing how dimly lit the corridors were. Why he didn't know. That had been the case the entire nine years he had been employed at Peterson Prison. Originally, he liked it that way. The overnight shift was usually low-key, which helped create a very tranquil setting. But the bottom line was it made him relax. At the end of the shift he had a short ride home, most of the time he could fall asleep quickly. Now that Michelle and the kids were gone there were no more distractions, not that it was ever a big concern. He truly missed living with his family. His life had to go on, but it would never be the same. No one could ever replace them, and he didn't marry Michelle because she got pregnant. It didn't matter what they disagreed about, he never had any desire to shout at her. She used to tell him that she loved the way he could get his point across without becoming hostile or aggressive, but not anymore. In fact, during the last few years they were together she stopped saying that. He completely understood why she left. The longer he worked as a guard, his enthusiasm waned. And even though the two of them still had their moments of intimacy, that wasn't a big deal, either. He never forgot the time she told him that there was no longer a sparkle in his eyes. He was already aware of that, but the moment she said it he knew it was the beginning of the end.

978 had to keep reminding himself to concentrate on the task at hand, hoping that might help him during this rough period in his life. Yeah, right. That works for someone like Will, where the combination of routines and a good nature created a decent balance. Nowadays he could barely hold enough interest to read the front page of a newspaper. For years he always checked the horoscope under his astrological sign to determine what was in store for him on that particular day, even if he didn't whole-heartedly believe it. Now just watching the reruns of his favorite television shows required too much energy. At this point it would take a miracle for him to actually stumble onto something remotely interesting. But he hadn't given up completely. He still thought that life was worth living for lots of other people. He remembered his mother saying it was easier not to care than it was to care. Unfortunately, he felt so detached from real life despite wanting the best for his both family and the few friends he had left. This explained why he was continually becoming more distant from everyone.

It just dawned on the poor guard that his mind was rambling on and on, which didn't mesh well with the thought process that was required for a good job performance. Only an hour had passed since he started his shift. The first patrol went smoothly, but he knew the more he dwelled on certain things that work would go by slowly. He was convinced it should have been a lot easier, especially considering the fact that he didn't feel completely cut off from the job. He definitely appreciated that because a two-week absence can really put someone out of a working mode, and people who work during the off-hours get affected the most. It only took a few minutes to complete the necessary paperwork, and when he turned right down the next corridor 401 was standing there waiting. He handed over the report, somewhat relieved, because now he didn't have to drop it off at the main office.

"So far so good?" asked 401.

"So far," answered 978.

"I'm glad to hear that. I forgot to tell you that the second shift searched D5's cell right before you came in tonight."

"Did they find anything?"

"No, they weren't expecting to."

"Is he allowed to go back there?"

"After his 72 hours are completed."

"Okay."

That was good to know, even though that was almost always the case. It also helped that the inmate's numbers had to be the same as their cell number. This was supposedly done to make the job easier for the guards, even though that was never officially confirmed. At this point, 978 honestly didn't care. He knew what the deal was, and he would always reach the same conclusion. It was just another formality, but he didn't want to dwell on such a minor detail. Unfortunately, trivial matters were becoming an obsession, and that certainly wasn't going to help in the present situation. The smartest thing to do was simply keep quiet and do everything by the book. Then again, his own guard number was originally invented for talking. Maybe he could teach himself the art of selective hearing. That way he could just tell his co-workers that he was unavailable and they would have to leave a message.

The exact time was 2am, which was when bars were supposed to close for the night. This meant almost nothing to 978, mainly because he was on duty. Visits to any after-hours establishments were more or less out of the question if you worked in any kind of law enforcement during the off-hours. Unless someone wanted to arrive at work intoxicated which would result in immediately disciplinary action, meaning an automatic three-day suspension without pay. That was considered to be pretty lenient if you were a first-time offender. For a brief moment he was blinded by white lights, than everything quickly went back to normal. It was just another drill. This specific drill was done to make sure the lights in the corridors were operational. The electrical systems needed to be fully functional at all times, and this routine took place twice a week on the overnight shift. That wasn't so bad. The second shift had to deal with it twice every night. It was also important to remember when this procedure took place who would be effected the most: the four prisoners who truly believed they could see the light. Maybe in their delusional states of mind they thought that God was showing some forgiveness, but who were they kidding? 978 knew full well that God had nothing to do with any of it. Only one person serving time in Peterson Prison's Psychiatric Unit was responsible for this.

Enter Jack Burton, better known as inmate number D7. At this point he had been locked up for eleven years, with only one more to go before being paroled. This was the man who was responsible for supposedly enlightening other inmates, at least from 978's point of view. He was best known to his friends, family, the outside world, and himself as the Zen Lunatic. Burton, D7, or the Zen Lunatic graduated magna cum laude from Boston College with a bachelor's degree in philosophy. For the majority of his life he was known to have very possessive behavior, and believed he had found his true calling after learning everything about Zen Buddhism. He became truly convinced that he could save the world by preaching to everyone about living in the moment. It didn't matter to him if it sounded crazy, especially since he thought the here and now should be the only purpose in life. He found it easy to prove that his obsessive personality paled in comparison to the fanaticism and narcissistic points of view displayed in the media on a daily basis. A close friend called him the Zen Lunatic as a joke, but he took to it very quickly. Granted, it may have sounded sinister, but it would grab attention.

978 saw D7 as someone who was unable to have any true friends. But his followers clung to his every word like it was gospel and did everything he told them to do. Judging by the crimes being committed, the situation could easily have gotten as bad as what Charles Manson's followers did almost a hundred years ago. Upon sentencing, the majority of people saw it as a good thing that no evidence could prove that anyone's lives were directly in danger. Just like Manson, he would be convicted of conspiracy due to his followers carrying out his orders. The majority of crimes committed were burglaries and car thefts. D7 felt it was justified because all of the victims supposedly had too much money and should be forced to live without some of their material possessions. But in the jury's eyes he was no modern day Robin Hood. He would sell almost all of the items his followers stole from homes in classified ads. The cars were sold to be stripped of all their valuable parts by corrupt garage owners so they could avoid paying higher overhead costs. It was a shame that none of those guys faced any criminal charges. A case like this one would have increased the public's awareness of the constant scams in the automotive industry. The least surprising aspect of this case was the fact that D7 kept all of the money made from everything stolen, yet somehow convinced his followers that they were doing what was right. 978 knew this guy was nothing more than a master manipulator.

In hindsight, it was probably a good thing that 978 hadn't followed the highly-publicized trial to closely. This was a situation where the information kept on file regarding the prisoner was more than enough. Besides, the guard thought that someone like D7 deserved as little attention as possible. The self-proclaimed Zen Lunatic created more drama than necessary, and had little or no chance of gaining any sympathy compared to an inmate like D5. This guy could have cared less about enlightenment, power was his big thing. Yet little did he know that political ties would make his theft ring come to a complete stop. His followers broke into the house of an ex-senator's daughter, unaware that she called in sick to work. Her car wasn't there, which would have made someone automatically assume she was gone. But she had brought it to a local garage earlier that morning to have minor repairs done, and the owner was a nice enough guy to give her a ride back since she wasn't feeling well.

During the break-in, she attempted to defend herself against Leroy, D7's number-one-thief, but was unsuccessful. Unfortunately for her, Leroy would hear her sneak up from behind, and the big brute turned around and knocked the baseball bat out of her hands. He proceeded to kick her in the stomach and sucker-punch her on the left side of her head. She quickly fell to the floor and became completely disoriented. Because of this, Leroy hoped that she would be unable to identify him as the attacker to the police.

That would not be the case.

Once apprehended, though, Leroy felt slightly relieved that the woman didn't sustain any serious injuries. With his height being six-foot-six and large gorilla-like physique, which had developed later in life due to complications at birth, made him look intimidating to almost everybody. And violence was not condoned, regardless of the criminal activity. However, it was this particular incident that would create major controversy and lead to the downfall of the almighty Zen Lunatic. It was hard for 978 to imagine what the trial was like. The tension alone in the courtroom probably cut like a knife, making it easy to think it could have caused internal bleeding. All of D7's followers pleaded guilty, but when he took the stand it was a different story. He did everything possible to be seen as the Zen Lunatic and not Jack Burton. He absolutely refused to discuss anything related to the crime, and tried to convince every person present at the trial to only think about the here and now. With both the prosecution and defense attorneys, he would answer questions with questions. He asked them if they even remotely cared about the case, or enjoyed dressing formally for work, and if they were truly happy with their chosen professions. He then told the judge that the case wouldn't have been that big of a deal if an ex-senator's daughter hadn't been the victim. This was the only aspect of the case that D7 would acknowledge. After that he attempted to point out every juror's physical traits and habits, than tried to guess what each of them did for a living. He decided that his encore performance would be to take a knife out of his pocket and attempt to carve the word Zen into the palms of his hands. 978 saw that as nothing more than a cheap ploy to live up to a criminal name he had grown to love, but supposedly he had also cut himself while awaiting trial and got described anti-psychotic medication, which he was taking even to this day. This circus act caused a panic among the jurors, convincing the judge to impose a sentence of no more than twelve years at the Peterson Prison's Psychiatric Unit.

In 978's opinion, the bastard got off easy. This was someone who didn't deserve to be called anything else but D7. Because referring to this lowlife by any other name, including his own, would thrill him beyond belief. He simply thrived on being the center of attention and was pretty much a charlatan who managed to convince at least for other inmates to hang on to his every word. D7 had concocted the idea that the light seen from the main entrance at night brought his followers closer to God. This concept he created was meant to be nothing more than a tool to manipulate others. Ridiculous stuff like this gave 978 good reasons to feel that he should not be referred to as Jack Burton, or the Zen Lunatic for that matter. He should be D7 and only D7 for the rest of his prison sentence, perhaps for the rest of his life as well.

978 started to reminisce about his time in college. He was

young and the possibilities seemed endless. Looking back now it may not seem like a whole lot, but it was fun while it lasted. A lot of it may have been because he wanted to be there, or that he wasn't completely caught up in the college lifestyle. He may have done his share of partying, but he had made the smartest decision by not living on the campus. It was only a twenty minute commute from home, and if his car broke down his mother could easily pick him up or drop him off at the train station. College was also the place where he would meet another close friend named Larry Denton, who was a communications major and also a really good guitar player. 978 was a mediocre bass player, and it wouldn't be long before they would hook up with a seventeen-year-old drummer named Eric Cormier. Their band would often play gigs at local bars and functions on campus. Most of the time, they just played their favorite covers with Larry and Eric sharing the lead vocals. 978 always found it difficult doing both the while playing bass, so he never seriously considered singing lead. Ironically, most of the original songs they wrote he came up with almost all of the lyrics. He also came up with the band's name: Curly, Larry, and Moe. Obviously it was taken from The Three Stooges. It worked because Eric always kept his head shaved like Curly, Larry already being named Larry, and 978 became Moe simply by default.

Nostalgia dominated the guard's mind at the present moment. 978 didn't even like the word. He kept promising himself he would concentrate on work and work alone, which was important since it was his first night back. As the time went by, it became more and more obvious that it wasn't happening. But thinking about college felt alright. Right now that relaxed his state of mind a lot more than carrying out orders in the prison world. Unfortunately, the rest of the night would consist of the same old stuff: Formalities. Still, the time he spent with Larry was something he never took for granted. Not only did they share a similar taste in music, but they were both lifelong fans of Doctor Who. Throughout his childhood he knew other classmates who liked the show, but he never thought he would become close friends with a fanatic. Then along came Larry. It was nice to talk to someone who knew more about the show than he did. Larry owned every episode available on disc, as well as some old merchandise like action figures and even some of the oldest shows recorded on videotape. Larry actually owned a VCR, which was surprising since those old machines were almost as obsolete as telephone area codes.

There was one Doctor Who episode, which originally got released as a feature film that 978 had a soft spot for. It was Doctor Who and the Daleks, starring Peter Cushing in the title role. Although not directly linked to the BBC series which premiered not long beforehand, there was something about the movie that drew him in. It was both intriguing and enticing. He thought it might have been because it was filmed in bright Technicolor, which made it special since the series never used that technique. 978 actually saw that as a good thing and it made the movie all the more special. He often wondered if he preferred seeing Peter Cushing in this along with some other roles he did in Hammer Films instead of his performance as Grand Moff Tarkin in Star Wars.

Regardless, the actor would always remain an icon of twentieth century films. Right now, however, he wanted to keep thinking about Doctor Who. The first thing that came to mind is how some of the actors involved in the show would react if they knew that there was still a devoted following. Of course that was one question no one could answer, especially since everyone from the original series airing from the early sixties to the late nineties had been dead for years.

For 978 the one name that always came to mind regarding the Doctor Who series was Jon Pertwee. This particular actor would play Doctor number three, and his absolute favorite. He had no idea as to why, not that he thought there needed to be a specific answer for that. But the episodes that comprised the story Frontier in Space ranked highest in his book, even if there were other Doctor Who fans that didn't think much of them, but he didn't care. He never even bothered to get Larry's opinion, not that his friend would ever trash any era of the show completely. 978 thought there had to be something special to it. Otherwise he wouldn't keep going back and watching it again. Maybe it was good that he didn't know the specific reason, meaning he should simply enjoy it for what it is. And for him, that was what entertainment was all about, anyway.

As most fans of the original BBC series knew, the actor that gained the most popularity from playing the character back then was Tom Baker. 978 also enjoyed Baker's portrayal of Doctor Who. Maybe it was because he took over Jon Pertwee's role. Or perhaps it had something to do with the fact that he played the part longer than anyone else. One also needed to consider that the guy also had great charisma as well. The two Doctors were similar to a certain extent. Both of them were very tall with thick, curly hair. However, Pertwee was considerably older than Baker, or at least it appeared that way on screen. 978 often wondered if the producers chose Baker to play the fourth Doctor Who because they wanted a younger, more eccentric version of the previous incarnation. If that was the case they did a very good job. Granted, 978 could never believe that actor Patrick Troughton won the part of the second Doctor Who due to a striking resemblance to the character of Moe from the Three Stooges, so that theory might be way off. Yet one needed to keep in mind that Elizabeth Sladen's ever-popular character Sarah Jane Smith had already been introduced before Baker came along, so he may have been chosen for being closer in age, even if only slightly more, than Pertwee.

978 also remembered that not long after Frontier in Space came out and Tom Baker took over as Doctor Who, the

villainous role of the Master would be taken over by someone else. The new Master was certainly younger than the previous one, but the resemblances between them were far more obvious compared to the third and fourth Doctors. He couldn't remember the names of the actors who played that part for the life of him, which was surprising since so many facts about the show would role off his tongue instantly whenever he and Larry met up and had in-depth discussion about the show. Of course he also had to consider the amount of stress he had dealt with recently, and his adjustment to life on the job played a big role in it. And he honestly couldn't imagine recalling stuff related to Doctor Who would be a contributing factor.

978 thought about when he and Will used to shoot baskets after school together, which made the Boston Celtics come to mind. He was specifically thinking about the Larry Bird era, long before he was born. Many fans still considered that to be the most magical time in the team's history, and he truly believed that was right. About a month ago he watched the disc of the 1986 championship series when the Celtics defeated the Los Angeles Lakers. Back then they could be compared to Beatlemania when it came to basketball. Even if you didn't follow sports at all, just by living anywhere in New England it was damn near impossible not to know what was happening with them. And it wouldn't be until 2008 when the team would win again, but supposedly that still didn't cause the same sensation compared to 1986. Unfortunately, this all happened long before the guard was born. But that didn't matter. If he could go back in time and sit in front of a TV set while these games went on, the excitement he would have felt at that moment would have been enough.

978 started to feel like all this contemplating of old sitcoms and sports games threw a monkey wrench into his thought process. Naturally, he had hoped for the opposite effect. Right now the only thing that might help would be a trip to the

employee's cafeteria for a glass of ice water. To most folks that may not sound like much, but in his case that could make all the difference in the world. This felt like a realistic goal: taking very small steps to accomplish a simple task. Of course something this tacky would make any therapist feel proud. Perhaps the guard discovered the true definition of self-help. Granted, half the night hadn't gone by yet. And 978 had no idea what he was up against.

4 •••

As 978 looked straight ahead, he saw a figure about a hundred feet away. This person walked towards him very slowly, which was somewhat nerve-wracking. With the lights being dim, it was pretty much impossible to determine who it could be. He decided to simply stop and wait for whoever it was to approach him. It turned out to be another guard, which he'd suspected all along. The closer she got, the easier it became to see her physical features. She was short, about five-foot-two, with blond hair she kept tied back, which convinced him it grew far below her shoulders. She probably used some hair gel. He felt a bit intimidated when she looked him in the eye. The piercing stare made him forget about her good looks. Finally, she decided to break the ice.

"I'm 609," she stated. "I'm new to the night shift."

"I'm 978," he responded.

"You just returned from a leave of absence, correct?"

"That's right."

"I'm just keeping tabs on everyone since I'm new on this time slot."

"Good idea."

The conversation ended at that point. 978 couldn't believe how cold and calculated this new guard sounded. He felt like he was talking to a robot, not unlike the voice heard over the intercom while checking in for duty. At least that machine thanked him at the start of his shift. That would probably never happen with this 609 he just met. After she took her eyes off him and moved on he noticed she wasn't wearing the required helmet, much less having one in her possession. The main problem, however, was the fact that he didn't feel like chasing her down because of it. He decided not to mention it to 401 or whoever was on duty at the main office. It was his first night back and he just wanted everything to go real smoothly, but all he could think about was that cold stare she had. It was as if she could see right through him.

978 checked the time. It was exactly 3am. In another hour he would be halfway through his shift. So far it had been a pretty slow night, which meant the level of stress would be minimal. The leave of absence probably helped, with the exception of the court date. He started to think about Doctor Who again. If he remembered correctly 2063 would mark the 100th anniversary of the series premiere. Granted, it was still early 2062, but Larry Denton would be the first to know about any official celebrations. He began reminiscing about an early episode starring William Hartnell, who played the very first Doctor, when the buzz alarm activated in the earpiece of his helmet. It would reoccur every four seconds, which specifically indicated that a camera in an inmate's cell had been damaged. Now he had to call in to the main office for confirmation and further instructions.

"978 calling in response to alarm, over," the guard stated.

"This is Staff Sergeant 101 at the main office," a voice responded. "You are required to report to White Room number one immediately, 978."

978's mood immediately changed for the worse. No one wants to help out in the White Room, especially after returning from a vacation or a leave of absence. Knowing it was D5 being held captive wouldn't make it any easier.

Regardless, he still felt bad for the poor soul. All Peterson Prison's Psychiatric Unit was succeeding at was making the situation for Gordon Lutz worse. It would take a few minutes to get there, which was fine since it most likely not a serious emergency. 401 had said earlier that no doctors were involved yet. D5 was probably felt more helpless than ever, possibly causing the feeling of deserving the name Lutz the Putz.

978 marched down the corridor known as number seven. All corridors had individual numbers, helping guards verify their specific locations at all times. It didn't take long for most guards to memorize them. The entire layout of the prison was in numerical order, making it easier to remember. After checking the time again, he estimated arriving at the White Room in another minute or two. He lifted his head up to look straight ahead and set his eyes on a tall, dark figure at the end of the corridor. It startled him somewhat, despite the fact that it was probably just another guard. Whoever it was vanished as quickly as they appeared, and after reaching the end of corridor seven, he looked down corridor number eight and saw no one. There was no time to investigate since he had to head in the opposite direction. 978 was expected to arrive at the White Room any second now, but he decided to contact this other guard for visual confirmation.

"Guard 978 calling on guard patrolling through corridor number eight," he stated. "Please respond."

There was no reply.

"Guard 978 calling Staff Sergeant 101 at the main office," he stated.

"Go ahead," 101 responded.

"Please identify guard patrolling through corridor number eight."

"There is no guard."

"Say again?"

"Repeat. There is no guard. There is nothing on report or any visual sighting."

Now he was spooked.

The corridors were very dark at night, but 978 refused to believe that his eyes were deceiving him. He had been working as a guard for almost ten years now, so he wasn't about to question what he had sighted. Perhaps 101 looked at the wrong monitor, but he didn't want to cause trouble. Was he being lied to? Not likely. What was the big deal about verifying the location of another guard? By asking himself these particular questions repeatedly he got scared of developing an obsessive thought process, which was something meant to happen only to the inmates. All he really wanted to do was concentrate on the current task. That is the only true expectation of any guard, which sounds very reasonable. It would only be another incident where D5 was acting out again, not considered to be a major crisis by anyone. As soon as he reached the end of corridor number one, he marched around the corridor and stopped at the front door of the main office to receive further instruction. 101 was sitting at the front desk, sorting out paperwork and keeping half an eye on the monitors.

"Are there any other details?" asked 978.

"Dr. Carlton and 609 are already at the scene," answered 101, looking up briefly. "They need extra assistance."

"Thank you, Sergeant."

"Report back here afterwards."

"Yes sir."

He immediately felt worse knowing he had to discuss the incident later.

978 only had to march maybe another forty feet to the White Room. It was a strange sight to behold. This particular corridor was a little brighter than the other ones, probably due to the fact that the door to the White Room was wide open. The light shining from the inside and the chattering he could hear was nerve wracking, but nothing could prepare him for what he was about to witness.

Upon entering the White Room, 978 immediately saw D5. He was lying on the floor with his hands tied behind his back. His right eye was as swollen as it possibly could get. He just barely managed to sit up and stare directly at 978. The most unusual aspect of this was the fact that D5 was still wearing his prison uniform. Any prisoner that got put in the White Room was required to wear thin white clothing. This was mandatory at any hospital, and Peterson Prison's Psychiatric Unit had to live up to that expectation.

978 got concerned when he noticed that D5 wasn't wearing a helmet. He didn't like it when inmates were forced to wear them, but it prevented serious injuries. He hated seeing the poor guy get hurt. Now he needed information from 609 and Dr. Carlton.

"Status report?" asked 978.

"D5 attempted an assault with a deadly weapon," said 609.

"How is that possible? His hands are tied!"

"You are about to see."

609 took out her mini-gun, which confused 978 since guards rarely, if ever, used this particular weapon. She slowly walked behind D5, leaned over, and untied his hands. She proceeded to walk in front of him and placed the mini-gun on the floor.

"D5," stated 609. "You must follow the instructions I am about to give you."

"Pick up the gun, stand up and walk over to Dr. Carlton and place it on her desk."

D5 slowly crawled forward, reached out with his right hand and grabbed the weapon then stood straight up. He moved toward the desk and was about to put it down before D5 got between him and Dr. Carlton. He started to step backwards, quickly becoming wide-eyed and shaking. It was obvious that he was intimated by her cold stare. Suddenly and without warning, 609 raised her right leg in the air and kicked D5 in the crotch. What happened next seemed impossible. D5 flew backwards across the room and his body slammed against the wall. 609 quickly marched over D5 and stood directly above him. Poor D5 was lying on the floor in a lot of pain and completely disoriented. When he was able to start focusing again, he looked up and saw 609 staring down at him.

"You made a crucial error," said 609. "Logic should have dictated that you should not have given the gun to Dr. Carlton. You had the chance to shoot me and win the gun. You have failed and are no longer an eligible candidate for the LEO1 project. You have outlived your usefulness. For that you will receive the death penalty effective immediately."

Within seconds 609 took out her standard gun, which is issued to every guard and expected to be referred to as weapon number one. She stepped on D5's neck, aimed directly at his head, and fired. The bullet hit him straight between the eyes, killing him instantly. What in God's name was happening here? This put 978 into shock.

"What have you done?!" shouted 978.

"It is very simple," answered 609. "He lost."

"What do you mean he lost?! He didn't have a chance!"

"There will be no LEO1 replicas made in his image and likeness."

"What the hell are you talking about?!"

978 had no clue what she was saying. He couldn't understand what he just heard. He quickly glanced over at Dr. Carlton, who just sat the desk and showed no emotion. Then two more gunshots fired, which sounded like they came from down the hall, possibly at the main office. He took out his standard gun, exited the White Room, and ran a short distance back down the corridor. He was only a few feet from the entrance to the main office where he truly witnessed the impossible. Everything that occurred from this moment on felt like it was happening in slow motion. A figure slowly marched out of the main office. 978 nearly froze when he saw this person turn to look at him. He thought he was staring at his

own reflection. Like him, this person had the same dark hair and eyes, facial structure, and standard uniform minus the helmet. To top it off he saw a small amount of facial hair around the mouth, like a goatee had been shaved off. This is exactly what he did a few short hours ago, right before leaving for work. He closed his eyes for a split second, but when he opened them again he knew it wasn't a dream. After this exact replica gave 978 a cold and quick stare, it slowly blinked its eyes before turning around and heading down the corridor. 978 looked in the main office and made a gruesome discovery. Staff Sergeant 101's body was faced down on the front desk with his head in a pool of blood. The poor soul had suffered the same fate as D5: a bullet straight between the eyes. 978 turned around and saw the replica marching further down the corridor slowly disappearing.

"NNNNOOOOOOOOOOO!!!!!!!!!" screamed out 978.

He fired four shots, not thinking that it was too dark to aim accurately. He quickly felt a hand grab the back of his neck, then got thrown to the left and smashed against a wall. He fell to the floor and dropped his weapon. He was disoriented, but slowly got on his hands and knees, and reached for the gun. A hand grabbed the back of his neck again. It was the worst pain he had ever felt. Then he heard a voice he immediately recognized give him a direct order.

"Don't even try!" demanded 609, forcing him to his feet. This was done by keeping a tight grip on his neck. Then Dr. Carlton appeared in front of him and leaned over to pick up his gun. She placed it in the left pocket of her white lab coat before vanishing from sight again. She was probably standing next to 609, who barked another order at him.

"Start moving!"

They started marching down corridor number one, the same direction his replica went. At least that's what 978 assumed it was. He had no idea where he was being taken, but noticed that at least four prison cell doors were open. The inmates were nowhere to be seen. These were the same ones who truly believed they could see the light, thanks to the self-proclaimed Zen Lunatic. Now he was worried that maybe D7 had been let out as well.

"I need the guards I requested earlier immediately!" commanded 609, who must have had a small audio transmitter on her uniform near her neck. When they passed D7's cell it was wide open and empty. Before he could continue contemplating what was happening, 978, 609, and Dr. Carlton, whose footsteps he could barely hear from behind, reached the intersection between corridors four and five. After stopping briefly, two guards appeared from the left, then two more from the right. All four guards stood behind them before continuing to march straight down corridor four.

There was no way for 978 to determine who the four guards were. He cringed at the thought of D7 and company running amok through the whole prison. Then he decided that he should be more concerned about what might happen to him. He was also worried about Will. Where was his friend? He doubted the guy had any knowledge about what was going on. What was worse was feeling like he was in a drug-induced haze. He had no idea where he was going, but it seemed to be taking a long time. Everything he witnessed in such a short period of time was barely sinking in. He was probably going into shock. Most likely due to the severe pain caused by 609's tight grip on the back of his neck.

All seven of them, 978, 609, Dr. Carlton, and the four guards continued marching down several dark corridors. 978 gave up trying to keep track of where they might be, except for staying on the same floor level. He was pretty sure they arrived at their destination, the exact time he didn't want to guess. They stopped in front of a huge set of double doors, both of which had small windows at eye level. It only took a few seconds to figure out where he was, even though the place was closed off at night. It was an area specifically used for the prison's general population.

Two of the four guards marched in front of 978, 609, and Dr. Carlton in order to unlock and open the double doors. Upon doing so they all marched in quickly. The further they traveled the lights turned on slowly and steadily. 978 had forgotten how large the place was. It must have been at least as big as the gym back in high school.

When everyone arrived at the other end of the general population area, 609 finally released her hand from 978's neck. The two guards in the front blocked another set of doors directly in front of them, which opened only seconds later. There was no way determine who walked in until the guards obstructing the view moved out of the way. The individual who came forward looked 978 straight in the eye.

It was none other than Dr. Fletcher.

978 was speechless. All this bloodshed had happened so quickly, with one person shot by someone who looked just like him. He might be in shock, but what happened was no hallucination. What was really going on? Now was the time to find out, especially since he was being confronted by the man in charge of the Care Control Division. Maybe he should ask why this guy didn't have an assigned number!

"Good to see you," said Dr. Fletcher.

"I'll bet," said 978, just barely getting the words out.

"I'm just glad you weren't caught in the crossfire. There is still some use for you. That is of course if you agree to certain terms."

978 just stood and stared at Dr. Fletcher. He didn't respond.

"I know this must be difficult," continued Dr. Fletcher. "But everything you witnessed tonight was the real deal. That's the trick to all of this. We are entering a new era of prison reform."

"By executing a prisoner on the spot?!" snapped 978. "You had 101 shot in the head! For what?! Where the hell are D7 and his followers?!"

"All of your questions will be answered in due time. I must warn you, everything you've seen so far is only a small handful of the changes being made. You did see Staff Sergeant 101 get shot by someone who is identical to you. Now take the time to look at the four guards who escorted you in here."

978 turned to look at all four guards, who were now lined up side by side. They were standing straight up, staying still, and looking forward like soldiers in the military. This was something Will was good at, but was not present at this gathering. He was afraid to ask where his friend was. It didn't take long to find out.

"401 calling in," Will's voice stated, easily heard over all of the guards transmitters. "Please respond."

"This is 840," responded the guard standing fourth to the right, whose real name was Steve Walsh. At least it sounded like Steve Walsh, stood like Steve Walsh, and even looked like Steve Walsh after 978 briefly studied what little he could see of the guard's facial structure.

"Rounds on the second floor are complete. I'm heading to the main office to drop off my report."

"Negative. There has been a weapons malfunction. A drill is also being conducted in general population."

"That must be incorrect, 840. Drills and actual emergencies do not occur simultaneously. But I will report to general population in order to receive further instructions."

"We'll be waiting, 401."

978 felt a chill all over his body. His friend was in trouble, and might be walking into a deathtrap without any warning. At the moment he was free from the painful grip of 609. The only chance he had was to put up a fight, creating an opportunity to get his hands on a firearm. He quickly ran up and shoved 840 in the chest as hard as he could. 840, more likely a replica, fell backwards and 978 snatched the weapon. He then fired several shots at the other three guards standing

there, who eventually lost their balance and fell to the floor. He turned around to find 840 standing up again but immediately fired a shot straight between the eyes, which was the same way D5 and Staff Sergeant 101 were killed. 840 fell down again, this time for good. A quick glance revealed very little blood flowing out and faint mechanical sounds. This wasn't the 840 he knew, or Steve Walsh. He didn't need to take a closer look to figure out this was something else entirely.

978 couldn't take any further action when 609 appeared in front of him. She charged forward and grabbed his right wrist, causing him to point the gun above him and fire several more shots, none of which would help his battle strategies. But he was quick enough to pull a blade out of his belt with his left hand. He aimed for the face and stabbed her in the chest area directly below the throat. She let go of him completely and stumbled a few feet backwards, allowing enough time to aim the gun at her head. There wasn't much ammo left, so hitting the intended target the first time around was a good idea. He wanted to kill her, or it, quick. Then again, that seemed to be the only real choice. But before he could pull the trigger the other three guards, or replicas, were back on their feet with their guns pointed right at him. It didn't matter what part of his body was shot, he was a human being, which meant he had a higher probability of dying right away. All he could do was drop the weapon and cooperate. If he was lucky maybe they would just lock him up.

Fletcher walked over to inspect 840. He looked disappointed and shook his head.

"I had very high hopes for this one," he said. "It looks like we'll have to replicate someone else."

978 heard the sound of footsteps. He turned his head and saw Will marching across the general population area. His friend had no way of knowing what was happening. It was simply a matter of being in the wrong place at the wrong

time.

"What's going on here?" asked Will, arriving where everyone else was.

"You already know," answered Fletcher. "It's another drill."

"In the middle of the night? In general population? What about that weapons malfunction?"

"Will!" shouted 978. "You've got to get out of here!"

"Mark," said Will, taking a closer look at 840's supposedly dead corpse.

"What's happening here? Walsh is dead!"

It was hard to imagine what was going through Will's mind. He rarely, if ever, referred to co-workers by their real names while on duty. It didn't matter what the circumstances were, even if it was a private area like the main office. This was definitely an exception to the rule. But there wouldn't be enough time to figure out how bad the situation was.

Will stood a short distance away from everybody. He couldn't keep himself from staring at 609. 978 looked over to find out why. It was a sight that would stop anybody in their tracks. 609 was standing up straight and still had the blade 978 had stabbed her with sticking out of her upper chest area.

"609," said Will. "What the hell happened to you?"

There was no response.

609 pulled the blade out and a dark liquid started slowly leaking out of the wound. It was similar to blood in color, but a lot thicker. 978 and Will kept on staring without uttering a single word. She looked over at the three remaining guards and gave them a single nod. Without hesitating, they raised their guns, aimed at Will, and opened fire. He received multiple shots in the chest and legs. He dropped to his knees and fell flat on his face. There was no doubt it.

Will was dead.

978 just stood still. He was in shock and completely unaware of everything around him. It was almost like being in a trance. He suddenly felt a sharp stinging sensation in the

back of his neck, most likely a needle injection.

Within seconds, everything went black.

5 •••

978 just barely began to open his eyes, and he felt disoriented. His vision was very blurry, possibly because of the bright lights around him, but that stopped bothering him in a short period of time. Standing in front of him were Dr. Fletcher and 609. It took a minute to realize that his hands were tied behind the chair he was sitting on. Standing directly behind him was Dr. Carlton, who hadn't even said a single word in his presence.

It didn't take long for the guard to figure out where he was. It was a conference room not far from the general population area, a place that was rarely used during the night shift. 978 only knew of it being used to interrogate inmates, which he could imagine might have been under slightly better circumstances. Maybe if the lights were dimmed and the air conditioning was on, it might have been more comfortable for certain inmates expected to answer serious questions. If the powers that be had brought D5 in here instead of the White Room, the poor guy would still be alive. But from what he saw, he honestly wasn't convinced that was just what they wanted. And at this moment, he thought nothing good could come from this.

"Finally," said Dr. Fletcher. "You're coming around. We've been waiting for you."

"You missed me, huh?" said 978, just barely. He couldn't believe he responded with a sense of humor.

He took his eyes off Fletcher and 609 for a moment to look at the clock on the wall behind them. It was 4:10am. He had been unconscious for at least an hour. But with everything that had happened so far, time wasn't important. Taking action should be. Fletcher and 609 kept staring directly at 978 for what seemed like an eternity. It was only for a few seconds, but the trauma and intimidation was consuming him to the point where he couldn't think about anything else. Granted, no one could blame him. He wouldn't expect any of the inmates in the Psychiatric Unit to handle this any better, and right now his life was at stake. It didn't take a genius to figure that out since three people had been shot in cold blood, and it still hadn't sunk in that his oldest friend was gone forever.

Fletcher turned his head slightly to look at 609, who was standing as still as a statue. 978 knew that the guy was about to say something. To be honest, he even looked somewhat relaxed. But there was nothing lifelike about 609, and it became obvious the longer she stood there. Her eyes displayed a cold stare, there was no sign of sweat, and he couldn't see if her chest expanded in and out in order to breathe. 978 knew that she wasn't human.

Okay then, what was she?

"It is time for you to leave," Fletcher said to 609. "Go report to your next assignment. It will be your most important one yet."

"Understood," 609 replied, without so much as blinking an eye. The facial expressions were cold and calculated, maybe even nonexistent. 978 compared it to a cat. She quickly turned around and exited the room, allowing Fletcher to focus all his attention on 978.

"What you are feeling right now is certainly justified. It is not often a guard has to deal with multiple assassinations, if ever. Especially if one of them happens to be an old friend, which I believe was the case with 401. Or should I say the late Mr. Grant?"

"Patronizing me isn't going to change anything," said 978.

"A lot of things have changed already. It doesn't matter how you are treated or whether or not you approve. In fact, things have changed so much there is no way of stopping it."

Fletcher couldn't seem to help himself from expressing a huge smile. With his full beard and heavy-set physique, you'd almost expect to hear a good-natured belly laugh. Unfortunately, in this situation it wouldn't improve matters.

"I take it you're about to subject me to an orientation?" asked 978.

"Absolutely," answered Fletcher. "This could be the opportunity of a lifetime for you. Of course that will depend on the decisions you make, which will allow your life to be spared, but more on that later."

"At least I'll die well-informed."

"Excellent. You're showing a positive attitude already. I will start by explaining what will interest you the most. It must be unbelievable to think of yourself as an assassin. I can't begin to comprehend what it felt like to witness a mirror image of yourself killing for no apparent reason. You will be happy to know that what you saw was no hallucination. It has to do with the technology that is being brought into all of the prison systems. Some information has been leaked on purpose, and you might have heard something about it."

"LEO1? Cyborgs, right?"

"You are very close. Cyborg projects are meant to help people with physical limitations, allowing many of them the opportunity to become super soldiers. I bet your second guess would be clones, which is also incorrect. Experimenting with clones has gone on for decades, which is how it should remain. Over time, they try to think for themselves and start developing physical and psychological problems. Eventually they become less and less manageable, making them expendable. But if you need some temporary cheap labor, they're right up you alley!"

"So far all you're doing is telling me what it isn't!"

"Alright, let's talk about the first prototypes that have been created. The results have been phenomenal so far. Seeing that guard who looked just like you would scare anyone to death. That must have been obvious after dealing with 609. These are the actual LEO1 soldiers, the ones that very few people know anything about. Are they cyborgs? No. Clones? No. The LEO1 title has been saved for the best one yet: replicas."

"So that thing that killed 101 was an exact replica?"

"Precisely. But there are still many things that need to be perfected. However, the results so far have been far better then we expected. More visible sweat and heavier breathing should be in effect with the first official batch. The traits they are developing are unbelievable. The physical strength they possess is beyond human capabilities, regardless of each individual body structure. What is even more amazing is the personalities are so similar to the people they are modeled after. Their programming absorbs the tiniest detail of whomever they are a replica of. The only difference is that they are much stronger willed, which is where I find fault. But there's always room for improvement!"

"Only for what you consider to be the perfect soldier! Not a human being!"

"You're missing the point. Human beings are only capable of doing so much in a lifetime. We don't live forever and during our lifecycle the potential slowly decreases. The age for retirement increased quite a bit throughout, but the government made the wise choice by stopping that. These days more people are being forced to retire earlier due to health problems. The human race is becoming obsolete, at least in its old age. We are far from facing extinction, but it is time for us to become more practical."

"You really think you're doing society a favor?"

"All that you've seen so far are three lives taken. Society shouldn't be a big concern. Right now you should be much more worried about what might happen to you. You have already been framed for murder, but that can be changed very easily if you cooperate. You cannot be programmed like one of the replicas, but if you're smart than you will comply. So you better think long and hard about it!"

While Fletcher kept carrying on, 978 took notice of the transmitter in his right ear. Normally it wasn't that big a deal since all employees were required to wear one, but in this situation something was different. Each time he spoke someone was communicating with him at the same time. The volume was kept up loud enough to the point where 978 couldn't figure out why Fletcher wasn't distracted by it. Unfortunately, it wasn't loud enough to figure out what was being said.

978 couldn't believe that Fletcher expected him to seriously consider going along with this crazy conspiracy. It was as if seeing his replica in action was supposed to be some kind of personal honor. He also couldn't believe that Fletcher was arrogant enough to think he was just take his friend's death like it was no big deal. From this point on 978 could no longer see this guy as a doctor, or as somebody in charge of something called the Care Control Division.

"You know," said Fletcher, trying to keep 978's attention. "I have always liked you. Both your work experience and the education you have received so far are very similar to my own background. If you play your cards right you'll be able to keep your salary and get sent back to college, courtesy of the Care Control Division. I might also consider hiring you as my junior partner."

"Really?" asked 978, in a somewhat agitated tone. However, he still thought it best to simply play along. "To me, it just sounds like you're expressing a very unique sense of humor. But please continue, because I am interested in hearing you out."

"Excellent. In fact, I'd like to point out that you are demonstrating one of your best qualities right now. It is always a wise idea to give any worthwhile situation the benefit of the doubt. There must be something that appeals to you."

"Only if it will keep more people from dying, and I'm not just saying that because my best friend was killed."

"To be perfectly honest, Mr. Grant was simply in the wrong place at the wrong time."

978 certainly didn't buy it, but Fletcher didn't have to know that. He started thinking about D5, who was now the late Gordon Lutz. That was one inmate who would have had a good chance to do better in life after getting paroled. He then thought about his own replica. That thing could be anywhere in the prison, or somewhere else, doing God knows what. Dr. Carlton had remained in the same spot without saying a single word. He could barely hear her breathe, which was the only indication that she might not be a replica.

"Remove his restraints," ordered Dr. Fletcher, causing Dr. Carlton to comply immediately. "It is time to take you on a guided tour. You have certainly earned the right to know much more."

Dr. Carlton walked up from behind, leaned over slightly then freed 978's hands. He heard a clanking sound against the back of the chair, which meant that his gun was still in her left lab coat pocket. He would have to act fast. It was now or never. The moment he stood up straight he turned slightly and quickly pulled the gun out of her pocket. He aimed it directly at Fletcher's chest and shot twice. Fletcher then fell backwards to the floor, causing a loud thud. 978 now knew that the old saying was true. The bigger they are, the harder they fall.

Despite the fact that Fletcher wasn't moving, 978 could still hear the guy breathing. He moved closer, looked down, and stared this monster straight in the eye. This was only the second time that 978 had ever shot somebody, the first being 840. Fletcher may have been defenseless, but he felt no remorse.

"It would have been interesting to see you as a replica," said 978.

"But that doesn't really matter now, does it? Getting shot and killed puts everything on hold. Which you are now finding out, aren't you?"

Fletcher breathed in and out, and continued to do so faster and faster. Then his eyes started to role into the back of his head, within a few more seconds they would close forever. There was absolutely no movement at all, except for the blood that was oozing all over his chest which quickly flowed down to the floor. 978 did just kill a human being in cold blood, but there was no need to be reminded of that. Since Fletcher was the mastermind who started all the bloodshed that occurred tonight, it only made sense to end it with him. Of course 978 knew that this situation was far from over, but hopefully ending it with the leader would put a stop to this madness a lot faster. It would only be a matter of time until some major disasters would occur outside the prison walls. Dr. Carlton then walked over and stood next to the guard.

"You're definitely braver than I am," she said very frankly, standing over Fletcher's body for a closer observation. "He was defenseless, but I was going to wait until he turned his back."

"That would have been easily justified," said 978, a little surprised that she finally spoke. "With all the trouble that has happened so far, he definitely didn't deserve to have his life spared. The only thing he would have been useful for was information. Can I assume you've been playing along with this scheme for some time now?"

"Yeah, pretty much."

Before the conversation could go any further, Dr. Carlton knelt down and searched Fletcher. She couldn't find a wallet, much less anything of interest in any of his pockets. The only thing that she found on him that had any practical use was the earpiece he was wearing, but that wasn't anything unusual. All employees, associates, or anyone affiliated with the prison system was required to have one. All guards including 978 had this equipment built into their helmets. Since there was nothing significant about it, Dr. Carlton could hardly call it evidence. However, she decided to hold on to it anyway. There was no real sense of intuition within her at that moment, but anything was possible.

"You should definitely hold on to that," said 978. "Fletcher must have been listening to someone important. I could hear someone most of the time. I couldn't figure out what was being said, but the volume was up really loud on that thing."

"There's only one problem," said Dr. Carlton. "This particular type of earpiece was cheaply made. You can't trace it back to whoever he was communicating with."

"That doesn't matter. Whoever he was talking to will probably try to make contact with him again. So you should hold on to it anyway."

"That's a good point. Still, I'm surprised that I don't know who he was talking to. I'll wear it for now. Whoever it is won't make it a top priority to come after me since I worked for Fletcher. But I don't think it will take long to figure out what happened to him."

"Well, I hope you have a good share of information, some worthwhile connections, and anything else that will put a stop to this."

"I certainly do, which is the reason why Dr. Fletcher wasn't needed as a tour guide. That was a good call on your part."

"Let's not talk about it. I don't feel bad, but I'm not proud of what I did. I think now is a good time to get moving."

"Call me Wendy."

Dr. Carlton took a minute to check the volume on Fletcher's earpiece. She noticed it was all the way up, making her decide to lower it to half of that. She then placed it in her ear, quickly adjusted it for comfort, than nodded at 978 to indicate that it was time to go. The two of them walked around Fletcher's body and headed for the door, ready to plot their next move.

6 •••

It didn't take long for 978 and Dr. Carlton to make their way back to the main office. Before entering, 978 simply dreaded the vision of seeing 101's dead body again. Much to his surprise, however, it was long gone. There wasn't a single trace of the corpse, not even a drop of blood. The guard turned his head to see how Dr. Carlton would react to this. She didn't seem the least bit phased, prompting him to ask some serious questions.

"Where's the body?" asked 978.

"Thanks to those three remaining replicas you dealt with in general population," said Dr. Carlton. "They were ordered to remove all traces of 101. His replica will probably be here by the time were gone."

"What about Will?"

"There is no replica of Will............at least not that I know of."

978 hoped for God's sake that was true, this would mean that his friend's reputation wouldn't be tarnished. Poor Will was simply in the wrong place at the wrong time. Both of them had respect for anyone who got killed in the line of duty. It came with the job, even more so with Will because of his military background. He may have lost his life early and unfairly, but perhaps it was a mixed blessing. Unfortunately, 978 would miss all the fun stories that Will told about his time in the service, which was somewhat unusual since there were no wars going on back then.

Dr. Carlton quickly made her way over to the main desk. She pulled out the chair and sat down. The moment she logged on to the computer 978 stood behind her and looked over her shoulder. He wasn't quite sure what she was trying to do, but he hoped she could get access to anything online that would put a stop to all this bloodshed.

No such luck.

"Are you able to make any major changes from here?" he asked.

"I can't override anything in the system," she answered. "But I can get those replicas to get rid of Fletcher's body, which will remove all the physical evidence that points to us."

"That's encouraging."

978 was tempted to ask if there was a replica of Fletcher, but quickly decided against it. If that was the case, he figured he would find out eventually. As much as he hoped there wasn't one, he was able to take comfort knowing that Will wasn't going to be recreated as a replica. At least as far as Dr. Carlton knew, anyway. Besides, he didn't want to deal with anything that reminded him of Fletcher. However, he appreciated the fact that Dr. Carlton was taking some responsibility for Fletcher's demise.

"Is there anything else you can do that will help?" asked 978.

"I can find out where your replica is," answered Dr. Carlton. "Other than that this system's options are very limited."

"Do you think it's still in the building somewhere?"

"We'll have an answer shortly."

Dr. Carlton kept busy working on the computer, doing things quickly while remaining at ease. Just watching her type seemed natural, which helped 978 keep some faith in this crazy situation. At this point he was almost convinced that she kept him from having a nervous breakdown. Or maybe it was because everything that had happened so far hadn't sunk in completely. He kept reminding himself to call her Wendy, but he still wanted to think of her as the good doctor. Then he considered the fact that it was still too early in the game to have complete faith right away.

It didn't matter.

Now it was time to hear the results.

"I've found something," said Dr. Carlton, a.k.a. the good doctor. "But you might not like it."

"That's okay," said 978. "A good doctor always tells the truth."

"According to this system you have left the building. It gets worse."

"Keep going."

"Your replica is going to continue to take over your identity completely. It even took your vehicle. Right now it is going to meet up with 609."

She was right. Everything was continuing to get worse. He would be more relieved to get diagnosed with a terminal illness. He also thought that if there was a way to give a replica a psychiatric evaluation, it would be considered a sociopath, and then some. Not to mention the fact that he knew there was a lot more information he would hear from the good doctor. If there was a plan, now was the best time to put it into motion. Especially after finding out it boosted his car, which was something he hadn't considered as a possibility until now.

"Those things can drive?" asked 978. "I still have my keys! So what you're telling me is they're smart enough to steal cars by themselves? I can't wait for you to tell me why I'm supposed to meet up with 609!"

"609's at the Boston Common," said Dr. Carlton. "The Governor is planning a speech for tonight. You and 609 have been given a special assignment to protect him. At this particular gathering there is supposed to be a lot of praise for Fletcher, who isn't expected to be there."

"Why on earth would I take on an assignment like that? All the years that I've worked here I've never signed on to do that kind of stuff! Why now? I didn't even vote during the last election!"

"That's very easy to answer. Obviously you're being set up. It says right here that you volunteered on your own behalf, which is something no one would have expected you to do. But due to the mandatory leave of absence you were required to take, one could assume you may have taken this assignment to earn extra brownie points. You most likely want to keep your job, especially considering the number of years that you've held your position. You should also know that Fletcher had your replica free John Burton and four other inmates. "

"What? Not D7! You're saying I let that self-proclaimed Zen Lunatic and his dumb disciples out of here? You have got to be kidding me! It's no secret to anyone I work with how I feel about that guy!"

"I know. But think about it. You'll be working at this major political function with D7 and his entourage on the loose. You released them, but they have to follow strict orders that you dictate. They must attend the Governor's speech and cause minor bloodshed."

978 had to take a few moments to take in all this information.

"Minor bloodshed?" he asked. "I don't get it. I mean, it doesn't make it sound any better. Assassinating the Governor doesn't sound minor to me."

"No one is supposed to die," answered Dr. Carlton. "But there will be someone getting hurt."

"I still don't understand this. Why would I go through all this trouble? I know I've been set up really good, but it just doesn't make any sense."

"It's all because of the recognition that Fletcher is receiving because of the efforts that have supposedly been made on his part when it comes to prison reform. Operating something called the Care Control Division sounds very positive to the general public, or anyone else for that matter. He also has his partner 609, and the last piece of the puzzle is you. There might be a lot of controversy after the chaos is all over. Just the simple fact that you're so out of place there will raise a lot of questions. You will also be held responsible for D7's escape from here. I'm sure you remember many years ago when one of his follower's broke into the house of a senator's daughter and assaulted her. The press will be able to point out the political connection right away, especially after finding out that both you and the Zen Lunatic clan were present."

978 started thinking about all the trouble that D7's followers caused in the past. He only thought about it because it was his first night back at work. Trying to remember the criminal history of as many inmates as possible helped him stay focused. The only problem was that these guys were unaware of the victim's political connection. Something else that weighed on his mind was the frightening replica 609. He started to wonder who she was modeled after. He quickly decided that he didn't want to know and kept his mind on the problem at hand.

"The victim was the daughter of a senator that D7 wasn't familiar with," said 978. "Do you really think it will be that big of a deal?"

"It's obvious that you didn't follow the case as closely as you should have," said Dr. Carlton. "That particular senator is now the Governor, and his daughter will be with him at the speech tonight. She is going to be shot at by someone you allegedly let loose. You could be charged with being involved in a conspiracy to commit an attempted political assassination!"

978 just stood there, trying to absorb all the information that was being fed to him by Dr. Carlton. He honestly didn't know what he was feeling, except for a few knots in his stomach. All he could hope for right now was not to throw up. However, in his mind it would have been easier to travel back in time and assassinate John F. Kennedy. Could it get any worse? Of course, it could always get worse. Yet he had

always believed that if you kept telling yourself it couldn't get worse it would. He knew he had a long road ahead of him. For someone who worked in law enforcement, it was hard to accept the fact that everything had been turned against him. He had always believed that the people working beside him would be allies no matter what. Now he had to face the harsh reality that the enemy truly came from within.

"The function will begin tonight at 7pm," said Dr. Carlton, in a very matter-of-fact tone. "The Governor will give his speech at 7:30, which is supposed to end at three minutes before the hour ends. Then, at exactly 8pm, his daughter will join him onstage. At that precise moment Jack Burton or one of his followers will open fire, but they have strict orders not to hit their so-called designated target."

"This is too much to take in," said 978. "I mean, what kind of deal did Fletcher give them? Besides me allegedly providing an opportunity for them to escape?"

"None, they're taking orders directly from you. Your replica to be exact, they'll think it's a conspiracy against Fletcher. If they have any doubt that will be gone when your replica says that you killed him."

"How could they possibly find out? They're long gone from here."

"The replicas have sensors in their memory banks, allowing them to instantly communicate with one another. The exact moment Fletcher's body is removed along with every ounce of physical evidence that would indicate a crime was committed all of them will be notified immediately. Your own replica will take responsibility for the vicious act and tell D7 and the rest of the gang. This will put fear into them, especially since they think the replica is you. This simple tactic is used to make them follow orders without asking any questions."

"That's okay by me. I actually see it as a positive aspect. I've always hated those guys."

978 never felt any sympathy for the so-called Zen Lunatic

or any of the weak-minded followers that got easily converted. It was nothing but manipulation from what he saw. In all honestly, he hoped that his replica would treat them worse than any prisoner of war in history. It probably wouldn't go that far, but they just might get frightened into believing otherwise. He started wondering what Will would make of all of this. The prisoner of war comparison wouldn't go over very well, especially considering the fact that no one in their right mind would show up to work expecting to be shot to death. A guy like that would never have gone along with any of this. Then again, neither would 978. It didn't matter what kind of an offer Fletcher made. All he knew for sure was that a dangerous replica of himself was on the loose and needed to do whatever he could to stop it.

"It's time to get moving," said Dr. Carlton.

"Are we taking your car?" asked 978.

"Yes."

"Don't you think it will look suspicious going through the main gate? It's still going to be a couple of hours before the night shift ends. You're aware of all the formalities. We'll be detained for God knows how long just for trying to check out of here early, especially since I'm a guard who is expected to remain on duty for the entire shift."

"We're not going that way. Our ride is in the garage."

"Are you talking about the underground garage? That place hasn't been used for years! Only the broken down vans originally used for prisoner pickups and transfers are stored down there."

"That's what everyone who works here is told. I'll bet the entire time you've worked here you had no idea that the garage was soundproof. It's actually used to store a variety of items down there. Just name it and you can find anything from artifacts, electronic parts, and bodies that should be buried in cemeteries. That includes D5, Staff Sergeant 101, Fletcher, and your friend as well."

978 couldn't respond. All these years had gone by and the worst kind of corruption was occurring directly beneath the ground he walked on. If he decided to stop caring and continue working here, he wouldn't need to travel to a grave yard to visit Will or Lutz. The next thing he knew his train of thought got interrupted when Dr. Carlton got offline and quickly stood up.

"Come on!" she said.

••• 7

978 had expected to take another long walk through some part of the prison. When Dr. Carlton made it clear that it was time to go, he thought she would lead him through a secret passage to the garage. He was right about that. However, he was very grateful they wouldn't need to travel a long distance.

Dr. Carlton started making her way toward the back area of the office. 978 followed her, passing by at least half a dozen cubicles that typically displayed small desks and computers. They were mainly used during the first shift, leaving only the desk by the front door. It was supposed to be occupied exclusively by a staff sergeant. The only exceptions would be a substitute guard if there was a meeting, a sick day, or a vacation. Staff Sergeant 101's replica was expected to appear any time now.

Once the two of them passed the cubicles they entered a dark room, Dr. Carlton then flicked a switch on the wall to turn on the lights. It was completely empty with white walls and a thin beige carpet. 978 quickly estimated it to be approximately twenty feet in both length and width. He immediately noticed a large black door with a metal handle directly ahead of them. They made their way over to it and Dr. Carlton pulled a large set of keys out of her pocket. She knew which key would unlock the door and quickly did that before pulling the door open so they could go inside. There were two switches on a panel to their left. The first one turned the interior light on and the second one turned off the lights in the other room. After shutting the door behind them, Dr. Carlton would take another device out of her pocket that resembled an old television remote control. Directly in front of them was a wall that looked like it was built from the same material as a garbage can. She pressed a button and the wall went up and disappeared instantly. If that wasn't shocking enough for 978, what he was about to see next certainly would be.

Now it was time to make the journey down below. Dr. Carlton began walking down an old spiral staircase with 978 following her from only a few steps behind. He knew this would take a while, but that didn't shake the feeling of disbelief. Spiral staircases were a rarity in this day and age yet here was traveling down one, and of all places it happened to be in a prison. Even though he started to feel a bit claustrophobic, he remained very intrigued.

Once they reached the bottom of the staircase, 978 saw an opening of what appeared to be another dark room. Granted, the lighting all the way down the stairs was brighter than any spotlight shined in his eyes before, which probably contributed to the eternally long climb down. However, the lighting in the garage wasn't much brighter than the prison corridors were throughout the night. He decided it was best to appreciate the fact that being down here would be an easier adjustment to his eyesight.

Upon entering, 978 thought the size of the place to be beyond belief. And that was just from taking the first few steps inside. He saw all kinds of clutter, a lot of which were storage boxes piled up against the walls. When he and Dr. Carlton made it to the end of the first section of the garage, they took notice of what looked like a corpse sitting up against a corner on their right. The strangest thing about it was seeing the right arm and head missing. What made it really eerie was the fact that it slightly moved back and forth, and a small amount of thick, red liquid oozed out of the arm socket and neck. Most people would be convinced it was simply blood, but 978 knew better. After everything he had been through, mainly fighting with those guards, he could easily determine what it was: another replica, more than likely a defective one. Right then and there he decided to look straight ahead and continue walking beside Dr. Carlton. He wanted to put it out of his mind. Besides, what did he really know about this stuff? Not much. And he preferred to keep it that way. Even though he knew it wasn't going to stay that way.

"So far this place is making me think of an old junkyard!" exclaimed 978, despite not wanting to say anything. "Were funeral plans made for the broken tin man back there? I'll bet there's a Frankenstein laboratory down here, too!"

"You should give yourself a lot of credit," said Dr. Carlton. "With all the stuff that's happened tonight, you have somehow managed to keep your wits about you. Your questions are valid as well. There were plans to remodel certain sections for repair and maintenance, including an area to continue building and improving replicas."

"So what happened?"

"There's already a location which is considered to be the main base of operations. It's a factory in South America where the replicas are being constructed. So far the public doesn't know anything about it. Not in the United States or the rest of the world for that matter."

978 was about to ask Dr. Carlton exactly where the base of operations was in South America, but figured that she would tell him eventually. He assumed it was probably in Brazil somewhere, but that wasn't very important right now. He was a lot more concerned about their current situation. Just

fighting these replicas and attempting to clear his name were the top priorities.

978 kept mulling over everything continuously. He figured that it wouldn't hurt to find out exactly how the operation was run. He knew even today, despite considerable improvement over the past several decades, South America would still occasionally be referred to as a shady Third World country. Perhaps there was a positive side to this, such as hiring natural born citizens for half-decent wages.

"Do they ever employ the local residents?" asked 978, sounding a little optimistic.

"No," answered Dr. Carlton. "Never."

"I think I've got it. They hire contractors straight out of Washington, right? They're all a bunch of white guys with the worst part being the fact that they can't speak a word of Portuguese or Spanish?"

"They don't even do that. There's a lot less humanity involved in this project than you can imagine. However, the picture in your mind is how it appears on the surface."

"Enlighten me."

"Remember when Fletcher talked about the advantages of cheap and temporary labor? Well, clones can come in very handy at times like this. For most of their lifespan, clones are obedient and have simple needs. But outside influences can cause them to start thinking for themselves. It sounds like a good thing, a human quality that comes from the heart. But I've witnessed it time and time again. They become more aggressive and self-destructive. This is definitely the one thing where Fletcher was right on the money. If you ever see them in action, you'll know what I mean."

978 saw this as the beginning of a long learning process. That might not be a bad thing. Perhaps it would take his mind off seeing Will get shot to death. He wasn't as concerned about killing Fletcher, because anyone who knew the whole truth wouldn't have any sympathy for the guy. However, he

knew he was facing an uphill battle trying to clear his name of murdering 101. He may even have to accept the fact that he might not ever be able to prove his innocence, especially considering that his replica helped D7, a.k.a. Jack Burton, or the Zen Lunatic out of this place along with the dumb disciples.

Upon entering the next section of the garage, 978 would take notice of the transport vans parked on each side. None of them looked much different than the standard vehicles the prison used today, but obviously they weren't being maintained. Even in the darkness anybody could tell that none of them had so much as been to a car wash. It seemed like such a waste for these vans to be left abandoned with no real purpose. Then again, the entire place was run down and had little use at this point. So why not leave them here to rot. There was only one parking space on the right that was unoccupied. 978 could see dirty tire tracks and decided to ask about it.

"I didn't think you could even start any of these vans," said 978. "But one of them was obviously taken. What's the deal?"

"The Zen clan is using it as a getaway vehicle," replied Dr. Carlton.

"Let me guess: per orders of my replica, right?

"You got it."

"At least those guys think they're taking orders from the real me. It's not what I had in mind, but it beats nothing. You don't need to remind me about their plans to sabotage the Governor's gathering. Do you have any idea where they might be hiding out until then?"

"No, the worst part is the fact that using a transport van is the perfect decoy. Anyone who sees it on the highway will assume they are guards on route to pick up a transfer from another prison. Your replica probably found extra uniforms for them to use, which means that no one will look twice."

"Not to mention the fact that they're traveling down the

road in the middle of the night, making it too dark for anyone else to get a good look at them."

"True. But there is a chance I might be able to find out where they are, especially since they were more than likely instructed by you, meaning your replica, to meet up at a rendezvous point."

"At the very least, it's a good start."

Regardless of 978's last response, despite sounding very positive, the conversation came to another grinding halt. This wasn't very surprising, especially since everything Dr. Carlton said would always come across very informative. It didn't even bother him when she referred to both him and the replica as one and the same. He came face to face with it when 101 got killed, yet still couldn't accurately describe to anyone how that felt. He also knew she felt bad about what she had just said, the look in her eyes was all the proof he needed. Regardless, he wasn't going to call her on it.

They continued to walk through the garage section by section. The two of them may have been moving at a decent pace, but for 978 it felt like an eternity. He knew that a lot of this was due to the fact that all of this was too much to absorb. Everything he was experiencing weren't your normal everyday occurrences. He tried to appreciate the fact that Dr. Carlton was with him remaining quiet and calm, most likely since she knew what had been going on for some time now.

As they reached the middle of the next section 978 briefly glanced to the light and something caught his eye. He thought he saw something in the very last window of one of the old buses that needed to be checked out. It looked like a head was leaning against the glass with some blood staining it, making him assume it was most likely a corpse.

"Check that out," said 978, in a quiet tone.

"What?" asked Dr. Carlton.

He pointed his finger directly at it, seconds after that he took out his flashlight and shined it toward the window.

"I see it," she responded.

"Is it what I think it is?" he asked.

"Probably," she said. "But I think we've seen enough."

"I want to take a closer look."

"That's a bad idea."

"It will only take a minute."

"I really think we should get out of here."

978 walked slowly toward the old bus. He made his way toward the door which was already open. His instincts told him to have the shotgun ready, so he did. He climbed the stairs, turned left, and looked straight to the back of the vehicle. With his left hand, he aimed the flashlight, and his right hand held the weapon. He took a few short steps, than shined the flashlight on what he had originally observed from the outside. The exact moment he set his eyes on the head he couldn't believe what he saw. It was his old friend.

"Oh my God!" exclaimed 978.

Before the guard could say another word he had another surprise. A growling sound occurred with a body rising up from a seat just slightly ahead of him on the right. He couldn't believe it. This thing with very pale skin and wide eyes stood up and stared right at him. It slowly made its way toward the aisle of the bus and moved toward him. As he began to take a step backwards the thing opened its mouth and made that awful sound again. There was no way to describe it. Growling would just be the beginning, hissing was also a part of it, but there was something else about it that sounded like it wasn't from earth.

978 couldn't wait a second longer. He aimed the shotgun right at the thing's chest and fired several times. At first the pale-skinned creature screamed out even louder than before, making him believe that all he did was aggravate it more. But a few seconds later it started shaking, almost like it was having convulsions. After that it raised its arms up and blood poured out of the eyes, ears, nostrils, and mouth. He was

getting ready to shoot it again until it let out one last scream and fell to the floor.

This was nothing like what the guard had seen before, but there was no time to think about it. He started to hear more sounds similar to what that thing made. It wasn't as loud but just as distinctive. It came from the left side of the bus about three seats away from where he was standing. Of course it turned out to be another one of those creatures he had just shot. It started to slowly rise up, but this thing didn't have a chance. 978 wouldn't even wait for it to stand up straight. He put a bullet into the left shoulder, which automatically threw it off balance. After that he shot the thing in the head before it disappeared behind the seat again.

At this point 978 didn't want to wait around for more of these things to shoot. He looked at Will for the last time, not that he really wanted to. It was just for confirmation. He quickly turned around and made his way to the door. As he rushed down the steps Dr. Carlton was right outside waiting for him. She had a gun drawn as well, so obviously she knew something about what happened. The moment he reached the bottom and stood in front of her she received an earful.

"WHAT THE HELL WERE THOSE THINGS?!" he shouted.

"Let's just get out of here," said Dr. Carlton, trying to stay calm.

"Do you know whose body was in there?! Will, for God's sake! Is that the best that can be done?! Just leave him with all of those monsters in there?!"

"I think we should go."

"That's easy for you to say! You weren't in there fighting off those abominations or whatever they were!"

978 and Dr. Carlton stood silent for a minute. He knew it was a good idea to try and calm down. But it wasn't long before something would grab his attention again. A large thumping sound came from inside the bus, but he wasn't about to go back in there a second time. The two of them

slowly made there way over to the middle section on the outside of the vehicle, which was near the same area where he had shot the second creature. They both took a few steps backward so one of them could shine a flashlight through the concrete wall. But before either one of them had the chance to do that the same creature 978 just shot in the shoulder and head burst its upper body right through the window. The impact was so strong it even tore pieces of the bus off as well, almost like a wrecking ball from a crane smashing through a concrete window. The scream the creature made was louder than what was heard the first time. However, 978 and Dr. Carlton wasted no time taking out their guns and firing several shots. The creature simply keeled over and fell out of the bus. Amazingly, its head hit the pavement first before eventually landing on its back, allowing the body to lay there facing up. It didn't move, which led them to assume that they'd finished the job. But they weren't about to take any chances. Dr. Carlton approached it first and lightly kicked it with the foot.

"It's actually dead this time, right?" asked 978.

"Yeah," answered Dr. Carlton. "But sometimes these things don't go down right away."

"I get it. The other one I shot in the chest multiple times."

"That what you have to do."

978 walked up next to Dr. Carlton and looked down at the creature. It reminded him somewhat of a vampire he saw from an old 1920's horror movie. The ears on it still looked human, but there wasn't much hair left on the head. The eyes remained wide open, and so did the mouth with all of the teeth showing. He was convinced the thing didn't die smiling, or smirking for that matter. He couldn't remember the name of that movie for the life of him. He was pretty sure it was silent. Almost all of those pictures were back then. Big deal, it was probably better that he didn't.

"Do you think there are more of these down here?" asked 978.

"I don't know," answered Dr. Carlton. "Let's not wait around to find out."

"These things don't get to the beach very often, do they?"

"Not really, no."

Despite the humor, neither one of them were about to get any laughs in. Another scream came from one of those pale-skinned creatures. This time it came from their left side about ten feet away. They turned to see the thing standing up straight and feasting its eyes on them, but it would only take a few steps forward when 978 and Dr. Carlton fired several shots in the chest area. Like the first creature he shot, it raised its arms in the air and let out the loudest scream possible before falling backwards and dying.

978 and Dr. Carlton would not take the time to inspect the corpse. They were pretty sure the job was done right this time, which lead them both to instinctively turn around and get the hell out of there. Neither of them wanted to talk about it, much less come face to face with another one of those things. However, at this point the guard was convinced he was ready for almost anything. He also remembered to keep in mind that the good doctor would fill him in with all the gory details eventually. All he had to do was ask. Not that he was in any hurry to.

The next section of the garage that they stepped into would stop the guard in his tracks. 978 eyes focused on something that truly excited and intrigued him. An immediate description would define it as a first class ticket out of this hellhole. It was an all black vehicle similar to one he had seen while watching an auto racing program recently. He couldn't imagine why it was left in a place like this. The name of the model had slipped his mind, but that didn't matter. Dr. Carlton would give him all the details.

"This is the 2062 SPY 6 vehicle from the Chandler series," she stated. "It can go from zero to two-hundred miles in fifteen seconds. There were some special modifications done in order to prevent people from seeing inside, which is an option you can program in on your own. The outside is bulletproof from all rifles and shotguns designed in the past decade. You'll find two of each of those weapons in the backseat, and there's plenty of ammunition included."

"I'm surprised the car itself doesn't have built-in weapons," said 978.

"It does, but they aren't loaded. We should do that, but there isn't enough time."

Dr. Carlton took out her television remote control look-alike gadget again, pressed three buttons which produced a beeping sound that was barely audible. The car started, the lights came on, and the doors opened.

"I'll drive," she said.

"Are you sure?" asked 978.

"Trust me, you need someone to navigate if you've never drove this before. Also, grab one of the guns out of the backseat before you get in."

He wasn't about to question her, so he quickly made his way over to the passenger door. He moved the seat forward and grabbed the shotgun that was immediately within reach. He was about to check to see if the weapon was loaded when he saw a group of guards running toward them ready to fire.

"Stop those two!" shouted a guard. "Shoot to kill!"

Without hesitating, 978 aimed the shotgun and fired at the guard that was closest to him. Luckily, the weapon was already loaded and hit the target twice in the upper chest, causing the subject to fall forward face first onto the pavement. He wasted no time shooting another one. None of the other guards were able to get many shots in, proving that neither he nor Dr. Carlton would wind up getting hurt themselves. She also got a rifle out of the backseat of the car and fired at these would-be assassins. Within seconds, four of these guards had been killed. Or at least they hoped so.

"Get in!" shouted Dr. Carlton.

978 did so almost instantaneously. However, he quickly realized that Dr. Carlton shifted the car in reverse. He looked back and saw the same guards they had just shot were on their feet again. She hit the gas pedal and backed up as fast as she could and pressed a switch that opened both windows.

"Get your gun ready," she said.

After giving him that order she backed up far enough to run over two of the guards. One had managed to get out of the way and ran over to the passenger side of the vehicle only to get greeted by several shots fired by the shotgun 978 was using. The guard Dr. Carlton missed completely marched over to the driver's side and got shot by the rifle she was now making good use out of. Unfortunately, she got surprised by two more guards that came out of nowhere. Thankfully, 978 timed it just right by standing up and forcing the upper part of his body out of the passenger window and fired several shots at them. All of which hit the chest and facial areas. Within seconds, they all dropped to the pavement again. He sat back down properly in the passenger seat and was ready to go.

"Let's get out of here," he said. "I don't want to wait around to see if those things get back up again."

"Me neither," said Dr. Carlton.

"Do you think that will happen?"

"From all the experiences I've had with the replicas so far, I'm sure it will definitely happen."

8 •••

When Dr. Carlton pushed the gas pedal to the floor in the SPY 6 978 estimated that they reached the exit of the garage within sixty seconds. He really hadn't paid much attention to his surroundings after the run-in with those creatures and the shootout with those guards. As expected, he couldn't to take his mind off discovering Will's body in the back of that bus. That might be normal, but in this case it will make it a lot harder to face what he was up against.

They couldn't have been more than twenty feet from the exit as the doors opened on both sides faster than the blink of an eye. 978 couldn't believe that he actually was able to catch a glimpse of the doors closing when he checked the rearview mirror. It didn't take very long for them to make their way down a dark and deserted two-lane paved road and up a short but steep ramp onto the highway. Dr. Carlton slowed down a bit, but not much. 978 thought this was kind of neat. It reminded him of the time when his father sat him down to watch the old reruns of the 1960's Batman television series starring Adam West and Burt Ward. This was especially the case when he remembered the Dynamic Duo receiving a call from Commissioner Gordon via the Batphone to report which arch enemy was on the loose that week. The coolest part, however, was when The Caped Crusader and Robin got into the Batmobile and zoomed out of the Batcave seconds later onto the main road and make their trek into Gotham City. Of course he couldn't forget the sign those guys passed by every time indicating their destination was only fifteen miles away. This was a great childhood memory. Unfortunately, that didn't make him feel like a real superhero.

The two of them had only traveled maybe a couple of miles down the highway. It would still be a while before the sun came up. For 978, that was perfectly fine. There were very few other vehicles on the road, but it wouldn't be long before every single lane got backed up by commuters living in the nine to five world of work. Just thinking about it made the guard appreciate being employed during the off hours even more. He never encountered a lot of traffic en route to the prison in the nine years of performing late night duties. The only exceptions would have been due to road construction or a major accident, like the tractor-trailer truck that tipped over three years ago. He remembered being stuck in traffic forty-five minutes, but since it was out of his control it couldn't count against him at work. The weekly paycheck was still the same amount. The only time he felt the daily grind was driving home from work after 8am, but even by then most of the traffic had decreased significantly. Besides, he didn't think it could be any worse than what happened during the night. Unfortunately, he started getting a sneaking suspicion all of that stuff was now behind him.

Dr. Carlton stayed occupied by keeping her eyes on the road. She made use of her right hand by operating the navicomputer. 978 hadn't been paying much attention to what she was doing, probably from the surprise of cruising along with this attractive doctor in the SPY 6. That was alright by him, especially considering everything that had occurred up to this point. He hadn't even asked her where they were going.

Now was obviously a good time.

"Where are we headed?" asked 978.

"My office," replied Dr. Carlton. "We should be there in another ten minutes."

"Your office?"

"That's what I said. Like a lot of doctors, I have my place for my own private practice. We won't be long, there's something I have to do there. The office is closed until the end of next week. I'm having a new alarm system installed, plus all my patients think I'm on my vacation."

"Some vacation so far, if they only knew the real truth."

"No kidding, maybe I should start to accept some clones and replicas as patients. I've had a lot of practice with them already, but one problem is that an entirely new billing system would have to be created. I don't know what kind of insurance they would carry."

978 glanced over at Dr. Carlton while she was talking and noticed her facial expressions didn't change much at all. She

remained very focused and serious despite the fact that the last thing she said was meant to be humorous. The two of them shared an important bond, they were human. That might not sound like a big deal to the world at large, but right now no one was going through the same ordeal that they were. At least not in this part of the world, anyway. Most people would not be able to grasp what was happening. It was hard to expect anyone to understand, just like Will having no idea what he had stumbled onto right up until the very moment he got shot. 978 didn't even want to start thinking about the construction of the replicas down in South America.

Dr. Carlton couldn't stop herself from thinking back to when she first became familiar with the Chandler series of vehicles. It was many years ago, 2055 to be exact. The SPY 4 prototype had just been introduced and she was receiving her first assignment from the government and certain people, one being Fletcher later on, would be very impressed with both her medical and technical background. One man she was only allowed to know as Lt. Collins said her credentials were so good that it qualified as a resume in and of itself. She found this surprising, especially since she had no experience in law enforcement or the military. However, she was intrigued by the challenge and signed on immediately. It wouldn't take long to figure out that it was a huge mistake. The more involved she got in these government assignments the more corrupt and unpleasant they became.

Luckily, there was one exception. Dr. Carlton had no regrets working with her first partner. His name was Greg Nelson, and he had just been released from federal prison after serving three years. An attorney who took his case for free was able to prove beyond a reasonable doubt that there was no sufficient evidence leading to his conviction. Nelson had been employed as a contract mechanic in the auto-racing industry for a number of years. His older brother Tom was a professional driver who gained worldwide media attention after being charged with possession of narcotics and smuggling firearms, but got released on $250,000 bail before vanishing altogether. The F.B.I. made every attempt they could to track down the fugitive, who had been frequently spotted in desert areas throughout Arizona, Texas, and New Mexico. The once nationally loved Tom Nelson had gotten involved in illegal drag-racing using dangerous weapons and hardcore drugs like cocaine and methamphetamines. Many of the places used for these deadly activities were military zones at some point in history, and had been condemned for years. There was no way to determine how hazardous any of these locations were due to testing all kinds of chemical weapons over the past several decades. Anybody who took up residence in these spots for long periods of time suffered severely. Those whose children were born there almost immediately developed brain damage or physical deformities. It was difficult to even think about everything that occurred out there.

Dr. Carlton was introduced to Greg Nelson through Lt. Collins. He had just been released from prison after his conviction was overturned. She was told that his attorney was able to prove that an associate of Tom Nelson named Gus Gardner made a false confession. Several months after the famous race-car driver had made bail and skipped town, the shady Gus Gardner had been arrested and charged as an accomplice. The lowlife was able to get a reduced sentence by presenting false evidence which supposedly proved that Greg was involved. Gardner was nothing more than a paper pusher whose best skill was falsifying records in order to pocket extra money or grease the palms of guys like Tom, who had the best connections when it came to drugs and weapons. Of course Gus couldn't forget to put aside a few bucks for a crack habit. Once Greg got released, he agreed to track down his brother thanks to a very generous amount of help from the government. This was how Dr. Carlton became involved. With medical school, internships, and other experiences she had very advanced skills treating patients who had been exposed to very dangerous amounts of radiation and all kinds of different chemicals. Lt. Collins was convinced she would be of great use to Greg working in the areas they were headed to. This was when she had her first introduction to the SPY 4 vehicle which gave her hands-on training. She has worked with these cars ever since.

The rest is history.

At this point, however, history was not very appealing to Dr. Carlton. She had recently learned that Greg Nelson had passed away last month after suffering from a long-term illness. He was just forty-seven years old, which was the only information she had so far. The worst part was the fact that she had had very little contact with him after completing the assignment. Until tonight he was the best partner she ever worked with, the only difference now being that she and 978 were partners by choice. She started remembering the loud sounds the drag cars made in the races out in the desert, which got interrupted by the sound of a low, rumbling engine directly behind them. A pair of very bright headlights turned on and this monster-sized vehicle was right on their tail.

Both Dr. Carlton and 978 knew exactly what it was: a prisoner transport van.

"No!!!" snapped 978. "Is that the Zen clan?!"

"It's the replicas!" exclaimed Dr. Carlton. "They probably started to follow us after we left!"

"How is that possible?!"

"They must have started tracking us with their neural networks being connected to all the computer systems! I didn't think they would come after us until the end of the shift!"

Before Dr. Carlton had a chance to put the gas petal to the floor, the van rammed them. The entire car shook, making the two of them feel like they were smack dab in the middle of an earthquake. 978 only had experience with transport vehicles during this first year as a guard. It was state-required orientation, but that never gave him any indication as to how powerful these things were.

He just found out the hard way.

The SPY 6 and the transport van were in the middle lane. Dr. Carlton refocused and picked up speed, then typing more information into the navicomputer before maneuvering into the right lane.

"What are you doing?" asked 978.

"Programming the system for automatic cruise control," answered Dr. Carlton. "The van will soon reach its top speed of 120 miles per hour. It will take a minute to set this to stay at 115 miles per hour."

"Why only 115? You said it can reach its top speed of 200 miles per hour in fifteen seconds!"

"Do you want to run away from the problem or get rid of it? We can use the guns to put them out of commission and keep dodging them until we do. I got out of the middle lane so we can stay ahead of them. We do not want that van to ram us off the road!"

Dr. Carlton steered the SPY 6 vehicle steadily upon entering the right lane. She didn't like the idea of playing cat and mouse with the transport van, but felt there was no other option. She quickly reached the speed of 115 miles an hour. This was just enough to stay ahead of those replicas that would stop at nothing to catch them and kill them. 978 immediately turned around to grab the rifle in the backseat, checked to make sure it was fully loaded, and turned off the safety switch. He stuck his head and the upper part of his body out of the passenger window and aimed the rifle at the windshield on the driver's side of the van. The bullets didn't so much as create a scratch on the service, but there was no time to think about that. Within seconds both vehicles were cruising alongside each other at incredibly high speeds, then the driver's door of the van quickly slid open. A replica dressed in a guard's uniform stood at the bottom step and jumped directly at him. 978 pointed the rifle at the replica's face and opened fire, shooting several times right above the tip of the nose. The impact shattered the eye shields and a portion of the upper right side of the helmet. The replica's facial structure slowly burned away, convincing him to shoot it one more time, causing it to fall face forward onto the highway. A brief glance would have shown the replica rolling over several times, but not enough time to see if it got back up, thanks to the SPY 6 cruise control allowing them to move at almost twice the actual speed limit!

After the replica hit the pavement like typical road kill, Dr. Carlton checked the rearview mirror and watched the van come to a complete stop. When 978 got his upper body back inside the vehicle she slowed it down and watched the van back up a short distance. Eventually it would stop and park sideways, covering both the middle and inside lanes. The replica that 978 shot was blocked from their vision, causing Dr. Carlton to stop and figure out what was happening. She turned the wheel to the right and pulled into the breakdown lane, shifted into park, and left the vehicle idling. Both of them opened the doors, stepped out, and looked back at the transport van which was approximately two hundred feet away. They took a few steps forward then moved closer to one another before standing behind the SPY 6. 978 glanced to his right and noticed Dr. Carlton using a small pair of binoculars.

"See anything?" he asked.

"Nothing," she responded. "My guess is they're removing all traces of the replica, regardless if it's still functioning or not."

"It won't be long before they start chasing us again."

"You got that right. Let's get moving. We don't have very far to go, so keep in mind that we have a very good chance of putting them out of commission completely."

"That's fine with me."

The two of them got back into the SPY 6 and drove off into the night. Dr. Carlton would only cruise slightly over the speed limit. She knew it wouldn't take long for the replicas to catch up to them. But like she had said earlier, it was better to diffuse the situation sooner instead of later. She started to feel a lot more sympathy for 978. This must have been the longest and most traumatic night of his life.

Dr. Carlton was beginning to wind down a little. It was a lot easier to focus on driving while relaxed, or as much as she could allow herself to be under the circumstances. Unfortunately, any sense of relief she might have felt vanished instantly. She checked the rearview mirror and saw bright headlights appear. The closer they got it was obvious who it was. This time the replicas were not about to make any effort to sneak up on them unexpectedly. They meant business, and obviously would not be considering the element of surprise.

"Our friends our back," said Dr. Carlton.

"So what do we do now?" asked 978.

"We put Plan A into effect."

"What we did before wasn't Plan A?!"

"No. I was acting on impulse. That wasn't any kind of plan. Now it's time for a real strategy."

"Which is?"

"I'll get into the right lane and put the car on automatic pilot. All the information I have uploaded into the navicomputer will keep us on the right course and we can fight both of the remaining replicas at the same time. Two against two should work better in our favor."

"Come on! They have twice the strength that we do and operate at speeds ten times faster than us!"

"Tell me something I don't already know! Remember what Fletcher told us, these models are still being perfected. You already put one of them out of commission, even if it's only temporary. The chances of disabling these other two replicas are just as good."

After everything Dr. Carlton just said, it wasn't helping 978 feel any more prepared, at least not mentally. Mentioning Fletcher's name was something he wished she hadn't done. The man was dead thanks to him, and he wasn't proud of the fact that he killed a man in cold blood. He actually felt a lot more resentment instead of guilt. It was bad enough that the guy was in charge of this sick operation, the worse part of it was being called the Care Control Division.

978 tried to keep in mind that the replica he shot between the eyes was not Steve Walsh. The real Steve Walsh was somebody who had a family and friends, but he didn't want to think about that. He could only begin to imagine what Fletcher told the toy soldiers to do with the poor guy's corpse. It still hadn't sunk in that his best friend was also dead as a result of this conspiracy. Then again, maybe it never will. Nobody really wants to believe that their best friend will be shot to death right in front of them, which could easily explain why opening fire on Fletcher wasn't eating away at him.

"Everything is ready," said Dr. Carlton. "It will take a minute for the car to stay at the programmed speed requested for auto pilot. Then we'll be able to stick our heads out the windows and start firing, and hopefully cause a little damage."

"It not just our heads that need to stick out!" said 978.

"You know what I mean!"

At this point 978 decided he was simply going to do what Dr. Carlton said without asking any further questions. Besides, she was the one who had the expertise with the SPY 6 vehicle and also knew the direction to go. Both of them prepared their guns, stood up off the seats, then turned around and leaned halfway outside the windows. He honestly couldn't fathom what she was thinking, but the impact of the wind was shocking. It didn't matter that his back was turned. But he knew that one thing was definite: this wasn't some rollercoaster ride at an amusement park.

The transport van caught up to them, and was approximately fifteen to twenty feet away. The distance slightly fluctuated while it continued to cruise in the middle lane. 978 and Dr. Carlton could easily see the two remaining replicas, one behind the wheel with the other in the passenger seat. They could be seen thanks to the vehicle's interior light being left on. Both of the replicas were wearing the standard guard uniforms and had their helmets on with the eye shields down. With the exception of seeing the driver's hands move on the steering wheel and the passenger turning his head to observe the intended targets, almost anyone could be convinced that these man-made soldiers looked like department store mannequins. 978 and Dr. Carlton were well prepared for this battle, but there was no way of knowing what might happen next. Life would be a lot easier if these things were only used for store security.

978 saw the replica sitting in the passenger seat begin to stand up. It started walking down the vehicle's sidesteps and slid open the door. It stuck the upper half of its body outside and made no attempt to hold on to anything. Then 978 and Dr. Carlton saw it take a gun out of a holster with its right hand faster than any outlaw in a western. Shots were fired which either hit the SPY 6's rear window or barely missed the two of them. Since the bullets didn't break the glass, there was a small feeling of protection. 978 had no recollection of Dr. Carlton mentioning the car being bulletproof, but liked the fact that it seemed to be the case.

Right now the two of them had to concentrate on their primary goal, which was to disable the van and its occupants. The simple thought of destroying those replicas was very appealing to 978. He aimed the rifle at the right front tire, hoping to cause the vehicle to tip over sideways. He shot twice, both times barely missing the intended target and hitting the pavement. There was a small explosion, making the van slow down and hit a brand new pothole created as a direct result of his actions. This would only last for a moment, which was disappointing. In recent years, a lot more effort had been made to fix the roads in Massachusetts. He didn't like the fact that all the work done to make it possible could be brought back to square one, thanks to him.

It didn't take long for the replicas to regain speed and catch up again. Now it was Dr. Carlton's turn to make an attempt, unaware that it would take a minute for 978 to figure out that she had thrown a small grenade the size of the palm of a hand. Like him, she was aiming directly at the passenger's side of the van. She threw another one of these grenades, but still missed the intended target. It caused minor damage, thanks in part to the explosion it created. Unfortunately, it didn't take her very long to figure out that the damage wasn't enough to stop anything or even slow things down. Almost instantly, the replica fired shots back. The bullets barely missed, either hitting the roof of the car or zipping past her or 978 by only a few inches. She took a couple of seconds to pull out another grenade and throw it at the replica as quickly as possible. But this time something unusual happened: it hit the target in the face and exploded on impact. The timing couldn't have been any better as the upper part of the replica's body caught fire, then fell out onto the road and got run over by the van's rear tire. She probably didn't permanently disable the thing, but there was little chance of it going anywhere for a while.

The last replica continued driving the van without being distracted. 978 and Dr. Carlton weren't sure what to expect next, but decided that their best bet was to keep shooting. Without consulting each other, they both thought the best thing to do was disable the vehicle. This time Dr. Carlton decided that the shotgun would be of better use to her. She got it out as fast and aimed for the front tire on the driver's side. While attempting to hit the intended target 978 shot repeatedly at the windshield, which was slowly beginning to crack on the surface with each bullet that hit it. But no immediate results came to fruition, despite being in the middle of a high speed shootout. It only got worse when the replica followed suit by taking out its own weapon and firing several shots. Now the SPY 6 had a windshield that was completely shattered, and the replica pulled into the right lane only a few feet behind it. At this point all of the broken glass had spread out onto the rear hatch which allowed small pieces of it to gradually fall off and land on the pavement, resulting in the possibility of some commuters receiving flat tires on their way to work tomorrow morning. Nevertheless, Dr. Carlton managed to shoot out the van's left front tire. Unfortunately, the last shot that the replica fired would hit its intended target: 978. The bullet penetrated the top of his right shoulder, causing him to fall back and drop his rifle, with his hands barely missing the pavement with the car still cruising at an insanely high speed. Just a few seconds after that Dr. Carlton aimed at the replica and fired one last time. The bullet hit the thing directly in the face on the right side of the eye shields, hopefully causing some serious vision damage. The replica turned the steering wheel all the way to the right before losing all control of the vehicle. Miraculously it did not tip over. However, within seconds it went off the road into a ditch.

Dr. Carlton immediately got all the way back into the car then quickly programmed it to slow down and come to a complete stop. She pulled into the breakdown lane and helped 978 get back inside then placed his left hand on his right shoulder in order to put pressure on the wound. She put the car in reverse and backed up to the area where the van had taken a plunge. In a matter of seconds she reached the designated spot before opening the door and walking a short ways further, eventually reaching the grass leading to the ditch area. She looked down to observe whatever damage was done to the van, just to see it explode within moments after laying eyes on it. The main concern she had now was not being able to see the replica. The darkness outside accompanied by the flames made it impossible to determine whether or not her intended target got destroyed in the crash.

At this point she decided she had seen enough and ran back to the car to find 978 standing outside the passenger door keeping pressure on the gunshot wound. He was a little bit disoriented, prompting her to take off her lab coat and give it to him, assuming he would know what to do.

"You'll be alright," she said.

She stood beside him and placed his left arm around her. She helped him get back inside the car by slowly helping him sit back down on the seat again, then shut the passenger door and ran around front and getting into the driver's seat.

"Are they toast?" asked 978.

"I hope so," she answered.

Dr. Carlton would rather have been able to give the wounded former guard a more concrete answer, but that would have been so far from the real truth. However, the situation was becoming a lot more optimistic. Then again, anyone witnessing that van explode would reassure almost anyone that they were ahead of the game. The real problem was the fact that no one had any idea how much damage these replicas could actually withstand. It was frightening enough to know that the ones they fought with were mere prototypes, and the newer models currently being built could be far more dangerous. Whatever the case might be, it remained to be seen. Right now, however, all Dr. Carlton cared about was getting to her office.

She had to help 978.

9 •••

Dr. Carlton started up the SPY 6 again. She put her foot on the petal and pulled out onto the highway, quickly leaving the scene of a so-called accident. The laws against doing that had been in the books for a number of decades, but in recent years they became a lot stricter. Naturally, that was especially the case if you worked in law enforcement. Of course this was an exception, and there was no time to explain it to anyone. If she or 978 reported this it would quickly be covered up and the both of them would be placed into protective custody. Granted, it was highly unlikely that they would be brought up on charges. There was a high probability of being permanently detained by a bunch of replicas that wouldn't let them out of their sight.

The here and now dictated that the two of them needed to get as far away as humanly possible. At the present moment the law didn't apply to either 978 or Dr. Carlton. However, they both knew that there would be dire consequences for their actions. No one had to inform Dr. Carlton how easy it was to have her credentials get flushed down the toilet. The Care Control Division, with or without Fletcher, made it clear from day one that it wouldn't be difficult to plant a story in the press which would declare a malpractice suit against her. The media would then broadcast the news worldwide in a matter of minutes, especially considering how well known the source had become.

Dr. Carlton was so preoccupied with her thoughts that she had barely noticed the sign for the next exit, which was the one she needed to take in order to get to her office. Only a couple of minutes had passed since she and 978 had left the scene of the so-called accident, but it seemed like an eternity. Then again, anyone who had to contemplate all of the recent activity they had gone through would probably not be giving any thought to looking at their watch. At this point it was all about soldiering on. The key was survival, an instinct that had quickly kicked in for both of them. But 978's wounds had to mend in order to move forward.

Only another minute or two had passed before reaching the next exit, which meant they would be at her office in no time. Immediately after Dr. Carlton turned off the highway and reached the end of the ramp she put on the directional and went to the right. The location of her office was only about a third of a mile up on the left hand side, but she didn't to take any chances by pulling into the front parking lot in a fancy car. She slowed down the closer she got and glanced over to look into the double-glass doors. The lights were on and Ryan was sitting at the front desk posing as a security guard. This was a good sign, because it meant that everything was in place. Ryan was simply helping her out until a new alarm system could be installed.

For Dr. Carlton and 978, the best decision would be to park the car at a place that was a little further up the road. As they made their way past her office, only a minute had passed before they settled on a parking lot at a small shopping center. A restaurant located near the front entrance was already open despite the fact that it was still dark outside. When she pulled she made a point of being as far away from that place as possible. She chose a space all the way down on the left end near the main road, knowing it would attract a lot of unwanted attention. It wouldn't take long for the SPY 6 to be traced back to the government, but it would take a lot longer to trace the vehicle back to them. This would allow her plenty of time to treat 978's wound and figure out what to do next. She also knew that someone like Ryan would do anything to help, regardless of the circumstances.

978 wanted to make every attempt possible to keep moving despite sustaining a serious injury, but he started

going into shock. Dr. Carlton opened the door to get out, and he did the same. He had to use his left hand while doing that, but continued to lose a lot more blood as every moment passed by. Dr. Carlton used the same device to lock the doors and set the alarm. It would take an entire wrecking crew to break into the SPY 6, which was good considering that vehicle stood out. She put the device back in her lab coat and removed her belt in order to tie all the guns together. Not exactly the safest technique, but it would make it far easier to carry all these weapons with one arm. Since 978 had such a dire need of emergency treatment she needed to have her other hand free in order to help him.

Dr. Carlton quickly made her way around the front of the vehicle to the passenger side to assist 978. Her lab coat was draped over his right shoulder, and she didn't check to see if he had tied one of the sleeves on the wound. It would be alright as long as it stayed on and less blood was being lost. She placed his left arm around her neck and the two of them started walking toward the right side of the shopping center. For a brief period of time they traveled on a paved walkway before stepping onto a grass area next to a building of some department store. Neither of them took notice of the actual name, not that there was any reason to. By the time they made it out back they set foot onto another paved area where a tractor-trailer truck was parked at the loading dock located right behind the restaurant. The engine was running and the lights were left on, and Dr. Carlton could barely see two men at the rear entrance talking. It was probably an early morning delivery, but the only thing that she worried about was not being seen by them, or anyone else for that matter.

Hope quickly became a reality. Dr. Carlton and 978 would set foot on another patch of grass which brought them to a dirt path leading up to a small wooded area. Within a matter of seconds the two of them stepped onto another paved area, this time a bicycle path, which lead them directly behind her office. Dr. Carlton started slumping to the left while 978 kept his arm around her neck. She did this thinking it might help him stay balanced, and the effort was proven to be successful as far as she could tell. As they began the trek to her office she only hoped that there would be no run-ins with anyone.

It was still dark outside. The best scenario for Dr. Carlton and 978 would be not to encounter so much as one jogger. She was desperately hoping that would be the case because there was no need for an innocent bystander to get involved, even if the person wanted to help. So far this particular bicycle path had lighted lampposts every one hundred feet or so, but was of little help considering it seemed dimmer than the lighting inside the prison during the night shift. The local police probably didn't want anyone down there at this hour, or at least that would seem like the most logical explanation. The easiest part for them, however, was that the path was as straight as an arrow. After a short distance 978 removed his arm from her neck.

"I think I'll be alright for now," he said.

"Okay," said Dr. Carlton. "But don't push yourself too much."

"It's not that far from here, is it?"

"No."

Despite sounding coherent and walking upright, 978 was still feeling very disoriented. Be he marched forward without complaining, hoping to reach their destination in no time. However, less than a minute would go by before something lying in the grass on the right that caught their eye, almost forcing them to stop immediately. Even with the dark skies still present, the large animal carcass laid before them as clear as day. It was lying on its right side with large chunks of fur and flesh missing, leaving 978 and Dr. Carlton to come up with their own conclusions.

"What is that?" asked 978, barely above a whisper.

"My God," said Dr. Carlton, almost stunned.

"It looks like a dog, or a wolf maybe. What do you think happened?"

"Someone got hungry, or very angry."

"But this has no predators around here, why would this be here?"

Dr. Carlton took a small flashlight out of her lab coat to examine the carcass more closely. She was unable to immediately determine whether the poor creature had been partially eaten or mutilated. She also had to consider the fact that time was of the essence, and 978 was the one that was still alive and had serious wounds which desperately needed to be taken care of. She wasn't giving the guy enough credit. He was standing still and in a lot of pain, yet he remained curious about this situation with the dead animal and did not complain the entire time.

When Dr. Carlton lifted her head to look up she moved the flashlight in order to focus where her eyes were looking. It was just a reflex which required no thought, but she didn't know if that was good or bad. What she saw would force her to investigate, even if there was no connection to the current scenario that she and 978 were in right now.

Dr. Carlton saw something sticking out from behind some bushes that neither she nor 978 needed to see, the lower part of another human body. The exact specifics would be legs and feet, which were covered by blue jeans and white sneakers. It was off the paved path, ten yards away from them at the most. Not a single word would be spoken by either of them. They just simultaneously began walking toward this corpse. At this point there needed to be a closer inspection. After everything the two of them had been through, it was almost mandatory. This situation probably had nothing to do with the conspiracy involving the replicas. Still, they both knew that anything was possible. Dr. Carlton and 978 were only a few steps away from the bushes that hid the rest of the body, but the brief period of time that passed to reach their destination felt like an eternity. All the other deaths they faced that night had to do with Fletcher's scheme, but what lied before them would offer very few clues, if any. No animals were supposed to be harmed in this conspiracy. In fact, animals weren't supposed to be involved at all. Then again, even Dr. Carlton knew she wasn't going to be kept updated on every detail. It didn't matter if she fully supported the LEO1 concept. Everyone participating in this deadly experiment was expected to follow orders without asking any questions whatsoever. Information related to the LEO1 protocol was only given out on a need to know basis.

A ruffling sound came from a bush on the right. Without warning, a tall thin figure jumped up and surprised them. This person wore very dark clothing and had an extremely pale complexion. He had very little hair and displayed a wide-eyed stare. A deep sounding scream would occur the minute he opened his mouth right before pushing Dr. Carlton to the ground, causing one of the firearms to go off immediately upon impact. The distraction it created for this maniac gave 978 a few seconds to take action. The former guard knew both arms were of no use thanks to the bullet wound, so a karate kick using the right leg would be more than suitable. By doing this the attacker was forced to take several steps back before falling over the bush he had jumped out of. Even though it had happened so fast Dr. Carlton was still able to look up and witness the whole incident. She was convinced that 609 had a worthy adversary in a human best known to the system as 978.

Luckily, this ambush wouldn't keep Dr. Carlton down long. In seconds she got back on her feet and pointed the rifle at the attacker, which was the one that fired off a shot when she hit the ground. The perpetrator got up at the same time she did. All it took was one bullet in the chest to fall again. This time he wouldn't be getting up.

She and 978 stepped forward to inspect the damage. All that remained was a large bloodstain smack in the middle of the sweatshirt this guy wore, other than that he barely let out one last breath before the life left his body. The most unsettling part being the eyes, which would stay open with the wide-eyed and obsessive glare he gave them at the beginning of their encounter.

This was enough for both 978 and Dr. Carlton. The best thing to do was leave and get to her office. Formalities should be dropped from this point on. Stuff like that certainly didn't apply to replicas. In this kind of battle, there was no such thing as fighting fair. Granted, who knew what this thing was that just surprised them? The last thing that caught their eyes was the object that their attacker carried in his right hand. He would slowly lose his grip of it when his pulse stopped and he breathed his last breath. It was definitely some kind of weapon, a wooden stick with both ends sharpened. A crude spear most likely constructed by the assailant himself. The deaths of both the animal and the poor soul partially seen sticking out from behind the bushes had to be his doing. Dr. Carlton and 978 knew better than to so much as debate it. But there was no reason to stick around to investigate. Nothing would bring any of them back, and they didn't have to remind themselves that their own survival came first.

No more killing.

Yeah, right. That was an understatement at best. Stopping all of those replicas was enough for Dr. Carlton, despite the fact that she had been involved in similar situations that were equally dangerous. She got into her line of work to help people, not hurt them. Whatever 978 felt at that moment had to be more than unpleasant, especially considering the fact that he shot Fletcher in cold blood. Granted, the bastard deserved it, so it's not bad for a first kill if you have no choice in the matter. It would be nice to think that the replicas don't count in this particular matter, but they were the ones who always fired first and were designed to look as human as possible. Adrenaline alone now kept 978 on the move. He simply marched on, knowing he was in good hands with Dr. Carlton by his side. Maintaining balance and enduring the pain was surprisingly manageable. But the best part was the fact that her office couldn't be more than a quarter of a mile from their current location. Luckily, they wouldn't run into anyone else on their little trek down the bike path, dead or alive. The same could be said for any large-sized wildlife, too. Deep down both of them knew that whatever happened to that furry creature was something that they really didn't want to know.

For 978, this early morning walk started to feel like an eternity. A lot of it probably had to do with the fact that he kept pondering everything that occurred only moments ago, but who wouldn't? Not to mention that it was impossible to ignore all the stuff that had happened throughout the night. This was absolutely crazy. Dr. Carlton knew that, too. So why did he continue to debate every single scenario that they had survived up to this point? The answer was simple: No one ever expects to stumble onto a sick situation like this. You'd think reaching that conclusion so quickly would make everything easier to process, but that was not the case. But how could 978 expect do that? Just seeing your best friend shot and killed right before your eyes was enough to send anyone over the edge.

If only he could've stopped it somehow.

Dr. Carlton softly pressed her hand on 978's left elbow. He turned his head to look her in the eye. She pointed toward an area to the left, which made him assume they were close to her office. He was right. She took the lead and he followed directly behind her. It turned out that there was no direct path to where they were going, making it all the more difficult with the bad wound. The thick bushes and sharp tree branches would be serious obstacles for the poor guy. Luckily the good doctor took the lead to make it easier. All she needed now was a large machete like the ones used by those explorers out in the jungle. Obviously, it wasn't that bad. Still, it would make things happen a lot quicker, and they both knew that time was of the essence.

The moment they hit pavement, 978 and Dr. Carlton moved across a small parking lot and headed towards a large door. A light was on above it and a dumpster was located about ten feet next to it on the right. 978 took notice of a large, brown pick-up truck parked in one of the spaces on the left. It belonged to the security guard sitting at the front desk. His name was Ryan. When they reached the back door Dr. Carlton checked her pockets but couldn't find the keys. It wasn't that big a deal since she knew Ryan had an extra set. Now all they had to do was walk around to the front entrance.

978 and Dr. Carlton made their way to the front of the entrance of the building in less than sixty seconds, which was amazing considering how serious his injury was. When they reached the corner near the front right side, across the road was something their eyes could only describe as an abomination. Or a replica, the one that Dr. Carlton shot just before that van crashed and burned. This particular LEO1 soldier just stood still and looked lifeless, which made sense since it wasn't human and merely an early prototype of what was yet to come. It still wore the standard guard uniform, yet no longer had the helmet on. Both the burns and thick red bloodlike liquid were obviously the results of being shot and the crash. However, the worst damage was around the right eye. Also, without any head or facial protection, the replica had dark straight hair and was clean shaven. 978 immediately figured out who this replica was supposed to be: night shift guard Eric Fox. He couldn't remember the guy's number, but he honestly didn't care at this point, either.

The replica started to slowly walk across the street. Anyone that was close to it might have been able to hear faint mechanical sounds of gears grinding when the legs moved. By the time 978 and Dr. Carlton were at the front entrance, it had stepped into the parking lot. Dr. Carlton banged her fist on the glass to get Ryan's attention, prompting the security guard to get up from behind the desk so he could rush to the doors and quickly unlock them. Once inside all three of them would make their way back over to the desk. Dr. Carlton then let go of 978, who leaned back against it. She removed the belt which had all of the firearms tied together, then picked up and shotgun and got ready for action.

"Who's that?" asked Ryan, pointing to the front entrance.

The replica had arrived at the front entrance, and continued walking towards the double glass doors without stopping. Then the unthinkable happened: it marched right through the left door, causing glass to shatter all over the floor. Before Dr. Carlton had the chance, 978 pulled out his mini-gun and shot it four times in the chest. It stopped moving, dropped to his knees, and fell on its back. The danger was over, but not for long. Dr. Carlton was about to help 978 into the chair at the desk to treat his injuries. As she got ready to do so, she turned around and noticed that Ryan had wandered over to the so-called body to inspect the damage.

"Stop!" she yelled out.

"He's dead," said Ryan.

"Get back!"

"Okay."

Dr. Carlton turned her attention back to 978 again, telling him that he would be alright. She promised she would take care of the bullet wound and that he should rest for a while. She helped sit down and prepared to take a closer look at the injury. But when she turned her around to see what Ryan was up to, she knew things were about to get worse. The guy had knelt down to give the replica a closer examination.

"Get away from him!" she screamed.

"But he's not breathing," said Ryan.

"No!"

Without any warning the replica's eyes opened and raised its left arm, then made a fist and punched Ryan in the right jaw. After that it gripped his shirt in the upper chest area and flipped him over onto his back. He was barely conscious and had no idea what actually hit him. The replica stood up again and walked toward 978 and Dr. Carlton, almost like the march of the living dead. Dr. Carlton picked up another loaded gun and got ready to fire. She aimed for the chest area and fired, which caused it to stop again. Now it seemed to lose its balance. She knew if she shot the replica in the same spot twice it might explode, which could cause them serious injuries or their own deaths. These sample prototypes always had a number of more weak spots, so she aimed directly at the face. The first shot hit the lower side of the face, the second hit the middle of the neck, and the final shot hit the forehead straight between the eyes. The results were thick red liquid leaking out, minor burns, and quite a few sparks. This time it fell on its right side, rolled on its back, and burst into flames.

It was dead, or at least very disabled.

Ryan slowly sat upright. He looked at the burning replica in disbelief.

He then stood up and walked over to the desk to help Dr. Carlton escort 978 into the room behind them where an examination table was located. 978, injured and exhausted, fell asleep moments after being placed on it.

10•••

978 slowly began to open his eyes. The first thing that would get his attention was the fact that he was now lying on a couch a short distance away from where the examination table was located. Dr. Carlton and her friend Ryan must have

moved him, because he couldn't remember doing that for the life of him. She must have taken care of his injuries while he was unconscious, especially since the upper part of his guard uniform or the clothing he had worn underneath were missing. He also had bandages placed over the wound and felt a lot less pain. However, what he appreciated more than anything was waking up on a comfortable couch. It was a lot nicer than lying down bare-chested on that stiff examination table. He had a bit of a chill, bit he still thought it could be a lot worse.

Before he even attempted to sit up straight, 978 could easily sense he had felt better rested. Perhaps Dr. Carlton had given him a really strong sedative, which would explain why he slept so well. He honestly thought that he would at least remember her doing that. Then again, he had never been shot before, or experienced anything that had occurred throughout the night. The lights in the room were still on. The moment he sat up, the first thing he did was check the time. It was 8:40 a.m. As soon as he set his feet on the floor the door opened and Ryan walked in.

"You're up already?" asked Ryan. "Talk about a real trooper, and to think you didn't have a career in the military like I did!"

"I can't see anything wrong with waking up to a compliment," said 978.

"The name is Ryan, by the way. I'm Wendy's brother-in-law."

"Nice meeting you."

As 978 stood up, Ryan started walking towards him. He noticed they were close in height and had very similar builds. However, Ryan looked a little older with slightly lighter-colored hair and a thin beard. He also assumed that the glasses were a regular fixture as well. After the two of them shook hands, 978 walked over to the door and peaked outside, where he could see Dr. Carlton out in the parking lot talking to a police officer. The replica, however, was nowhere to be found.

"We removed what was left of that thing so she could report all that damage done to the door as vandalism," said Ryan.

"Good idea," said 978.

Before 978 moved away from the door, he took notice of how gray and cloudy it was outside. That was alright, though, because at least he was able to catch a glimpse of the daylight. But what he really wanted to do was remove the rest of his guard uniform. Why not? He already knew there was nothing that could convince him to work in the prison system again. He also started to wonder what the next move would be. Which he bet was something that Dr. Carlton would include Ryan into as well. That was okay by him considering that the guy had already spoken so openly and proudly about being in the military. So much for a proper introduction, but that was alright. The more help the better.

Dr. Carlton had finished talking to the police officer. She waited until he got back into the cruiser and drove away before turning back toward the building and making her way back inside. She would soon enter her back office and shut the door. This time she had her hair down. It was dark, straight, and long enough to exceed slightly past her shoulders. In 978's eyes her skin looked different somehow. Probably most likely due to the fact that everything they had done together had so far occurred in dark areas throughout the night.

"Glad to see you're up," said Dr. Carlton. "You look better now than you have all night."

"Thanks to you," responded 978.

"Not entirely, you can definitely hold you own. I also had some help from Ryan here. By the way, Ryan, this is......."

"We've already gotten acquainted."

"Oh.......alright then, there's something we have to show you. It's not going to be pleasant."

"Nothing I've seen so far has been."

"That's a good point."

Dr. Carlton and Ryan took the lead and 978 followed directly behind them. They headed for the door at the rear of the office they were in with the examination table. She turned the knob to open it then walked right through. The other two did the same only moments later, bringing them to a back hallway. 978 looked forward and immediately focused his eyes on a large door, which brought him to the conclusion that it was the rear entrance he and Dr. Carlton originally attempted to go through. Almost instantly he recalled that she couldn't find the keys, forcing the two of them to go to the front and have Ryan let them in. Of course he couldn't forget the business with that replica of Eric Fox who tracked them down and smashed through the glass doors.

This was not good. That deadly incident was now replaying in 978's mind in its entirety. The whole thing occurred hours ago, and that deep sleep he had wasn't helping him either. But how could he stop all those racing thoughts? Or let his defenses down. Ryan probably knew quite a bit about post-traumatic stress disorder. It doesn't matter how well you fought in the battlefield, or if you won the war. Even the biggest victory ever doesn't make it easier. When a soldier opens fire on the enemy for the first time, there's no going back.

You just don't turn it off.

The next sight 978 would lay his eyes on would only add fuel to the fire. Dr. Carlton and Ryan turned left to lead him to a large steel crate with the top taken off. Ryan looked down inside, then slightly nodded expecting him to follow suit. Dr. Carlton flicked a light switch on the wall to make it brighter and easier to see what they wanted to show him.

The sight caused him to remain speechless. No one could describe this. Much less process it right away in order to come up with an accurate answer as to what it was. Of course he recognized it as what was left of that replica, because if this was the real Eric Fox it would be an actual corpse, and human for that matter. Even if someone could take a human body, turn it inside out, and sever the limbs, it wouldn't look like this.

The red, thick bloodlike liquid which brewed inside all of the replicas captured the eyes more than anything. 978 didn't have the first clue what that stuff was or how it worked, but it had flowed all over the bottom of the crate. He estimated the amount to be close to six inches, and more of it was coming out of the disassembled remains of this mechanical double of a human being. Whatever this stuff might be, these replicas definitely required a lot of it. Dr. Carlton would certainly have more information on the subject, but he knew that there wasn't any time for her to get into a detailed explanation on replica mechanics. He would eventually learn everything he needed to, it was just a matter of when.

The one thing 978 didn't want to learn was how Dr. Carlton and Ryan tore this thing to pieces and crated it. Maybe this was the closest thing to a funeral service for the average replica. The crate could be considered a coffin, despite the large size of it. Just from a quick glance 978 honestly believed at least three adult sized replicas could easily fit into this crate, possibly one or two more, regardless if they had been disassembled or destroyed. No worries, he thought, it's not like a proper burial would be necessary. Replicas didn't require family, friends, much less a cemetery. Then again, they may if those surrounding them are convinced there the real deal. Most people aren't checking someone for a pulse or listening to their heartbeat on a day to day basis.

There was also something about this situation that 978 appreciated to a certain extent. There was no smell, at least not a distinctive one. Not even a bad smell, for that matter. A replica without an odor, so there's something that works in their favor. Victims of traumatic events often remember stuff like that, and it can be either good or bad. Unfortunately, the worst part is that the instant recall might occur at any time throughout the rest of their lives. He didn't have to wonder why there were so many people out there who couldn't simply let these go. At least this time he had an advantage: NO FOUL STENCH ONBOARD. But deep down he knew it wouldn't decrease his memories at all. Even if he developed permanent hysterical blindness, he would always remember this vividly.

Right now, the sight that 978 beheld had to be the ultimate blend of man and machine. Of course that wasn't a compliment, and these types of thoughts only came to him because of everything that he'd seen that night. For someone who had just set their eyes on what was inside that crate without any prior knowledge of replicas, chances are they would simply remain speechless. Seeing all that thick red liquid or the strange inner-mechanical parts is one thing, but the severed limbs of what look like human remains are a sight that would devastate anybody. Even 978 knew that if he'd been shown this before last night he would have been unable to comprehend what was going on. Not that he really wanted to at this point, either.

When 978 looked up he turned his attention back to Ryan again, who had lifted up the seal off the floor to cover the top of the steel crate. He took a step backwards to move out of the way. It didn't appear that this guy needed any assistance, which was fine by him. Leave it to someone who knows what they're doing to take care of the job at hand, especially since both Ryan and Dr. Carlton had far more knowledge about this than he did. At the moment he just watched the former military man carry out the task, which obviously wasn't difficult. But 978 thought it best to find out every possible way to destroy, or at least contain, a replica. He then took notice of these handle-like devices, three of each on all four sides of the crate. Ryan just pushed each one up and pressed forward in order to fasten down the seal completely. Anybody could figure out how to do this, but luckily there was a little more to it. Ryan then placed four locks on top of the crate, with 978 quickly finding locations for each one on all four sides. On the surface there was nothing that appeared unusual about the locks, which looked no different than the ones that simply required a set of keys to open them. He could easily think about the locks that got used with bicycles, lockers, or freezers. It really didn't seem like that big of a deal. But after Ryan placed each one where they belonged, 978 took notice of Dr. Carlton's brother-in-law pushing small red buttons on all of them. This prompted the former guard to ask questions.

"What are those for?" asked 978.

"What do you mean?" Ryan asked back.

"The little buttons on the locks."

"They're for explosive devices."

"You mean the locks are explosive?"

"No, they're safety triggers to an electronic connection located inside the crate, which is explosive."

"That sounds a bit confusing."

"That's the idea."

978 watched Ryan finish placing all the locks where they needed to be, as well as press the tiny red buttons on the right side of every one of them. After that was done the former soldier moved to the front of the steel crate where an electronic combination was located on the top right side then proceeded to push seven different numbers and pressed enter. 978 heard distinctive tones for each number despite the fact of how quiet the sounds were. About thirty seconds later he heard a deep, mechanical voice which most likely came from a tiny sound device on the crate that he was unaware of. It simply stated: LOCKDOWN COMPLETE.

And that was that.

"I guess you could call this the modern technological version of King Tut's Tomb," said Ryan.

"Maybe," said 978. "I know they didn't have explosives back then."

"Yeah that's true. Even if they did, they probably weren't

going to use anything that would deliberately destroy those beautiful pyramids."

"I would bet those people from Ancient Egypt could still teach us a thing or two about that stuff, and vice versa."

"Perhaps and more fun, exploration would be cool. Just don't believe in curses, right?'

"That might help. It's too bad it doesn't apply to the replicas. Curses aren't needed with those things."

978 waited for a response, but nothing came out of Ryan's mouth. He started to think that he might be developing a quicker understanding of a replica's methods of operation. Maybe a little bit too soon. But there was no other choice. He decided it was best to return to the discussion of the steel crate again.

"Don't you think this is going a bit overboard?" asked 978. "I mean, the thing is completely destroyed, right?"

"You never know," answered Ryan. "Not to mention the fact that all the evidence needs to be hidden."

"Remember one thing," added Dr. Carlton. "The technology used to create the replicas is always being improved, so you never really know how powerful each one will be whenever you have conflicts with them."

After everything he just saw, 978 really didn't want to be reminded of that. But Dr. Carlton was only looking out for him, so he wasn't about to debate with her over this particular issue. Right now the only thing that racked his brain was what happened a little while ago. She had begun to introduce him to Ryan before he cut her off by clearly stating that it was unnecessary. He started to wonder exactly what words would have come out of her mouth. Would she have just referred to him by his first name or his guard number? He didn't get to tell Ryan anything when the guy made his introduction. Dr. Carlton had told him hours ago he could call her Wendy, and he hadn't even done that yet. He knew he had to stop thinking about the one thing that kept screwing him up:

Formalities. So far the two of them worked well together, and Ryan would undoubtedly be the extra hand they needed. Almost half the morning had gone by. He was surprised that he didn't feel hungry yet.

"Ryan," said Dr. Carlton. "Are all the weapons in your truck?"

"Everything is ready to go," he answered.

"Good. As much as we all need the rest, this is not the right place for it."

Neither 978 nor Ryan made any comments. They didn't need to, and it took long enough to hide the remains of the replica and clean the floor by the front entrance. Nothing could be done to hide the damage to the front entrance. The best thing anyone could have done was to just clean up the shattered glass as quickly as possible. The reason why Dr. Carlton contacted the local police was to make sure it didn't seem like a big deal. She made it clear in her statement that no other damage had been done to the property and nothing was stolen. She allowed the local authorities to think it was just kids causing mischief or something. She wasn't fond of trying to shift the blame onto someone else, but it was the best story she could come up with.

Dr. Carlton also started to think more about Ryan's involvement in all of this. Despite his expertise in securing the replicas into cold storage, he still didn't know about them. The first honest to God conflict he had had was just with the one that smashed through the front entrance only a few hours earlier. At least the art of optimism offered some relief by having the ability to lock those things up. That was the best skill to have since it was the closest guarantee to their disposal, which appealed to him more now after being assaulted by this one while simply conducting a closer examination. She started reminding herself of the fact that he had served twenty years in the Air Force before meeting and eventually marrying her sister. Also knowing him to be a standup guy was the reason he had no reservations about being face to face with a replica, and she knew he would always be helpful and look out for her best interest.

Now 978, Dr. Carlton, and Ryan had to leave the office. When Ryan opened the door leading to the rear parking lot, the three of them headed straight for the pick-up truck. 978 hadn't noticed that it was a four-door vehicle the first time around. This suited him well. All he wanted to do was climb into the backseat and rest more. Considering everything that happened throughout the night, operating on a need to know basis was something he could deal with for the time being. The moment that he and Wendy had reached the passenger side of the truck, she opened the rear door for him.

"I'm sure you wouldn't mind having some extra space for yourself," said Dr. Carlton.

"You got that right," responded 978.

"Are you exhausted?"

"Not completely, but I could use a little more rest."

"Good idea."

978 quickly stepped up into the backseat of the vehicle and shut the door behind him. Dr. Carlton got into the front passenger seat and Ryan entered the driver's side and started the engine. 978 sat close to the right but laid down on his left arm and back. He wasn't going to risk resting on his right arm or shoulder. His wound was well taken care of. The last thing he wanted to do was subject himself to further injuries.

While 978 was engaged in a light siesta he kept overhearing bits and pieces of Dr. Carlton and Ryan's conversation. It wasn't very difficult to follow since their main topic of discussion was the replicas. But the most important part of the subject that would get his attention was Dr. Carlton talking about South America, specifically mentioning the Rio down in Brazil. The replicas were being built in various locations in and around the city, but the main factory and headquarters was a short distance outside there in a somewhat isolated area. She offered no explanation as to how these machines were imported back to the United States. Granted, since the replicas are programmed to copy all human traits, it could only get easier for them to function among the living without being detected. The last thing he heard before dosing off completely was Ryan saying something about a good buddy of his who resided down there.

11 •••

The place had obviously been abandoned for a long time now, and it was a part of Boston that Jack Burton, the self-proclaimed Zen Lunatic, wasn't familiar with. The more he thought about it the more he came to realize that he had been raised by a well off upper middle class family. Attending Boston College was definitely a privilege, and he was starting to see that now more than ever. What also began to hit him was the fact that back in his heyday when he had his followers involved in criminal activity like theft they weren't in much danger. This was because none of them were ever sent out to areas like this. For the most part they were stealing from people that already had too much, or at least that was what their beloved leader wanted to believe. A rundown part of a city like this was beneath both him and anyone else involved in his little revolution. Unfortunately Mr. Burton had no idea that he'd actually developed that mentality until now. Maybe there wasn't much he could have done about his obsessive thought process, but perhaps being so preoccupied getting educated at such a prestigious institution like Boston College kept him from seeing how the other half lived.

Zen Buddhism had definitely taught him everything necessary about living in the moment and at the present time that was more important than ever, because right now he needed to find out why he was trapped in this predicament for both his sake and his cellmates. He didn't even contemplate the fact that these other guys were his devoted followers. All five of them were forced into this crazy situation for the long haul regardless of the circumstances, all thanks to none other than 978. That itself was something which simply didn't register, especially since the guard never acknowledged him. The lack of communication throughout his entire sentence in the Peterson Prison Psychiatric Unit was more than enough to convince him, and the Zen Lunatic did not like being ignored for any reason. Naturally, it was a complete surprise that someone like 978 would let him loose.

However, Burton had to consider what the true motive would be for 978 to break him out, because the guard had never mistreated or insulted him in any way. The lack of communication simply displayed a strong lack of interest, especially since he figured his much publicized profile in the press would intrigue anybody. 978 was the first person to prove to the self-proclaimed Zen Lunatic that this would not always be the case. Granted, he knew that some people just weren't impressed very easily. There were also other inmates that were great storytellers who made up stuff very quickly and spontaneously and sounded exciting. Unlike him, though, none of it was true. Perhaps these guys weren't viewed as a real threat to the powers that be. Guards like 978 had probably viewed them as nothing more than entertainment.

Now Burton started remembering that 978 had never really expressed a sense of humor. Not around him, anyway. He also had to keep in mind that people didn't always see entertainment as an outlet specifically for laughs. Then again, when was the last time he saw a guard laugh in front of him? Never, they probably couldn't, but inmates didn't get any kind of classroom lecture or orientation regarding what a prison guard's code of conduct was supposed to be. The only rules inmates learned were the ones the guards said to follow which mostly stated what not to do, unless it was a direct order from a guard or another prison official. For most of the new guys it sounded easy enough, but the longer their sentence was nothing seemed easy.

Now Burton started thinking about the most important subject in the present moment. 978's expected arrival was very soon, and both he and his fellow prisoners had to be ready for anything. This was the only time he had ever tried to think of himself as D7, the official number he had to respond to while being locked up. He didn't have a choice in the matter, nor did anyone else doing time in the Peterson Prison Psychiatric Unit. Then again, he also had to keep in mind that it wasn't a rule that applied specifically to those who were sentenced to that particular section of the jail, if you were put behind bars that's how it went.

978 would only refer to Burton as D7, any argument against that was non-existent. The guard may have taken him out of jail, but that made no difference whatsoever. The two of them never communicated very well, but that was always the case. But now it had gotten to the point where he was truly scared of this individual. All 978 had to do was just stare him in the eye. The look on the guard's face was cold, empty, yet somehow full of rage at the same time. Almost like a hulking behemoth that could break him into pieces, making it abundantly clear this was not the guard that everybody knew. Yet he also knew that nobody could truly answer how this man could drastically change for the worse overnight and instill fear in others without any real effort.

The five escaped prisoners were no longer required to wear the prison uniforms. 978 had other ideas, and had other outfits ready for them when they first arrived at this place. Outfits weren't the best description, since that sounded to formal, especially for Burton. After serving several years in an environment where he was only supplied with one basic wardrobe and referred to as number D7 by law had had its effect. However, it was a bit surprising considering how adamantly he was opposed to that. At least he had been in his own mind the entire time he was locked up, and it didn't seem to matter having these four other guys who idolized him as the Zen Lunatic. All the leadership skills that he had before were long forgotten, but he couldn't let his disciples know that. Lucky for him so far they had not asked for any guidance. None of them would be given any direction at all until 978 would make his presence known again.

That time was now.

The sound of an automobile engine was the first sign of 978's arrival. D7 assumed the guard returned in the same vehicle used to assist in their escape, not that it made any difference to him. He wasn't expecting this so-called visit to be pleasant, and the same feeling was probably shared by the rest of the guys. Next there would be dead silence, but less than a minute later came the sound of a door being pushed open then slammed shut. A gut instinct told him not to head in the direction where he heard the guard make a dramatic entrance. 978 would find him, as well as the other four prisoners who had no choice but to participate in this escape.

The self-proclaimed Zen Lunatic would have taken some comfort when his fellow escapees, or disciples for that matter, gathered around him to wait for 978 to appear.

Not this time, however.

He would be taking orders, like the rest of them.

Hell, he barely even took notice.

This situation obviously called for a leader, something that just came natural to D7 in the past. This time, coupled with the fact that he and the other escapees were now dressed up to look more like a motorcycle gang, could be viewed as a golden opportunity for him. But right now a big part of him wanted to go back to prison to finish his sentence and forget about all of this. 978 had just marched into the room then stood in front of him like a drill sergeant demanding his full attention. D7 decided simply to stand up straight and look the guard straight in the eye, which he knew would be expected of him anyway. The four other guys followed suit.

"D7," said the 978 replica, staring him in the eye. "I'll bet you never thought I would put some charlatan like yourself in charge of anything. What's even better is you'll be assigned to an inside job and you have to answer to me! But don't worry. The rest of the guys will still act as your disciples. Best of all, I'll expect them to call you the Zen Lunatic! From this point on every job that you take on will serve a larger purpose than filling your own pockets. Enlightening, don't you think?"

"I guess it should be," answered the Zen Lunatic, albeit reluctantly.

"It better be! This is what you've always wanted and what you've always done! Now you're unable to see things clearly? Pitiful! Now if you don't act as the leader, there will be consequences!"

"Like what?"

The replica quickly grabbed D7 by the neck. The grip felt like a metal vice slowly closing in. He was trapped and completely helpless. Unable to move, drop down, back up, or force the hand off his neck. This thing that was supposedly 978 did not blink its eyes or display any change of color or expression its facial structure.

One of the other escapees, Patrick Hoyt, decided that the Zen Lunatic he practically worshipped had had enough. He thought that this incident warranted proving himself as a valuable asset. He quickly ran over to try and pull his leader free without any success. He then grabbed hold of the 978 replica's right arm that held D7 by the neck, but it didn't budge. He clenched his fist and punched it upside the head. It turned its neck to the right and stared him in the eye, let go of its prey, and punched him in the face. He immediately fell down, and before he could react he got picked up by the neck at least a foot off the floor. He would never find out how long it lasted, but seemed to start losing consciousness right away. After that he was thrown backwards, his feet slipping on the floor first before going down and slamming the back of his skull. The massive shock of this monster's actions had woken him up completely. But before he was able to so much as sit up the replica marched over and stepped on the stop of his chest, then pulled a gun out and shot him in the head.

That was the end of Patrick Hoyt.

978 just stood over the body and showed no expression. Within a few seconds the guard, who was really a replica, marched right back over to the other escapees and stood before them, displaying a wide-eyed blank stare. As soon as the mouth opened the sound of rage was recognized by all of them.

"Let that be a lesson to all of you!" exclaimed what they thought was 978. "Do not question me! Do not ever make an attempt to interfere with anything I do! There are only four of you left! I can continue to decrease that number with no effort whatsoever! The proof lies before you!"

The four escaped prisoners watched this replica they recognized only as 978 turn around and march off. That was the last time they would see of him until nighttime at the Boston Common. They just stared at Hoyt's lifeless body until the Zen Lunatic snapped out of it and quickly decided what to do by motioning to Johnson, a follower, to come forward.

"Let's decide what to do with the body," said Zen.

"Good idea," responded Johnson, with his slightly noticeable foreign accent. He was half Native American and half Jamaican. He'd spent the ten years of his life in Jamaica until his parents decided to move to the United States. He was six feet four inches tall, with long dreadlocks that extended far past his shoulders. Originally he thought that he was strong enough to take down 978, but after looking at what was left of Hoyt he was glad he didn't try.

Zen started thinking about stuff they could use to contain the bloody mess of Hoyt's remains. Technically, the poor guy was still in one piece.

Being able to recognize the fact that the body stayed intact did nothing to diminish the horrible sight of the former prisoner's gunshot wound to the head. It wouldn't take very long for the blood to flow over the eyes, which remained open. More dripped off the sides of the cheeks onto the floor, while the rest of it would spread down to the neck and upper chest area. All four guys, Zen, Johnson, Rod, and Sid, were probably glad that this wasn't part of a cleaning detail back at the prison. Yet the inevitable task remained of wrapping up their poor mate's corpse, if you will.

Zen quickly glanced around the room they were all in. This place was unknown territory to them, just a big warehouse none of them had ever ventured into before, and probably never would have if it hadn't been for 978 coordinating their great escape from the big house and escorting all of them here. Of course that had to be the most polite way of describing this particular scenario, and being polite was something they had no use for after considering what had just happened. But Zen knew they should show more respect than just simply leave Hoyt's bloody remains lying on the floor for some stranger to discover and risk being traumatized by the incident. They needed to get organized and put everything together. He wanted to make a contribution to this case by making sure his former cellmate was prepared for an autopsy and a proper funeral. That way it would be easier for the authorities to conclude what happened here.

He couldn't believe it.

The war hadn't begun and already a casualty had taken place.

Zen finished his visual scan of the room and took notice of a bunch of boxes. The wooden crates were all stacked up against the wall and piled up high enough to almost reach the ceiling. The cardboard boxes had all been placed in front of the crates at numbers equaling far less with some of them being torn open as well, convincing him to search through those first. It wouldn't take long for the four of them to examine the contents and find items deemed useful, in his mind at least.

"Let's see what we can find in those cardboard boxes," said the Zen Lunatic. "It shouldn't take long to look through them."

All four of them wandered over near the wall where the boxes were located. They quickly began to open the flaps or tear tape off if it was necessary, then dug their hands in and rummage through the contents of each package. They weren't taking a long time or even attempting to do a particularly thorough job, but they knew neither of those opportunities available to them. They could only do things as quickly as possible with their best efforts. Luckily 978 had left, so the guard was unable to watch over what they were doing. Not that he would have approved or allowed them to pay respects to someone killed on the front lines, especially if it was a guy like Hoyt whose life was lost by his own hands. Suddenly one of the guys discovered some useful items.

"I got something!" said Johnson, pulling some white bed sheets out of one of the boxes. "These should work."

"That's probably the best stuff we can use," said Zen, agreeably. "We just need to make sure that we do a real good job wrapping the head, that way more blood won't get all over the place. Those sheets will definitely not that good, especially compared to the bandages used in the infirmary back at Peterson. But let's do the best we can. I also think that we should cover the entire body and make sure we place his prisoner identification on the chest area when we're done. That way whoever winds up finding him won't just stick a John Doe tag on him."

"Who should we expect to find Hoyt?" asked Rod.

"We'll contact the nearest authorities with the

communicator that 978 gave us. We can give them the address here as were leaving."

"Aren't you worried that it will look like we did it?"

"At this point it doesn't matter what we do, everybody will still see us as criminals. This communicator links us directly to 978, who will be on duty tonight at the Boston Common. Someone in law enforcement might use as evidence that could start a criminal investigation against him."

Or it, Zen thought to himself. Had 978 been a sick monster the entire time? He kept thinking about how he had spent most of his life trying to convince people that he was a great spiritual leader. Now a life had just been taken by someone who represented the justice system. This guard he only knew as 978 could not be human. Maybe the reason the guards were only known by their numbers was because they were mechanical abominations. Then again, could the prisoners be looked upon with any higher regard? After all, both numbers and letters were their only forms of identification to the rest of society.

Zen, Burton, or D7 as he was known to by just about everyone in the past several years, couldn't believe the thoughts that were going through his mind. The impact of medical treatment had never occurred to him at all during his prison sentence. He actually mentioned the infirmary when deciding what to do with Hoyt's body. What really shocked him was that he truly cared about making sure that Hoyt, a fellow prisoner as well as a follower of his had been prepared for funeral-like arrangements.

He had to ask himself: Was he a guru or EMT?

This time he couldn't believe it.

He was taking action, literally, with his own hands.

Zen and Johnson decided to use three large single white bed sheets to wrap Hoyt's body from head to toe. The cleanliness of the sheets was a bit of a surprise, especially considering that they had been tucked away in some old cardboard boxes in this rundown building. However neither one of them made a point of saying anything about it, probably because they really just wanted to concentrate on the task at hand.

Moments after completion of the wrapping job, Sid suggested folding Hoyt's uniform and placing it next to his body. The other suggestion of tying his identification around the neck was rejected quickly. The four of them thought that particular idea was somewhat redundant, and really no better than a toe tag. It seemed best to simply place that on the top of the uniform, which was probably the most respectable thing that they could do with the exception of a burial and a tombstone. Hoyt was laid to rest on the top of a large, wooden crate with his uniform and identification placed beside his head. At least the four of them could say that there was a little justice on their behalf.

Zen reached the conclusion that the best thing they to do was contact general emergency services regarding Hoyt's body. Rod checked outside to find the name and address of where they were. It didn't take him long to find out what he needed to. There was a five by three plaque located outside the truck delivery doors on the right. The placed was called the Washburn Warehouse on Myrtle Street, founded in 2029. Thirty three years didn't quite make the place ancient, but it looked like it had been deserted for twice as long. It wouldn't have been surprising to learn that the whole neighborhood was condemned.

Before the guys departed, Zen decided to use the communicator 978 had given him to report where to find Hoyt, than leave the device behind so the authorities couldn't track them. He simply could not believe that his conscience started to get the better of him. No man could do what 978 did to Hoyt. Not a human being, anyway. He knew that for sure.

"How about a eulogy?" asked Sid.

"Don't even go there!" snapped Zen.

"Maybe now he sees the light."

"Get over it! 978 literally tore the life out of him! Is that a good way to go? I don't think so! Think about what were supposed to do tonight. I can't even begin to imagine what will happen to us. My release at the beginning of next year was definite! I wasn't required to attend a hearing with the parole board! Now it's over for me, and all because of that 978! That psycho guard or whatever he is now wants me to be the first and only candidate for his own version of death row! And I'm forced to be a leader in a situation that I want nothing to do with!"

Sid was speechless. He could not believe what he was hearing. Zen was supposed to be the one who had all the answers. He still believed that, probably because he always needed the most guidance. Right now it seemed like his beloved leader could use a few pointers, but no sound advice came to mind.

Johnson, Rod, and Sid all lined up to stand next to one another. They faced Zen himself. The three of them then turned their heads to quickly glance at each other, than looked forward again. The tension could be felt easily. Hopefully, that feeling would subside shortly. Still, someone had to break the ice.

"This is an experience that none of us ever thought we would have to go through," said Johnson. "Each of us has fallen on hard times before, but nothing like this. Most of it we've been told was our own fault. Now we're in a situation to make the best decision possible, on where we can make a difference."

"You've got to be kidding!" shouted Zen. "Make a difference? You make it sound like we're able to do something noble! There's nothing beneficial in staging an assassination attempt!"

"Zen, you don't understand. From now until early tonight, no one is standing over us. We can't be traced if we leave the communicator with Hoyt's body. We can do something else other than shooting an innocent bystander."

"I think I'm starting to get an idea where you're going with this."

"Who says we can't pick and choose our own targets? We can easily fire a few random shots in the air, that's all it takes to cause a crowd to panic big time. Naturally, the guards are supposed to protect those with political power. Since 978 will be present, I say we should shoot mainly at him. Maybe that could help expose the prison reform proposal for the scam it really is."

Zen didn't feel the need to respond. He loved everything that Johnson was telling him. The four of them now had this golden opportunity. Why not go after the one who dragged them into this mess? The thought of destroying that monster known as 978 was nothing short of beautiful.

All this time, Zen had spent every moment convincing these guys that he was some guru who could lead them to true enlightenment. Now one of them, Johnson specifically, shared wisdom that could actually change things for the better. Perhaps he was a better inspiration than he realized, but right now he was just happy that there was a possible solution to this problem. He didn't want to take any credit. Not yet, anyway. But before he could say anything, he was about to receive more praise than ever. He honestly thought there would be a serious power struggle between them after everything that was said. He couldn't have been more wrong. In the past several years while sharing neighboring cells, the guy did express a lot of faith, which he assumed was in him. Now he was about to find out why.

"Don't you think all of this could be happening for a reason?" asked Johnson. "Your entire life you have always needed to be in positions that demanded leadership. It has also been important for others to believe in you. In the past these traits are what got you into trouble, now you have an advantage. In a way, you can redeem yourself by the actions you take from this point on. I don't know if that's something you want to do, but I think it's a better choice than being one of 978's disciples."

"We'll get into trouble no matter what we do!" answered Zen.

"At this point, an eye for an eye is justified."

"Don't look at it that way! Like I said there could be a reason for all of this, destiny perhaps!"

"I don't know. It's one thing to believe in luck, fate, or destiny, but don't always count on it!"

"Yes. But making a decision is your own choice, and once you follow through with it the best you can, at least you know you tried!"

It remained unlikely either one of them knew they were sounding so rational. Then again, it would be difficult for anyone to really sense that after being locked up for so many years. One can only hope to get even a slightly better perspective in a situation like that, regardless of their state of mind. However, this discussion they just had would hopefully change things for the better. If they survived this ordeal and no one else outside their circle could figure it out the worst thing to happen was getting put back where they came from, and Peterson Prison's Psychiatric Unit was a lot better than any other part of the facility.

Zen picked up the communicator and called emergency services. The instant reply was a female voice with a somewhat mechanical tone. He said Hoyt's name, than gave the address. The moment he heard the two words "message received" he turned off the communicator and placed it on top of Hoyt's chest. Zen, Johnson, Rod, and Sid quickly walked over to the delivery doors where the motorbikes were parked. Zen opened the doors and got on the first bike, Johnson followed next, Rod third and Sid fourth. They started their engines simultaneously and rode off into the sunset.

••• 12

978 had engaged in yet another argument with his now ex-wife Michelle. Of course engaged wasn't the best word to use in reference to situations like this, even if you're simply having a difference of opinion with a partner. Still, he had always been sensitive about this stuff, and it didn't matter if he could express it or not. And in his mind Michelle would always be his partner, at least in this lifetime. Children alone can do that, but he knew that was only one small portion of it in this case. Case, there was a term he could easily find himself sensitive to, and one he would never want to say in front of Michelle. There were endless problems between them, but they weren't crimes that needed to be solved where someone just simply documented everything in a police report only to be stored into some file cabinet at the end of the day and collect dust. Michelle would describe it that way, even though he never used that particular word. He knew this woman too well.

978 slowly started to realize that there was something different about this argument. It felt like he was on the outside looking in, and moments later he figured out he was right. He had been watching both himself and Michelle fighting, and this time it was worse than ever. The two of them had rarely raised their voices at each other, and that's exactly what they were doing now. At first he couldn't so much as a single word they were saying, and that's when he pieced it all together. He wasn't the one who was fighting with the women he still loved, but the replica she believed was Mark Allen Royce. Not 978, as everyone else referred to him as at Peterson Prison while on duty as a guard in the

Psychiatric Unit. That included his old friend Will, whom he was supposed to think of as 401. Now he couldn't call the poor guy anything, except dead.

When the argument turned audible in his ears, 978 could only watch helplessly as his replica stared straight into the eyes of Michelle. What made it worse was she had no way of knowing that it wasn't him, as it was also wearing his regular clothes instead of the guard uniform. Not that it made this mechanical monster any less intimidating, even through his own eyes. He never pictured himself talking to someone that he truly loved in the manner that this replica was. He had always been straight up with people in his personal life, but not overly demanding, controlling or unreasonable in any way. He now had to witness this demonic image of himself doing precisely that telling the light of his life how things were going to be whether she liked it or not. This barely registered with 978, especially since he always valued Michelle's freedom. It reminded him of the fact that he never once objected to looking after the kids, even if he only got five hours of sleep. But the change in his personality could not go unnoticed no matter how fair he might have been. The last thing he heard her say to what she thought was her former spouse was that the job was killing him.

"You're wrong," said the replica. "It's killing you!"

978 watched the replica grab Michelle with its right hand by the neck and strangle her with almost no effort. Her daughter Samantha and their young son Paul stood only a short distance away watching and displayed no emotions whatsoever. He didn't even want to consider the possibility of young children being replicated, especially their own. The next thing he realized was that he couldn't move or speak, having no more power than a fly on a wall. He also figured that buzzing around a replica's head would have very little effect on the situation and accomplish little more than being a distraction to Michelle, giving what he saw as an opponent

the upper hand. He couldn't believe his thoughts were this clear, which reminded him of how helpless he really was. He did everything he could to let out the loudest scream possible. Nothing worked, but he could feel vibrations occurring in his body. He started to tremble, then there was a loud bang and his eyes opened. He was lying in the back seat of Ryan's truck, which meant he just had a bad dream. They probably hit a pothole or something. He hadn't thought much about Michelle or the kids until now, which wasn't surprising considering how crazy the night had been.

He couldn't explain any of this, so there was no point trying to contact them. He also knew that if any information got leaked, chances are no one would ever see his family alive again. Maybe that was the reason why Fletcher had asked him about the divorce.

"Nice to see you're up," said Dr. Carlton, looking back. "How's the wound?"

"Not bad," said 978. "I'm not even feeling that much pain, at least not physically."

"That's good. I figured you would wake up after we hit that bump in the road."

"That's what you like to call it?"

"Whatever."

He honestly had no idea what got him to ask her about something as trivial as a pothole. Then again, he had just woken up from a nightmare so there was no reason to analyze any words that came out of his mouth. Still, he didn't really want Dr. Carlton knowing where his head was at emotionally, especially after that reference about pain. He knew that she understood which was all that mattered. This particular experience could be described as an intense transition, of which he was only beginning to feel the effects. At this point only God might know the lifelong damage it would havoc compared to a bullet wound. The brief moment that 978 saw Dr. Carlton's eyes in the rearview mirror, there was an obvious look of concern. Yet he kept asking himself the same questions over and over again. How long had she been playing the game with Dr. Fletcher? This replica conspiracy had been going on for a while now.

Originally, 978 hadn't thought much about where they were heading. Part of him wanted to crawl under a rock and die. He knew at this point that he and Dr. Carlton and Ryan were all fugitives. That was his take on it, anyway, especially considering the fact that his replica shot and killed Staff Sergeant 101 and freed prisoners he never wanted to give the time of day to. All replicas had been programmed with the traits of whoever they're modeled after. However, after what he had witnessed along with what little information he had, nothing could make him believe that his replica was connected to him in any way. The only option available now was to reexamine everything in his life. Whatever he found stimulating before had now diminished. The very brief moment that he stared that thing straight in the eye, he saw what he had become. The answer was a cold, calculated monster. Although these things were mechanical, they could blend into the human population without anyone knowing. While mingling with everyday people, they could learn their weaknesses and attempt to ambush and destroy them. If that happened, it wouldn't take long to start a revolution.

978, Dr. Carlton, and Ryan needed a good plan. They had to find a way to prevent any bloodshed from occurring at the Boston Common. Despite having a lot of faith in his two new allies, 978 honestly thought that tonight's event could go even worse than Fletcher had planned it. What would stop the Zen Lunatic, or his own replica, from killing the Governor or anyone else present at the gathering? Nowadays wounding someone simply isn't enough. Throughout America's history, Lincoln, JFK, Vietnam, the on and off Gulf War, and 9/11 were events that had the largest impact. Even when Ronald Reagan was shot and wounded in 1981, there was less and less talk about the incident over time. This was especially true once the President's two terms in office were completed. The most bizarre aspect of the whole scenario was the man responsible for the attempted assassination claimed to have done it for Jodie Foster. That must have caused severe psychological trauma to the poor woman for quite some time, regardless of her political views.

978 began to realize that his thoughts were starting to wonder again. He needed to stay focused on where he was. Now was not the best time to be grieving, even though he had every right to. One of his oldest and closest friends was dead, but hopefully his family was alright. He knew the smartest move would be not to contact them, especially if that was their only chance of staying alive. This was the one time where he could actually convince himself that ignorance was bliss, at least in their case. It was time to ask Dr. Carlton for an update.

"Where are we headed?" asked 978.

"Ryan's place," she answered.

"How much further is it?"

"About twenty minutes. Are you feeling alright?"

"Yeah, but what do we need to do at Ryan's place?'

"We need to do as much planning and preparation as possible. We've got some decent weapons in the back, but I don't know how much stuff we need. Naturally, security we'll be tight at the Governor's speech. It's going to be very difficult to sneak around the Boston Common without attracting attention. We'll have to find easy ways in and out, and we've also got the entire day to ourselves. A couple of hours to rest will be good for all of us, that way we'll be able to keep our heads clear and concentrate better when tonight comes."

That was all 978 needed to hear. Dr. Carlton was obviously on top of things from the get-go, and Ryan was the type of person who could keep it together under the toughest circumstances. However, he still wanted to know more about the construction of replicas down in Brazil, as that was the biggest piece of the puzzle. But Dr. Carlton was right by saying they all needed their rest. He also knew that she would probably reveal more information sooner than later, even if he didn't ask more questions. Now he felt strangely calm, like the calm before the storm. The feeling didn't last long, however, as his relaxed train of thought would suddenly come to a screeching halt, and that was the only way to describe it. Ever since he woke up from that horrible nightmare he had just continuously contemplated whatever was going on around him or within him. He knew it had to be some type of lingering paranoia, and who could blame him? Even if he got several more hours of sleep at Ryan's place, there wouldn't be any true sense of relief. He also knew that he had a long road ahead of him. The same was true for Dr. Carlton and Ryan. Would this madness ever end? Would 978 ever have any closure? With everything that occurred up to this point, it might take the rest of his life. He could truly imagine still struggling with these issues even on his deathbed.

Whether people realize it or not, most events that occur in their lives are not planned. It doesn't have anything to do with destiny. Nobody can predict anything with one hundred percent accuracy, much less count on anything or anybody. 978 didn't choose to be in the predicament he was in, and there was nothing that could be done about it. Now he needed to be a fighting soldier, far better than those LEO1's expected to take over after his retirement. That was supposed to sound sarcastic, at least in his mind. Everyone working at the Peterson Prison facilities was supposed to buy into the belief that the replicas were the answer to everything. 978 took some pride knowing that Fletcher would never see that day, now he had to find a way to put a stop to all of it.

The madness was far from over.

••• 13

The Governor checked the time on his watch again, which was now exactly 5pm. He usually didn't mind coming to the Statehouse, but for some reason it didn't do anything for him, at least not today. Still, it's not like he was feeling under the weather, tired, or even in a bad mood. He just couldn't focus as well as he wanted to, but he also didn't want to worry about it. He knew the most crucial time he needed to concentrate would be tonight during his speech, which was scheduled to take place in a couple of hours outside in the Boston Common. He kept thinking to himself how nice it would be to just walk outside ten minutes before his time to go on, quietly make his way through the crowd towards the stage and do his thing. Of course that would never happen. It was a waste of time fantasizing about it, especially if you were a politician.

It should have felt like another typical meeting inside the conference room where the Governor, as always, was sitting at the head of the table. They were doing exactly what they were supposed to, discussing plans for tonight's speech which represented all the parties present. But only a selected number of them were going to share the spotlight with him, one being his daughter and two prison guards he only knew as 978 and 609, who Fletcher had specifically assigned to this particular event. He didn't understand why he couldn't use his own guards. Fletcher was supposed to attend the meeting, the one guy who could answer that question. Then again, he was able to reach a logical conclusion. By using prison guards for tonight's security would help reinforce the proposal of prison reform, especially if Fletcher himself introduced these two guards at the meeting as being just that, but that wasn't going to happen.

Now the Governor's job had become all the more difficult. He had no idea why Fletcher couldn't make it to the meeting. Stuff like that usually didn't bother him, especially since he found out early this morning. That was more than enough time to regroup due to a sudden change of plans. But due to the subject matter of tonight's speech, the guy needed to be here. It had been public knowledge for a long time that Fletcher was in charge of the Care Control Division, making it clear who the brains were behind the operation. He saw it as a necessity to be there considering the importance of the issue, and the guy had every right to take credit where credit was due. Delivering a speech may have been on of the Governor's stronger qualities, but wasn't thrilled about putting words into somebody else's mouth. Even though he was convinced that Fletcher trusted him completely, he was more comfortable with the idea of people speaking for themselves, especially in politics. Postpone tonight's speech started to sound appealing, but not on such short notice. There were only a few hours left, and he had to consider the fact that thousands of people were already en route for the sole purpose of tonight's gathering. He did not want to create unnecessary overcrowding in an already overcrowded and hectic city.

Now, what would be a typical move by the Governor, it was time to prioritize. He had gone through all of the necessary motions and details with everyone present, the only thing that needed to be done was a quick review of everything that had been discussed. That was easy because the meeting hadn't lasted very long, especially after considering the fact that tonight's gathering had been planned for the last three weeks. That took a lot of weight off his shoulders. Granted, it didn't take a genius to know that planning any function so far in advance would usually allow it to be far more organized. Then again, he liked to pride himself on having that quality in him that liked to stay ahead of the game. At this point he knew he wasn't about to leave any stone unturned.

"I just wanted to tell all of you that I am very pleased we were able to get through this meeting quickly and efficiently," said the Governor "I like it that way, but most of you already knew that. Now everyone here is updated on current events, so you will know what to expect tonight at the function which will be right outside. Dress warmly, especially since spring has only begun. Unless there are any questions, then it's time to go until you hear from me again."

The last part when he stated to dress warmly he adlibbed at the very last moment. He wanted to end things on a lighter note. Of course he wanted everyone in his presence to take the subject matter and tonight's function seriously. Still, he felt the need to express some optimism in the most subtle way possible. Humor would have been nicer, but he also had to consider the fact that discussing anything involving the Care Control Division was new to everyone, including himself. A lot of information remained unknown, mysterious, and somewhat intimidating.

The first person to get up and leave the meeting was the Governor's daughter. She hadn't spoken so much as a single word throughout the entire meeting, not that she was expected to. She was not happy being there, and didn't dress as formally as everyone else. Even though she expressed no emotion and appeared content, he knew his little girl too well to know that wasn't the case. Still, it was best to let her go and have some time to herself. That would make her more calm and relaxed. All the other parties present stood up, organized their paperwork, checked briefcases, and straightened ties before heading to the doors to leave. The only two that stayed behind were these guards only known as 978 and 609, who had been required to do so. He hoped that some small talk would help break the ice, but honestly didn't think that would happen. The answer came quickly once the two guards marched over to the head of the table. They both took seats, one on the left and the other on the right. If he didn't know better, the Governor might have expected them to state that he was surrounded after seeing their cold stares directed at him.

"I know you're both clear on how everything will be set up tonight," stated the Governor. "The exact time my daughter walks off stage the two of you will stand by either side of me. About ten feet on each side, I believe. Then again, I'm sure both of you are familiar with the standard procedures at these events."

"You are correct, Governor," responded 609 who, like 978, was really a replica.

"Please, call me Ron. I'm perfectly fine being on a first name basis. Even Fletcher doesn't need to know. It certainly wouldn't be the crime of the century. By the way, have either of you been in touch with your boss today?"

"No."

"So you're both sure that there's nothing else he wanted to discuss with me about tonight? The entire concept of this Care Control Division is mainly about him. Everybody knows that. Is there any possible way to contact him?"

"No. He has been called away. There has been a death in his family."

Of course there was no truth to that, but the replicas had been ordered to tell the Governor that in case any questions were asked. He wanted to probe these two more, hoping to get more information. However, it was obvious that wasn't going to happen. The cold stares along with the cut and dry statements he had heard so far clearly indicated that the answer would be no.

"I wish I could at least talk to him," said the Governor. "But I respect his need for privacy. Please tell him to contact me the moment you hear from him."

"Yes, Governor," said 609.

He wanted to remind both of them to call him by his first

name, but quickly decided not to make a big deal out of it. As long as all the orders were being followed, then nothing else really mattered as far as he was concerned. Still, he couldn't figure out why these guards wouldn't make any effort to be more surface friendly. 609 only spoken to him in a very dry and stiff tone of voice, and 978 hadn't so much as uttered a single word. All three of them would remained seated for maybe another minute at the most. The two guards didn't even blink their eyes. All the Governor saw them do was briefly glance at one another before getting up from their seats and walking away, without saying anything! Talk about getting the cold shoulder! Perhaps they were under strict orders from Fletcher to be that way.

Whatever the reason is, the Governor decided, it only created an uneasy feeling.

Welcome to the concept of the Care Control Division. For Fletcher, that might be the name of the game. Being a no-show at the meeting, as well as tonight's gathering, only served make things more mysterious, suspicious, and intimidating. At this point the definition of the title felt like a contradiction, at least as far as the Governor was concerned. All he could do now was put on a fake smile and give the best speech possible when the time came, which was exactly what a politician was supposed to do.

At least old Ron knew he could do his job.

••• 14

978 just started to wake up from his fourth siesta, if you will. He was grateful the last two were by choice, and this time he woke up on a very comfortable sofa. The television was on at a very low volume, and his boots and socks were on the floor. They were placed below where his head was resting,

which was good since that was where he remembered leaving them. The only thing disturbing was the odor from it, making him want to thank God ten times over that no one else was in the room right now.

He started to sit up straight and began wondering where Dr. Carlton and Ryan might be. He heard some noise coming from the kitchen area located behind him on the right. Obviously the best thing to do was go in there to investigate. Upon entering, he saw Ryan standing over the stove boiling water. He also took notice of a small portable radio on the table, with the volume turned up just enough to be audible. But he didn't see Dr. Carlton anywhere, yet decided it wouldn't be long before she would make an appearance. The two men immediately locked eyes anticipating a conversation.

"Where's Dr. Carlton?" asked 978.

"Upstairs," answered Ryan. "She just went to use the bathroom. I just finished boiling some water, you want coffee or something?"

"Sure, coffee."

"You got it."

"The television was on when I woke up, and I also heard the radio. Is there any news that's significant?"

"Not yet, but I expect that there will be any time now."

"It might take longer than you think. Only the replicas know for sure that Fletcher is dead. I'm responsible, they also know about my alleged participation at the Governor's speech tonight. That needs to be covered up for now, maybe even permanently."

"You think so?"

"Absolutely, right now my replica is with the Governor, so everybody needs to think I'm still alive. However, I'm also supposed to be helping out a group of escaped prisoners. An assassination attempt is being made under my direct orders."

Of course 978 knew it wasn't really under his direct orders, but all he needed to do was look in the mirror as a frightful reminder of what he had seen last night. A deadly machine was out there somewhere that had been created in his image, but certainly not in his likeness. These things were supposed to be referred to as replicas by everyone involved in this conspiracy. He figured that whoever constructed the first batch of them would have been at least smart enough to keep them from operating in the public eye. Any kind of breakthrough in science required all kinds of tests for safety purposes, supposedly. Well, that was what 978 had been told most of his life. Maybe this was why the central base of operations was located in South America. Who knows?

978 began to see that Ryan's house was similar to his grandparents' house in Arlington. It was the last house that they lived in before retiring to Florida. Both of these places were relatively small, including a second floor with two bedrooms and two bathrooms. He would stay there about once a month, especially after his father died. He never asked his mother why that was. Maybe she needed time to herself, or perhaps she thought that an occasional change of scenery would be good for him. Whatever the reason might have been, he didn't mind. Despite the nice things they said about his dad, however, he always sensed they were never close. It happens sometimes, especially with in-laws.

While 978 was busy reminiscing he barely noticed Dr. Carlton walk into the kitchen. However, he heard footsteps coming down the stairs. He started to wonder why he didn't anticipate her making an entrance, even though she wasn't trying to attract attention. He reminded himself that his thoughts were scattered with everything that was going on, but maybe the paranoia was decreasing because he was beginning to trust Dr. Carlton and Ryan. Of course he had to keep debating if that was a good thing, which made him decide to concentrate on the moment. He was mainly interested in hearing what Dr. Carlton would contribute to the conversation, hopefully stopping him from entering that mode of constant contemplation.

"I'll give you a little credit, Ryan," said Dr. Carlton. "The bathroom is clean, but it could use an air freshener."

"Why's that?" asked Ryan.

"Use your imagination."

She smiled briefly after responding, both Ryan and 978 figured out what she was getting at. It was just a joke, probably to help lighten the mood. This was especially good for 978, thinking that it would help him relax more, and the trust would hopefully continue to increase. A little bit of faith would be nice, too.

"How's the wound?" asked Dr. Carlton, locking eyes with 978.

"Okay, I guess," answered 978. "To be perfectly honest, I hadn't been thinking about it. I'm not all that concerned. You've done a really good job taking care of it."

"I'll check it again later."

978 felt relieved. He could sense that Dr. Carlton was looking out for him. It also felt good that she showed a sense of humor during that brief conversation with Ryan, no matter how subtle it was. Maybe now it will be easier to discuss business.

"What time is it?" asked 978.

"About four," answered Ryan.

"Then we still have several hours until the Governor's speech. Have either one of you started making plans?"

"Ryan has plenty of ammo for our regular firearms," said Dr. Carlton.

"I have loads of stuff in the basement that we can make good use of," added Ryan. "Does a flamethrower strike your fancy?"

"Do you really think that would be the smartest choice?" asked 978.

"Think about it," said Dr. Carlton. "How often are flamethrowers used in any battle? The replicas won't expect anything like that. Even if they aren't completely disabled afterwards, the damage on the surface will be impossible to hide."

"That's a good point, but there are a lot of things to consider. Our main goals are to stop the replicas and the Zen Lunatic gang. Weapons like flamethrowers could cause serious harm to the crowd."

"That may be true, but remember Fletcher has already clued me in on everything. The crowd has never been the intended target, especially not in the early stages of planning tonight's event. The crowd and the media are only supposed to be witnesses. However, if we pull this off there will be more questions than answers from every party involved. Even if we only fire bullets at 609 and your replica, it won't stop them. The media will capture everything on film. This could blow the whole scandal wide open."

"You definitely have a clear view on this. It's giving me a better idea about what we should do. We all know there will be a lot of questions asked as to why I was allegedly present at this function in the first place. Also, seeing this guard who is supposed to be me getting shot without being seriously injured will raise a lot of eyebrows. The tabloids dream about stuff like this, but this time it's for real. I might be able to clear my name quicker, but I still have to consider what I did to Fletcher."

978 felt a finger tap his right shoulder, he turned around so that Ryan could give him his cup of coffee. He looked down to make sure it wasn't black.

"You wanted cream in that, right?" asked Ryan.

"Yeah," answered 978. "Tell me, Ryan. How is it possible for you to be in possession of a flamethrower in this day and age?"

"By spending twenty years in the Air Force, where I made a number of connections during that time, most of which I've kept. You'll never believe half the stuff I get my hands on. I'm convinced everything I have will eventually be needed. For all we know our little showdown tonight could lead to a revolutionary war or something."

"You're making it sound glamorous. Let's just hope it doesn't come to that, not now, anyway. We'll cross that bridge when we get there."

"This is obviously a situation that no one has any real control over, I mean there's no way to know for sure how this will turn out. Because with those replicas, it's still unknown what the real deal is. Even Wendy can't tell you exactly what to expect."

"You're right about that," said Dr. Carlton.

"What are you saying?" asked 978.

"That we can only do the best we can. This is something that no one has ever encountered before, so we'll just have to wing it."

"This is too much, man," said Ryan. "Back in the service when you went to war you just shot the enemy and they went down. Now we've got these replica things that are beyond super soldiers, what's next?"

978 didn't feel thrilled with what he was hearing, but he didn't have anything to add to it. The three of them could only work with what was available, including their own skills and motives. For him it was about stopping his replica, Dr. Carlton's smarts along with working alongside Fletcher, and Ryan's expertise with weapons and defense tactics. There wasn't enough time to create the most brilliant strategy, but they had the edge to make a difference. There are times when you can change things for the better, even if it's only a little bit.

"Let's take a trip downstairs, Ryan," said 978. "Show us what you got."

"You bet," said Ryan. "Just taking what we need and some very brief planning will be more than enough."

Ryan turned around and took a few steps toward a door

behind him. He opened it and flicked a light switch on the wall. He started to make his way down stairs, with 978 and Dr. Carlton immediately following him. Even this reminded 978 of the grandparents' place, which wasn't a bad thing. Ryan slid a large curtain open on his left, soon entering and pulling a small chain to turn on a ceiling light, something you never see anymore.

978 had to take his concentration away from the light, so to speak. He was now setting his eyes on some kind of arsenal, which also reminded him of an old storage space. The weapons and boxes needed to be dusted off, which wasn't surprising since this was a special occasion. He looked over at Ryan, whose eyes glowed with anticipation. The expression that Dr. Carlton displayed wasn't either good or bad, but Ryan had been part of her family for quite some time. Chances are this most likely wasn't a big secret to her. The best part was that most replicas did not have access to anything like this, at least not right away. Ryan may or may not have been ready to give them any kind of crash course or orientation, but was the first one to speak.

"Let's get started!" stated Ryan, as if they were about to prepare for battle.

"I take it you don't want to do any spring cleaning first?" asked Dr. Carlton, sounding a little sarcastic.

"As long as we choose the right weapons and they work okay, who cares?" asked 978, who felt anxious again.

"You make a good point," said Ryan. "Everything should work fine, but you can't always be sure. So I'll at least show you how to do safety checks, load ammunition, and store a whole lot more extra ammunition."

"We will definitely need the extra ammo considering what were up against."

"A little faith would be nice, too," added Dr. Carlton.

Ryan immediately picked up the guns that were in sight and started to inspect them. He told 978 and Dr. Carlton which boxes to open, which indicated it would not be difficult to find what they were looking for. It was pretty easy to figure out what everything was, despite the fact that Ryan was the only real weapons expert.

978 started to think about Will again, wondering if his friend ever had moments like this while enlisted. All the questions he wanted to ask but never could. At least the present company surrounding him was about to give him some firsthand experience, even though he wasn't particularly enthusiastic about it. But right now the only thing he could do was deal with whatever got thrown in his direction.

978 came across a large wooden crate on his left. He took a crowbar that was lying on the floor to open it up from the top. When he pried off the cover and looked inside he instantly knew what he was focusing his eyes on: two flamethrowers. He leaned over to take one out and placed it on the floor. He glanced over at Ryan, hoping to be enlightened a little more about this dangerous weapon.

"Take both of them out of the crate," said Ryan. "I actually have four of those, but we're only going to take those two. The plan is to only use one, but we'll bring a spare just in case one doesn't work."

"When was the last time you used any of these?" asked 978.

"Never," answered Ryan.

That didn't sound so bad to 978. Granted, all three of them may have been preparing for combat, but it was somewhat relieving to know Ryan wasn't going into battle every week. Then again, with the large number of connections this guy had might prove otherwise. Of course being in the Air Force for twenty years would most likely allow somebody like Ryan easier access to things like flamethrowers. Maybe Will would have benefited more and survived by staying in the Army, but he didn't want to think about that.

Ryan started inspecting the two flamethrowers. He had to

do it fast, but was very thorough. These things were some of the most dangerous weapons to handle, especially for civilians like 978 and Dr. Carlton. Of course wearing a backpack with a hose that shoots fire sounds dangerous to any normal person, but this was far from a normal situation. He then did a brief demonstration on how to both operate and conduct a safety check with the flamethrowers, but remained undecided as to who would be the primary user.

"Are either of you afraid of fire?" asked Ryan. "You should be if you have any brains whatsoever. Obviously as kids you were taught not to play with matches."

Both 978 and Dr. Carlton briefly smiled and chuckled a little, it was easier working with a weapons fanatic with a sense of humor. Having someone like Ryan on their side reassured them that they could survive this battle. Whether or not they would win the war was a different story altogether. All 978 knew for sure was that they could only take this one step at a time.

"You know there's going to be a high amount of security," said 978. "Don't you think it would be easy to spot someone walking around with a flamethrower on their back?"

"Not if we set it up right," answered Ryan. "Or at least we won't be spotted right away. We'll insert the weapons into regular backpacks and walk around with those on. We'll also wear street clothes, displaying the typical look of college students. I know we're a little older, but at least we won't look as suspicious. Besides, who would honestly expect to see someone carrying around a flamethrower in the Boston Common?"

"I hope we'll only need to use them tonight," said Dr. Carlton.

"I don't know about that. It may cause significant damage to those replicas, but anything else we'll only be able to find out as we go along."

"I got my hopes up too soon."

"Not necessarily," said 978. "This is the first time that we'll be taking action, at least as far as the public will know. If we accomplish anything tonight, we will have made some progress, which is better than none."

Ryan made his way over to the closet door. He opened it and pulled out three outfits that looked like a cross between both exterminator and radiation suits. He walked back over to 978 and Dr. Carlton and handed one to each of them.

"What could we possibly need these for?" asked 978.

"For our trip into the Boston Common tonight," answered Ryan.

"I thought you that wanted us to make our best attempts to look like college students."

"We will."

"You're losing me."

"The route we'll take to get there, we might need these. We're not driving directly into the Boston Common. Instead we're going to park my truck at the shopping center near the Cambridge Station. The subway line is what we'll use as the main route to get there."

"You mean Old Alewife? That place has been condemned for years!"

"I know."

"Didn't you hear about a bunch of fires that got started down there by some militia supposedly? And then there were those kids who wandered into the tunnels. Only one girl was ever seen again, and she claimed that her friends were killed by some mutant-like creatures!"

"That gives us several more reasons to bring these suits and flamethrowers! I also have night-vision goggles along with the other weapons that we're taking with us. It may not be the safest route to travel, but we'll be far more prepared to face whatever is down there, along with what we're up against at the Boston Common!"

"It's not what I had in mind!"

"Did we have any of this in mind?! If you have a better suggestion, I'm all ears! I knew guys who were part of the search team who tried to find those kids. Do you know that they found? Absolutely nothing! The girl who survived was institutionalized for a long time after that!"

"Anybody would have to be if they went through what she claimed to have gone through."

"True. But there was no evidence found to support those claims, and the subway line is the best way to go if we wanted to avoid detection. I also know the guy who's in charge of security at the Cambridge Station. He's on duty tonight, so I'll go visit him up in the tower. If we can time it right, I'll be able to distract him long enough so you guys can sneak through the train yard. It will be easy for you guys to find a way to get inside the condemned Alewife building. As soon as a train pulls in, Gary will have to make sure that the passengers arrived safely. Then I'll meet up with you guys as fast as I can!"

"This Gary," said Dr. Carlton. "Is he an old war buddy?"

"Yeah," answered Ryan. "You might say that."

There had been enough discussion. At least that was what 978 started to think. They needed to pack up everything and go. Right now time was the number one priority, leaving them very little room to be able to stop and question everything. No matter how they felt, circumstances were not going to change. All they could do was move forward.

"Do you want to start loading up your truck?" asked Dr. Carlton.

"Yeah," answered Ryan.

"I thought so. Even with all this stuff, I was pretty sure you weren't keeping a tank down here."

Good old sarcastic humor. It never sounded so precious until now.

15 •••

Ryan pulled his truck in a space in the middle of the parking lot and shut the engine off. The three of them were at the Fresh Pond Mall and it was a little after five in the evening. It didn't take long to get there, but for 978 it felt like an eternity. The place was crowded, mostly due to the start of rush hour traffic. None of them were thrilled about that, but they had the advantage. It was busy enough that most people would not spot anything suspicious.

978 started to feel a bit nostalgic. His grandparents' old house was close by, and he also took notice of the movie theatre that was there. He started to remember when his father took him to the weekend matinees when he was really young. That was over thirty years ago, making the memories seem somewhat surreal. He didn't know for sure, but as far as he knew the mall and theatre had been there for over a century. It felt good to know that some things never change, even if it's a corporate consumer haven like a mall. This made 978 realize that the times people cherish can occur almost anywhere.

978, Dr. Carlton, and Ryan exited the truck and started gathering their so-called baggage out of the back. That specifically meant four suitcases and two large backpacks. Two of the suitcases held various weapons, the other two held the exterminator-like outfits and extra changes of clothes. The two backpacks carried the flamethrowers, which prompted 978 and Dr. Carlton to put them on quickly. Ryan wanted to say something, but decided that they were just being cautious. This was a new experience for them, and he didn't see the need to question his new partners if they were preparing themselves the same way many his fellow soldiers had. He figured that they deserved a lot of credit for being willing to carry these unbelievably dangerous weapons on their first mission. Everything was in order. 978 and Dr. Carlton were both wearing the backpacks and carrying a suitcase. Ryan grabbed the other two suitcases that held the rest of the weapons. It was very unlikely, but he found it easy to imagine a scenario where they could be stopped and searched. It might not look suspicious crossing the street near the bridge by the train station, but you can never be too careful.

"I'm going to call Gary," said Ryan, taking a phone out of his pocket. He pushed a button, most likely for an automatic dial, than put the phone up to his right ear.

"Cambridge Central Tower, Gary speaking," a voice answered.

"What's up, Boudreau?" asked Ryan.

"Ryan?" asked Gary.

"You got it!"

"What's up? You old scruff! I haven't heard from you since the New Year started! How long were you in Rio?"

"About three weeks."

"Three weeks? You're just getting back to me now? Sorry I couldn't go with you. That buddy of mine I hired hurt his back pretty bad. Other than that, you know the gig here is okay."

"How's he doing?"

"He hurt both disks, so I doubt he'll be back anytime soon. You know you're always welcome to come back, but we don't need to discuss that if you don't want to. We need to get together, and I mean sooner instead of later."

"I'm just up the street at the mall if you want to talk for a few minutes."

"That sounds good to me. You know how to get back up to the tower, don't you?"

"You bet."

"I'll be here."

"Alright, I'll be there soon."

Ryan shut off his phone and put it back in his pocket.

"We're all set," he said.

"Sounds easy," said Dr. Carlton.

"It should be. We'll walk over to the station and I'll leave all the stuff with you guys."

"He'll spot you. Won't that look kind of suspicious?"

"Not really, he'll just think I was trying to be helpful."

Ryan knew Gary would not view anything he did as suspicious, the simple reason being that he'd never lied his friend before. Of course there was a first time for everything, not that he wanted to start now. He didn't think he had much of a choice, because his good friend didn't deserve to get stuck in the middle of all this chaos. This was someone who was in a good place in life with a lovely lady to come home to every night.

978, Dr. Carlton, and Ryan only needed to wait a minute or so for the lights to change at the crosswalk. They quickly rushed across the street and headed toward the bridge. There was a set of stairs where the bridge began which lead down to the train station platform, and within a short time they arrived at that particular destination. Ryan handed over both of the suitcases he had been carrying to 978 and Dr. Carlton. He extended his right hand toward them so they could both shake it. This looked good since he wanted Gary to think he was helping two strangers.

"I'm going to head over to the tower so and talk to Gary for a while," said Ryan.

"How can we be sure what the right time will be to sneak over to Old Alewife?" asked Dr. Carlton.

"Is your phone on?"

"Yes."

"Your number is on my automatic speed dial. As soon as you hear it ring head over there quickly and start getting ready."

"How long do you think you'll be up there?"

"It will definitely take time to make our way down the

subway tracks, but we still have a few hours before that function actually starts. With any luck, we'll get there a little early."

Luck was almost nonexistent in 978's vocabulary. He hadn't had much since leaving Ryan's house, and gathering all the weapons was a very frightening reminder of what they were up against. Preventing disasters at political functions was not something he did on a regular basis, much less coming face to face with his own replica. Was there any chance of knowing how tonight would turn out? Of course not, and he could also think of plenty of other places he would rather be. But the only thing he could do was stay with Dr. Carlton while Ryan talked his friend and wait for her phone to ring.

When Ryan reached the tower he opened the door and made sure to lock it once he was inside. He assumed that Gary left it unlocked since he was expected, but decided to be cautious. He quickly made his way up the stairs to the top floor. The entrance to the main security office was a large set of double doors, which Gary was required to keep locked at all times. Ryan pushed the buzzer, and within seconds his friend came out and greeted him with all smiles.

"How are you, my good man?" asked Gary. "Come on in and have a seat, we haven't talked in ages!"

"Thanks," said Ryan, making his way into the office. He sat in a chair next to a set of windows so he could see 978 and Dr. Carlton, but made sure not to look outside just yet.

"Were those friends of yours?"

"What?"

"That couple outside, you helped them with their luggage."

"No, I was just giving them a hand."

"Typical of the old scruff, you'll give the shirt off your back to just about anyone!"

"It depends on the weather."

The two of them shared a laugh for a moment, but quickly began to talk again.

"So how's Janice doing?" asked Ryan.

"You know me," said Gary. "I can't complain. She doesn't object to me doing the occasional night shift, plus it was our anniversary just last weekend."

"What's it been? Eight years now?"

"You're right on the money. What about you? Seen anyone lately?"

"No not really."

"I know you still talk to that sister-in-law of yours, the doctor. What's her name?"

"Wendy."

"That's it."

"Yeah, she's doing alright."

"Hook up with her, or maybe she has some single friends."

"Come on, Gary! She's my wife's sister!"

"I know, but if I remember right she's not shacked up with anybody. It was just a suggestion."

"No one can replace Marie."

"I can't imagine anyone replacing Janice, either."

Ryan was relieved that they reached an understanding. He didn't want the entire conversation with Gary to be one big debate. His friend meant well, so there was no resentment building up inside. Tonight was going to be hard enough without arguments from others. He felt bad deceiving the guy, but there was nothing he could do.

"Something on your mind, Ryan?" asked Gary.

"No," answered Ryan, half-heartedly, trying to think of something to say. "Are you still able to watch movies here?"

"You bet! The only difference watching them here is that you can't get drunk throughout the night!"

The two of them shared another laugh, convincing Ryan that the plan would go smoothly.

"It doesn't take much to keep us entertained," said Ryan.

"That's probably why we always got along with the wives so easily," added Gary.

"This is true. I honestly don't remember Marie complaining very often."

"Yeah, I guess you're ready to settle down once you start slowing down."

"That makes sense."

Ryan wasn't thrilled to talk about the wives, but the conversation was heading in a positive direction. Still, he knew that he needed to think of something to talk about quick to keep Gary distracted. That something suddenly came to mind.

"I was wondering," said Ryan. "How is this television and monitor system set up?"

"The way it's done," answered Gary. "Guys like you and I can't go wrong."

Ryan knew this might take a while. Now it was just a matter of when would be the best time to signal Dr. Carlton. It wasn't very long. Within seconds Gary rigged it to see the regular television on every monitor. He pulled the phone out of his pocket then quickly remembered that he had to turn it back on again. He hoped his friend would be too preoccupied carrying on about all the fancy details regarding the whole television and monitor system to hear the faint chiming sound which indicated that the communication device came back on. To his relief the answer was affirmative, prompting him to press the call button and place the phone back in his pocket. Now he could simply play along and just listen to his friend's conversation to occupy another couple of minutes. The channels changed regularly by the remote control that Gary was using. A movie here, a talk show there, and some reruns before finally settling on some cop show they both liked. After a few minutes Ryan looked outside and set his sights on the train station platform. He saw at least six people, but 978 and Dr. Carlton were nowhere to be seen.

"When's the next train supposed to arrive?" asked Ryan.

"Any minute now," answered Gary. "How many people did you see down there?"

"There were at least six."

Ryan didn't want to give an exact number. He wasn't too concerned about that. The only thing that mattered was if 978 and Dr. Carlton made it into the Old Alewife building undetected. He peaked outside again and saw a light off in the distance, and the expected train was arriving.

"The train's here," said Ryan.

"Right on schedule," said Gary. "Take a walk down with me. I need to talk to the conductor and you know I can't let you stay up here in the tower alone."

"Sure."

Ryan followed Gary outside the office doors. They quickly started to head downstairs, making Ryan curious if his friend remembered leaving the television broadcasting over the monitors. Normally he would have said something, but this would not be one of those times. He started to worry when they reached the bottom floor and Gary opened the door to head over to the platform. There was a chance Gary would notice that 978 and Dr. Carlton were not present among the rest of the passengers. The two of them would be easy to spot due to the large amount of stuff they were carrying. Luckily, when they reached the platform everyone waiting for the train had already boarded. He felt relieved. Then a man with dark hair and a moustache in a black uniform stepped down from one of the passenger cars and immediately extended the right hand out to shake Gary's.

"What's up, captain?" asked the conductor, with an Australian accent.

"Same old stuff, Quinn!" answered Gary.

"That's what I thought! Here are those inspection papers ya need."

Quinn reached into his right jacket pocket and pulled out two sheets of paper. He unfolded them and handed them to Gary.

"Who's your friend?" asked Quinn.

"This is an old friend of mine, Ryan Richmond," said Gary. "We go way back together during our time in the Air Force. We met overseas only to find out he grew up two towns over from me!"

"Like they always say," said Ryan. "It's a small world!"

"Pleased to meet you," said Quinn, shaking Ryan's hand.

"Same here."

"Any friend of Boudreau's is a friend of mine. It's smart to connect with folks who are always nice. Better luck than I had in recent years."

"It wasn't always like that for me," said Gary.

"Live and learn!" stated Quinn. "That is something you have always been able to do."

"C'mon, Quinn, lots of things have changed for the better in your life as well, especially in the past few years."

"Yeah, I know. Well, it's time to get a move on. Until next time Gary. Ryan, I hope I get a chance to talk to you soon. Now off I go!"

Quinn climbed up the first step of the passenger car and grabbed on to the railing. As the train departed he leaned out slightly to wave goodbye. Ryan started to think about how that was always done in the old days.

"Great guy," said Gary.

"I noticed the Australian accent," said Ryan. "How long has he been living in the States?"

"It's been a few years now. He came over here permanently after his divorce. I guess he needed a change of scenery. I'd rather deal with the climate in his home country myself. This was probably the best way to move on with his life."

"It makes sense."

The moment the train was out of sight Ryan and Gary started walking back to the tower. There was a little daylight left, which meant that Ryan would find an opening into Old Alewife easily. He also hoped that both 978 and Dr. Carlton made it in alright, and were getting prepared for the big trek down the subway tunnels and waiting for him.

"You want to come back up?" asked Gary. "I'll make some coffee."

"I'm all set," answered Ryan. "I need to get going."

"That's cool."

The two shook hands. Gary opened the door and headed inside. Ryan knew it would take a minute for his friend to get all the way upstairs to the main office. At that exact moment he made a break for it. Thank God for Gary's trust, along with leaving the regular television broadcasting over the monitors.

16 •••

It didn't take long for Ryan to find an opening that would allow him to get into the Old Alewife building. He was just grateful that he didn't have to force his way through a crawlspace or something. All the hectic stuff he'd endured over the past twenty-four hours was enough for now. The last thing he needed to cope with was claustrophobia. Then again, the majority of the subway tunnels weren't exactly filled with wide open spaces. But this was another mission where he would simply do what he had to do. Upon entering, he immediately looked around and above him. There were many cracks high up on the walls and the roof. A little bit of light was shining through, meaning he was setting his eyes on the last of the sunset. If the place ever got demolished it would truly see the light.

In a short time the sun vanished completely. Ryan was about to take out his flashlight, but he heard a spark and some mumbling voices. He looked toward the direction of a large staircase which would lead down to the old subway tracks that were no longer being used. He walked over and stood at the top of the stairs when he saw exactly what he expected to see,

978 and Dr. Carlton. The two of them had lit a flare so they could see what they were doing. Ryan had made it downstairs by the time they had their protection suits on.

"What's going on, guys?" he asked.

"Now I really feel like an exterminator!" answered 978.

"You're telling me!" added Dr. Carlton.

"Maybe this would have been a better career choice. I wouldn't have made much money or receive job stability that a guard gets, nor would I be forced to battle replicas! You can also get away with murder, at least when it comes to bugs!"

"But they keep coming back."

"But you can kill them again. Wait, now that I think about it, because of that there would be job stability!"

978 and Dr. Carlton shared another laugh. This was a bit of a relief for Ryan, especially since none of them knew how this expedition down the tracks would turn out. They were armed, but this could be far beyond dangerous. Those years in the Air Force he never thought that he would get involved in a situation like this. Not then, not now, not ever. But he knew he couldn't tell 978 or Dr. Carlton that. He had to remain strong tonight.

Ryan took the last protection suit out and started to put it on. It would only take a few minutes to get dressed since he'd worn the outfit before, even though it was a long time ago. Now came the time to decide who was going to carry certain weapons. 978 and Dr. Carlton were already putting the backpacks on again which carried the flamethrowers, just as they had upon arriving at the mall. As much as he could appreciate the incentive, Ryan still thought he should say something.

"Are the two of you sure you want to carry those things all the way down the tracks?" he asked.

"Definitely," answered Dr. Carlton, with 978 nodding in agreement.

"That's good enough for me. It shouldn't take long to sort out the rest of the weapons and divide them amongst ourselves. I just hope that we have enough time to figure out what to do when we arrive at the Boston Common."

"You're right," said 978. "Especially since we need to consider who to watch out for, we'll need to keep our eyes peeled for the Zen gang."

"I almost forgot about that. With any luck, maybe they'll be sticking out like a sore thumb."

"That would definitely help."

"Just remember those guys are still taking orders from the replica," said Dr. Carlton. "So it would be a smart if we didn't stick out at all."

"Remember what I told you before," said Ryan. "The moment we're above ground we'll have the protection suits have and have plain clothes on. Those backpacks will help us look like college students, only slightly older."

"I can say I loved medical school so much I wanted to do it twice."

Those last words said by Dr. Carlton and Ryan were meant to be dry humor. But despite all the quick planning, there was no room for error. Ryan knew this situation would be no different than any other military strategy, he just hoped that the first situations would be the right ones. Still, could all three of them trust their instincts? He thought so. It was easier to accomplish something when you believed in yourself and the others who supported the cause. But there was something more to this mission than most that convinced him they could win both the battle and the war.

Ryan reached back into a suitcase and took out three pairs of goggles. They were used specifically for enhanced vision and protection in dark areas, and deserted subway tunnels were more than appropriate. In all honestly he could not remember the last time he used this stuff, except the fact that it was while he was still in the Air Force, a long time ago. He tried on a pair, then handed the other two to 978 and Dr. Carlton.

"I didn't know we were going skiing," said 978, sounding sarcastic.

"Just try them on," said Ryan. "Then look for a small switch on the upper right side."

"Wow! We definitely won't need flares or flashlights anymore!"

"Exactly, and we won't attract attention to ourselves either."

"But you said we wouldn't have that problem down here."

"We shouldn't, it will just be easier than using flares or flashlights."

"I believe it," said Dr. Carlton, almost immediately after testing her goggles. "I just hope these things don't run on cheap batteries."

"Far from it!" stated Ryan, rather proudly.

After another few short minutes all three of them were suited up and prepared. Of course Ryan made sure they conducted a safety check with all the weapons. Venturing down these tunnels, no one could be totally sure what would happen. Perhaps nothing, but it would also be one less task to perform once they reached their stop at the Green Line. Now it was time to go, so Ryan heading over toward the edge of the platform where the tracks were. 978 and Dr. Carlton followed him from behind.

"Now it's time to take our first leap of faith!" boasted Ryan, jumping off the edge of the platform and landing on the subway tracks.

"You won't hear me shout the word 'Geronimo!' with any honest to God enthusiasm!" said Dr. Carlton, following suit.

"I'm still convinced that a train will come," said 978, leaping down right after Dr. Carlton had done so. He still had some vivid memories of taking the train into Harvard Square as a teenager, quite often with Will tagging along.

"It doesn't matter how dark it gets down here," said Ryan.

"I'm sure you remember how loud those trains were, if one was coming you would definitely hear it."

"True."

"How about a ghost train?" joked Dr. Carlton.

"Don't get me started! We'll have enough problems dealing with the technological horror of fighting those replicas! We don't need to make up supernatural garbage on top of that!"

"Maybe it will help if we all agree right now that none of us believe in ghosts?"

"Amen to that!"

After 978 made that last remark the silence between all of them was louder than words. He thought about what he said before that. It must have sounded like an over-analytical scientist on the edge of a nervous breakdown. Dr. Carlton would have been far more in the right to talk like that. Then again, he was only beginning to realize what he was up against. Maybe now she was slightly impressed if what he said grasped the basic concept of the replicas. Perhaps he was more technologically inclined than he once believed, but how much of it did he really want to know?

Even though all three of them had just completed a final, but fast inspection, they were still taking mental notes of the weapons on them. Dr. Carlton had the least to worry about: with the exception of the big flamethrower, she only had one handgun, a couple of mini-bombs, and some extra ammunition. 978 also carried his share of mini-bombs, along with two pistols and a 2050 hunting rifle. The rifle had always remained very popular among gun enthusiasts, the large bullets it fired along with the speed and impact could instantly kill a wild animal or a human with just one shot. Out of the three of them, Ryan looked the most convincing as a super soldier. Along with his favorite machine gun, the vest he wore over the protection suit which carried many explosives, and a belt which held guns in separate holsters. Last but not least he'd put strap-on Velcro on his legs that held various blades, and the backpack he'd put on would contain items that 978 or Dr. Carlton knew nothing about. Just judging by their appearances one might suspect that they were about to engage in an all-out war, which wouldn't be far off.

Now it was time to forge on ahead. The only thing they could was try to keep a steady pace, especially since their purpose for being down in these tunnels was not sightseeing. The goggles did drastically improve their vision, but didn't help much with colors or details. What you would see with these things on were either light grey or dark green. If you were unsure of what was approaching you would have to think fast and rush to judgment. That was how things were in heavy combat. In a way, these circumstances made Ryan feel right at home.

978 knew it would be quite a while before all three of them arrived at the Boston Common. The best thing to do was try to clear his mind and continue moving forward. This got him to think about meditation, which was something he didn't attempt to do very often. He envisioned himself riding a bicycle on a path in a wooded area. Not a bad picture. However, the subway tracks were unbelievably dirty and the tunnels were too dark, even with the fancy goggles on. The last thing he thought about was how quiet the overnight shift could be at work. He just desperately wanted to think of anything to help him stay calm.

Dr. Carlton seemed to have the best head on her shoulders. Of course wandering through dark and condemned subway tunnels wasn't her idea of a good time, all she could do was go with the flow. That was what got her through medical school, but there was nothing to indicate if the same attitude would do any good here. She started to have a bad feeling about this, an intuition of some sort. She may have had the right idea about just going with the flow, but was convinced they might encounter something far worse down here than anything that will occur later on tonight at the Governor's speech. The first sign of trouble slowly surfaced in front of them in the form of a light-colored furry carcass on the tracks.

"Check that out," said 978, speaking barely above a whispering tone with some intensity.

"What is that?" asked Ryan, stopping and looking down at the carcass with Dr. Carlton right behind him.

"It looks like a dog, maybe a husky. Possibly it's a wolf? I don't have a clue."

"Look at the blood, I think it's fresh. I'd swear there are big chunks of flesh gone, and maybe some bite marks, from what I can see. You're the doctor, Wendy, what do you think?"

"I don't know," said Dr. Carlton. "I did pretty well in medical school, but I wasn't studying to be a veterinarian."

"Could you determine what species the bite marks came from?"

"I don't know, I think it would be too difficult to figure that out right away with all the blood soaked into the fur."

The real truth was that Dr. Carlton didn't want to know. It's very easy to determine whether bite marks made by humans and animals, despite having very little experience with dentistry. However, the moment Ryan handed her a flashlight she kneeled down for a closer look. The answer was obvious, but she didn't want 978 or Ryan to know that.

"What do you think?" asked Ryan.

"I don't know," answered Dr. Carlton. "But we shouldn't worry about it. Let's keep moving, we have a long way to go."

Dr. Carlton was now convinced that she didn't have a grip on reality. She was in denial, and didn't have it in her to speak up. She tried being rational by telling herself that this was an isolated incident, but it didn't make her feel any better. She thought it best to take the handgun out and keep her finger on the trigger.

978, Dr. Carlton, and Ryan continued to travel down the

old subway tracks and stayed close together. They were all a lot more nervous than before, even if none of them were willing to admit it. However, despite their grotesque discovery, 978 started to think that Ryan had forced them to over prepare. Carrying these dangerous weapons down these deserted tunnels would make anyone uneasy. Not to mention the fact that maybe it wasn't unusual finding an animal carcass down here, and Dr. Carlton said there was nothing to worry about. He definitely trusted her opinion, but noticed that her examination was very brief.

"Are you alright?" asked 978. "I'm sure examining that dead animal back there was pretty gruesome."

"I'm certainly not going back to check it again!" stated Dr. Carlton, sounding a bit defensive. She knew that 978 and Ryan had trusted her analysis, but that didn't mean she was telling the truth.

"I'm sorry. I guess I'm a little freaked out by it."

"Same here," she responded.

"Don't count me out!" added Ryan.

Now the three of them started to pick up the pace, almost to the point where they started jogging. This would help them reach their destination a lot sooner, but the most important thing was trying to get through this underground dungeon quicker. They didn't want to think about coming back afterwards, especially Dr. Carlton. There was the remote possibility that they might not need to, depending how everything turns out tonight.

It didn't take 978 long to figure out exactly where they were, because the goggles made everything distinctive enough to realize that they had just passed through Davis Square. Of course just about anybody could have since it was posted on the walls, along with a lot more graffiti than 978 remembered. But it had been almost twenty years, so what could he expect? The best thing to do was remember the good times. Right now, however, time had taken on another meaning altogether. Tonight it was a matter of life and death.

978, Dr. Carlton, and Ryan were approximately midway through the tunnel between Davis Square and Porter Square. 978 felt a bit relieved knowing that when they arrived at the next stop there wouldn't be this huge crowd of tourists or college students wandering around, not that it bothered him much to begin with. If it was a big deal to him he would never have agreed to present himself as a college student at the speech happening in a little while. He could do far worse if he considered that a replica was out there impersonating him, which he did. Especially since its' assignment was to protect the Governor at all costs, supposedly. But right now something far more problematic was about to occur. The three of them could hear a fluttering sound along with some small chunks of the ceiling falling on the tracks. This was all happening about twenty to thirty feet ahead.

"What was that?" asked 978.

"I don't know," answered Ryan. "Wendy, did you see anything?"

"No," answered Dr. Carlton.

Immediately after Dr. Carlton spoke she wanted to eat her words. She looked up at the ceiling and swore she was setting her eyes on some kind of creature with wings, larger than any bird she had ever seen. The chest of this thing was slightly moving in and out, most likely since it needed to breathe. But the sounds it made came out like a cross between a deep groan and a light growl. She shined the flashlight Ryan gave her closer to the central area of this unknown specimen, thinking it might be either hibernating or chained to the ceiling.

She was wrong on both counts.

The creature spread open what could only be determined as bat-like wings. What Dr. Carlton first thought was a supernatural abomination remained perched on the ceiling about fifteen feet ahead of them. She shined the flashlight a bit further down directly into its eyes. She then saw wide eyes and large mouth open with a screeching sound to match its terrifying appearance before it started to fly and charge towards them.

"Look out!" screamed Dr. Carlton, then aimed her handgun and fired three shots. The first bullet hit the bat-like creature in the chest. The next one hit its head, directly between the eyes. For some reason, unknown to her, the last shot she took toward the ceiling above, causing more chunks and debris to land on the creature which was lying dead on the tracks in front of all three of them.

978, Dr. Carlton, and Ryan rushed over to this bat-like creature they hoped was dead.

"You're a better shooter than you realize!" said Ryan, attempting to observe the winged thing.

"Never mind that!" snapped Dr. Carlton. "Have you seen anything like this? It's huge!"

"A fruit bat, maybe?" inquired 978. "Those are supposed to be big."

"I can assure you," said Ryan. "This is bigger than any fruit bat."

"What do you think it is, then?"

"It's bigger than any fruit bat you'll ever find, especially around here. This particular one is roughly the same size of the bats that were being studied in the labs a few years back."

"Are you saying that this thing is the result of a military experiment gone wrong?!" exclaimed Dr. Carlton.

"I'm not sure. As far as I know bats like this one had been originally discovered and captured in Central America. A couple of guys that were still working on the base when I retired got assigned to look after these creatures. It was shut down very quickly without any explanation."

"So they just let these things loose? How did this get down here?!"

"I have no idea, but I do know that you won't learn about

this on any nature program!"

"I think we should just keep moving forward!" snapped 978, more or less cutting off their argument. He didn't see any point in debating over this thing that was dead, hopefully. There were simply wasting valuable time. He also knew that there was no turning back no matter how much he wanted to. It was difficult to imagine how Ryan felt at this moment, especially considering the fact that the origin of the creature was a giant bat, supposedly.

"You're right," said Ryan. "We should go, but not yet."

"Why not?" asked 978.

"I want to take a few minutes to examine this thing. Since we have a doctor in the house, we should take advantage of the possibility that we might learn something."

"I told you before," said Dr. Carlton. "I specialize in human anatomy, and replicas to a lesser extent. No animals have been replicated, at least not to my knowledge."

"But there has been a massive amount of cloning throughout the past several decades. Everybody knows that. It's also much easier to control clones of animals instead of humans. You only fired two shots, and that thing went down pretty quickly."

"You forgot something," said 978.

"What's that?"

"The specific areas on the creature's body that the bullets penetrated, one hit the chest, a fatal spot, and the other one right between the eyes, which practically guarantees death."

"True. But I think we should consider ourselves lucky. Those things are known to ambush prey a lot quicker compared to the attempt on us. At least that's what I learned from those guys working in the labs a few years back, and from the small amount of research that I had done on my own. Like I said before, the operation got shut down quickly without any explanation whatsoever. Of course that's nothing new when it comes to experiments involving both the military and the government. The thing that troubles me is when the operation got shut down the laboratory is automatically required to be quarantined until enough gas is released in order to paralyze the creatures, and eventually kill them. The one thing that's never discussed is the disposal of the carcasses. You would think that these things would be stored and preserved and put in a place like Area 51 or something, obviously that's not the case."

"It looks like the subway tunnels are being used as the local dump to dispose these things. And apparently some of them were still alive when they got dropped off."

"Let's just hope there aren't any more of them," said Dr. Carlton.

"Same here," added Ryan. "But he's right."

"Right about what?" she asked.

"There could be more of them."

"So you're saying we might have to keep an eye out for these things all the way to the Boston Common?"

"I don't know. But I think we should take a minute to examine it a bit closer. Maybe it'll give us an idea of what were up against."

"If you say so," she said, albeit reluctantly.

978 wanted to add something to the discussion, but couldn't think of anything. He just wanted to move forward, but Ryan was right in saying that they might learn something from this incident. As to exactly what he had no idea. Despite how crazy this particular incident was, he had some serious doubts that they would encounter another one of these giant bats down here. Unfortunately, there was no way to know for sure. They also had to consider the fact that they might have a run-in with something or someone else even worse. Of course he wasn't about to mention that to Ryan or Dr. Carlton or attempt to guess what that something or someone might be.

Now it was time for a closer look. Both Ryan and Dr. Carlton kneeled down to start conduct something that was considered to be far from any standard procedure. This abomination bared no resemblance to any kind of bat they had seen before. Then again, none of them had ever taken the time studying these creatures. So what did they know? It started to feel like they were forced to make baby steps when it came to every aspect of this ordeal. It would be absolutely justified to lose patience, but they couldn't afford to at this point. Many lives were at stake, and for some it was over already.

Time was crucial.

Ryan shined the flashlight on the spots that Dr. Carlton inspected. At least that was the only word which came to mind while looking over the creature. She honestly didn't know what to do, except take a small blade to cut the thing open to determine if it was a clone. But something like that would take time, and sarcastically thought to herself that she might as well spend the entire night performing open heart surgery. Medicine and technology had become far more advanced in this day and age, but that didn't make the process any quicker.

However, Dr. Carlton came up with an idea. For some reason, she had remembered to bring a stethoscope with her. She knew that the creature hadn't moved an inch since she'd shot it, and it wasn't breathing either. She decided that the only reason to deal with this thing was if it had any signs of life, and the heartbeat seemed to be the best thing to check. She looked up at 978 to give him instructions.

"Take a gun out," she said. "And keep it pointed at this thing."

"Are you sure about that?" he asked.

"Just do it."

"You got it."

She didn't need Ryan or 978 to waste their time and energy trying to turn this thing over. In this day and age certain types of stethoscopes could check for a heartbeat from both the front and back of humans and animals, and the one she had on her could do just that. The best part about using this particular model was the fact that it could detect a heartbeat very quickly with all large-sized creatures whether they're humans or animals.

Dr. Carlton put the earphones on, which she thought was the best part about using this thing. Unlike other stethoscopes, the hearing equipment for this was almost exactly like what was used for listening to most types of audio sounds such as radio frequencies, music recordings, or even the close-caption devices for the deaf in order to watch television. She felt a lot more comfortable, especially since she honestly had no idea what to expect from this creature which all three of them could only describe as a monster-sized bat.

It only took another minute or so for Dr. Carlton to discover where on the back area of the creature where she could read the heartbeat. Now it was time to listen closely. That came easily because, like every medical doctor, she knew what the standard heart rate was right off the top of her head. Also, no one had to remind her that time was crucial, and not just for herself, but 978 and Ryan as well. She took three minutes to make an exact reading, which she determined as normal. What she was unable to figure out for the life of her was that the creature showed no other signs of life. How could it possibly have a normal heartbeat?

"Wait a minute," she said to herself.

"What is it?" asked Ryan.

"These goggles have micro-lock connectors, right?"

"Of course they do."

"Are any of them operational?"

"They all are, but mine should be the easiest one to use. Why, do you want to look up something?"

"Yeah, but can it also do a scan-analysis and get an answer back in a short amount of time from your computer?"

"Sure. Let me guess, you want to find whatever information

there is on this thing, right?"

"Yes, can you do that?"

"You got it."

Ryan moved a little closer to the creature. He twisted a small button located on the top right side of the goggles he was wearing, not even a millimeter away from the lens. The only indication of technical activity occurred when a light green glow came from the eyes which only lasted about twenty seconds, not that any of them kept track of how much time it was taking. Dr. Carlton had more knowledge than 978 regarding how these goggles worked, but she was far from being any kind of expert, at least compared to Ryan. But that wasn't important right now, as long as Ryan knew how to work the thing and retrieve the information that she needed at the moment.

Dr. Carlton knew they had a serious problem on their hands. She was unable to detect any signs of life with this creature except a normal heart rate, a normal human heart rate to be precise. The main reason she asked Ryan to do a formal scan-analysis was so she could determine the origin of the species, both the type and location, whether it came out of Central America or whatever.

"I got something," said Ryan.

"What did you find?" asked Dr. Carlton.

"The information I have here indicates that this creature originated as a Big Brown Bat, most commonly seen around Nevada."

"You mentioned Central America earlier. Does it mention that area at all?"

"Give me a minute, I'll log on to specific areas."

Ryan twisted another small button which was directly behind the first one he used for the scan-analysis. This particular button simply made an arrow move up and down a small screen, after finding the specific option required for information. Last but not least you push the same button and log on to that particular site, and with the right set-up access will always be granted with no problem whatsoever. This equipment that's still used on many kinds of eyewear to this day are modeled after older prototypes of technology but remain very effective if they are taken care of, which was something Ryan always did thoroughly.

"It does mention Central America," stated Ryan. "They do exist down there, but they're extremely rare. There's no other information beyond that. Can you think of anything?"

"Maybe," answered Dr. Carlton. "The first theory that comes to mind is migration, but I'm not sure if that applies to both bats and birds. Try to remember I didn't study to be a veterinarian. I know that the climates in Nevada and Central America are extremely hot, so I guess we should forget that migration theory altogether. But it's obviously not impossible for these types of bats to find a way down there."

"The full scan-analysis is complete."

"What have you got?"

Ryan waited couple of more seconds to see a full reading displayed, but he didn't respond right away. If he didn't have the eyewear then it would have been obvious to see his reluctance to answer.

"You're not going to believe this," said Ryan.

"What is it?" asked Dr. Carlton.

"The reading equally divides the creature's body structure into three separate types."

"Go on."

Dr. Carlton already knew what two of the types were. She just wanted to hear him clarify all three, just to be convinced that she wasn't crazy.

"We already know the first one," he said. "The big brown bat, but this is where it gets bizarre. The second one is human, which is tough for me to accept despite suggesting that possibility already. But this last one, I know I said that stuff was going on in the labs back at the base, proves to me that those eggheads did not know what they were dealing with."

"Alright," said Dr. Carlton. "What is it then?"

"It's like I said, those lab geeks obviously didn't know everything, so the last part can't be specified."

"What does it say?"

"That's very simple.......unknown."

"Unknown?"

"That's right, so it could be anything. I can't even get the computer to break down the components for the last part, so there are no records of it anywhere."

"That's just great!" snapped 978. "So you're saying that whatever it is could range from some unknown alien DNA to a replica structure?"

"Now take it easy," said Ryan. "You've been through enough already and in a very short amount of time. We're here for you and we also want to help. You've kept yourself together real well, sometimes better than I did during my entire twenty years in the service. If we're able to make it through this alive you'll deserve some kind of honor from the service."

978 stayed silent. Ryan had a point. There weren't that many people around who went through these experiences like this within a period of a day or two. He'd already survived a gunshot wound. But it felt far worse just knowing that his replica killed Staff Sergeant 101 in cold blood back at the prison. All he had to do was look in the mirror to see the face of a murderer. Luckily for him there wasn't a massive quantity of reflective surfaces available in the subway tunnels. However, having his right foot placed on this creature's carcass while aiming a gun at it wasn't exactly a pretty sight either. There was no way to have a full view of this thing due to the darkness, and now knowing that a portion of this creature's genetic structure was unknown made it even more nerve-wracking.

"I can tell you this much," said Ryan. "It's almost impossible for this creature to have any type of replica structure. The scan-analysis would have indicated that. Not to mention the fact that animal replication is still in the infancy stages, and I hope to God it doesn't get beyond that in our lifetime. The unknown component is definitely from a living organism, as to exactly what that is I have no idea."

"I can tell you one thing," said Dr. Carlton. "So far this creature is not showing any signs of life, except a regular heart rate."

"That's strange. You'd figure being down here for so long it would've been in hibernation."

"It's not a bat's heart rate that I'm reading."

"What is it then?"

"A human heart rate down to the exact count per minute, what I can't figure out is how this creature is technically dead. There's no breathing, there's nothing."

"As much as I trust you're judgment," said 978. "That stethoscope or whatever it is, are you sure it's working right?"

"Yes," answered Dr. Carlton, not sounding the slightest bit annoyed. "I'm positive. It looks like this creature is defying all logic in regards to medical science, and you can thank people like myself knowing that it's the result of human tampering."

"Don't be so hard on yourself," said Ryan. "You didn't have anything to do with these kinds of experiments. It's like I told you before, I knew stuff like this was going on back at the base. I should have done more to find out what was going on."

"You might not be here with us right now if you had," said 978.

"That may be true. But I might have been able to do something which would have stopped it altogether. You're right, though. I probably would have been thrown in prison for the rest of my life, that or gotten killed as a result of it. I would have chosen the latter."

"I'm sure we'll learn a lot more about this in the near future whether we like it or not," said Dr. Carlton.

"I hope so, said Ryan. "But only if we can put a stop to it."

"That's wishful thinking," added 978. "For now anyway, let's take it one step at a time."

If the three of them put some thought into exactly where they were, then there should have been a time limit placed on sharing their infinite wisdom with one another. Of course there's nothing wrong with being a little bit introspective when attempting to carry out the plans they made. Also, with the exception of the mutant bat-like creature attacking them, these deserted subway tunnels weren't such a bad place to concentrate better. God willing there would be no more run-ins with a big brown bat/human being/unknown mixed abominations that could easily attack and eat them alive. There best bet however, was to be ready for anything.

978 took his right foot off the creatures back then placed it onto the ground, about two inches away from the subway rail. He briefly looked over the carcass before looking up and Dr. Carlton and Ryan to put his two cents worth in again.

"You know something?" asked 978. "In most cases I'd feel bad about shooting any animal that's as wounded and immobile as this one. But as far as I'm concerned, this is an exception to the rule. Like you said, Doc, this was the result of human tampering. Let's not forget the fact that this thing is technically dead besides the heart rate, a human one by God!"

"You got a good point," said Dr. Carlton. "I can't bear to look at this thing anymore. Do your stuff so we can move on."

"My pleasure!" boasted 978.

"Let's step back a few feet," said Ryan to Dr. Carlton, who stood up and followed his lead.

978 placed his right foot on the bat-like abomination's back a second time. He pointed his gun with his right hand toward the upper part of the back, directly below the neck area. He thought if this thing came back to life again a gunshot wounds in the back and neck area would at the very least leave it paralyzed. Not to mention the fact that if there

was anyone else crazy enough to trek through the Old Alewife subway tunnels then it would be easier to spot this creature lying on the tracks, much unlike the danger the three of them faced when it flew down from the ceiling to most likely ambush and destroy them. None of them wanted to consider the possibility of being this animal's next meal. That wasn't the worst of it either. Since they were able to determine that this creature contained at least one-third human genetic components, it wasn't just a carnivore, but also a cannibal.

Next the unthinkable happened. The back of the creature that 978 had placed his right foot on rose several inches into the air, indicating that it was beginning to breathe again. This startled 978, which showed as soon as he took several steps back. Why he didn't fire his gun at that moment was beyond him. The last thing he wanted was for this creature to wreak havoc upon them again, much less anyone else. But it would become far worse in a matter of seconds. The sounds that came out of the creature's mouth were beyond belief. What 978 heard while it breathed in and out was something that reminded him more of a bull than a bat. This forced 978, Dr. Carlton, and Ryan to contemplate what the full genetic structure of this creature might be. After all one third of it was unknown, causing even more confusion. Especially now with this bat-like abomination that made sounds of another animal which it bared no resemblance to. At this point they knew there was no rational explanation. The three of them looked up and locked their eyes on one another. It only lasted for a few seconds but it felt like an eternity. It seemed almost incredible when someone actually spoke up.

"Go ahead," said Ryan to 978. "I'm not going to stop you."

"From what?" he asked.

"Shoot it!"

978 took another couple of seconds to aim the gun at the upper area of the creature's back, but his enthusiasm diminished the moment this thing started sounding like a bull.

He told himself none of that mattered now, and to get on with it. One shot and the breathing slowed down, but it didn't stop completely. He placed his foot on this abomination's lower back again, ready to fire. Right when he was going to pull the trigger the creature made another bull-like sound. This time it was louder than ever and the screeching tone hurt all their ears. At this point all three of them anticipated this thing to rise up again and demolish whatever was in the way, prompting 978 to raise the gun higher and put a bullet in the back of the head to guarantee death. He shot the creature in the head, and for a brief moment after that there was an awkward silence between them.

None of them could have predicted what would happen next.

Bolts of electricity shot up from the subway tracks which looked like lightning, striking the creature and causing 978 to fall off the back again. The sensation he felt was indescribable. It kind of felt like being ejected from an Air Force fighter pilot's seat, which made sense considering the fact that he had also been thrown back several feet. The protection suits the three of them were wearing prevented any risk of being electrocuted. Dr. Carlton and Ryan quickly rushed over to 978 to see if he was alright.

"If that's as close as I'll come to getting hit by lightning," said 978, as he began to sit upright. "That's fine by me!"

"Are you sure you're alright?" asked Dr. Carlton.

"Yeah," he answered. "Probably thanks to these protection suits!"

"I thought they might come in handy," said Ryan. "But I didn't think it would be for something like that."

"At this point we should be ready to expect almost anything," said Dr. Carlton.

"You got that right. We've really got to watch it now."

"What are you mean?" asked 978, getting frustrated. "We almost got ambushed and eaten alive by this giant bat thing!

And I more or less just got hit by lightning! Don't get me wrong I'm very thankful we brought these protection suits with us, but what else should we watch out for?!"

"Lightning may have only struck once," said Ryan. "But that's all we needed to see to reach the next conclusion."

"What?" he asked.

"I think I know where he's going with this," said Dr. Carlton. "These subway tracks are operational."

"That's great! So you're saying we should prepare ourselves to get hit by a train?!"

"I don't know about that," said Ryan, trying to stay calm. "But there's obviously some type of human activity happening down here. I haven't heard of any plans to reopen this subway line within the next few years. So the military could be conducting experiments down here."

"Like this thing," said 978, pointing at the carcass. "Great. I'll try to look on the bright side. Maybe you'll run into some old war buddies and have a few drinks!"

Ryan wasn't sure if 978 was beyond frightened or merely displaying a sarcastic sense of humor. It was probably a bit of both. There was no time to figure that out now. The best thing to do was move forward and be prepared for anything, even if it meant being hit by a train.

••• 17

As the three of them continued hiking down the subway tracks, 978 began feeling a lot less nostalgic. The anticipation inside of him was something he hoped would diminish completely, mostly because of what just happened. It was pretty much impossible to believe further encounters with whatever was down here would be anything worthwhile, except for actual survival. He tried to ignore the slight adrenaline rush flowing through his body, which wasn't a big deal compared to the sensation he felt a short while ago. He still longed for the edginess to subside altogether, so he tried not to be so hard on himself. But with everything that already happened, and would most likely continue to happen, that was definitely a lot to ask.

The next destination was Porter Square, which in this day and age was nothing to look forward to. 978 tried to take comfort with the thought that there were still a people around his age who could cherish many good memories of that place the way he did. Many of these stops, particularly Harvard Square, had been staples for a countless number of New England folks as well as tourists from all around the world. Sadly, those days remained in the past for quite some time now.

When 978 looked up he could see an opening at the end of the tunnel, which was obviously Porter Square. He hoped they could stop there and rest for a few minutes if there was time. What also needed to be taken into consideration was a very strong possibility of encountering more giant bats. That creature was more than just a bat, but there was no point dwelling on that fact. Nothing could be done about that.

Upon entering Porter Square all was quiet and some of the lights were actually working, albeit dim and flickering. This made it far easier for the three of them to see, prompting them to remove their goggles. 978 still clearly remembered the mechanical voices heard over the intercoms on the trains stating which station you arrived at. That was probably the only technological thing he could think of that didn't intimidate him right now.

"Now arriving at Porter Square!" announced 978 with a mix of humor and sarcasm.

"I want to stop and rest for a few minutes," said Dr. Carlton.

"You're a mind reader!"

978, Dr. Carlton, and Ryan climbed up off the tracks and onto the platform. Dr. Carlton immediately took off her backpack and sat down on the floor. 978 felt he only needed to take a couple of minutes to stretch the legs, and didn't want to stay there too long. Ryan walked over to the nearest bench and sat down just to catch a second wind. It wasn't as easy as it used to be, but the majority of people don't make plans to spend their retirement trekking through deserted subway tunnels. Brazil began to sound far more appealing at this moment. However, that thought would quickly perish after looking down on the floor by the left side of the bench.

"Get over here," said Ryan. "The two of you should take a look at this."

978 and Dr. Carlton quickly gathered whatever stuff they'd put on the floor and made their way over to the bench where Ryan was sitting but had stood up by the time they got there. He then pointed his finger down to the floor at a gruesome sight that none of them wanted to see. There was blood, and lots of it. The really nasty part was the trail of it leading away, giving the distinct impression that a human body got dragged around.

"This is not good," said 978.

"Do you think the blood is fresh?" asked Ryan.

"It might be," answered Dr. Carlton. "I don't particularly want to stick around and find out."

The three of them began to hear strange noises. It would have been nice to think it was just some buzzing sounds being created by the electricity that was barely functioning, but that couldn't be the case. They turned around and looked straight ahead, their eyes focused on a short man standing in front of them with a medium build carrying a large torch. He had dark, disheveled hair and the widest set of eyes imaginable. The skin was so white that it looked like he hadn't seen the daylight in years. The clothing he wore was a torn short-sleeved t-shirt and jeans with large ripped holes by the knees. To top it off, he had very large bare feet. None of them had a clue what to make of this strange sight.

"CREEP!" this thing shouted out in a very low, almost belching kind of sound. In all honesty, 978, Dr. Carlton, and Ryan weren't quite sure what this so-called creature actually said. But Creep was close enough, and a perfect name for him.

Another creature began to emerge not very far behind Creep. He was tall, bald, and as skinny as a rail. An appropriate name for this thing would be Stickboy, who only wore an old pair of shorts. He carried a wooden spear in his left hand. His right hand dragged a body by the hair. He was still too far away to determine if it was male or female. But Ryan quickly came to the conclusion that the blood by the bench most likely came from that particular corpse.

"NEW BLOOD!" declared Stickboy, in a hissing tone. He then dropped the corpse and gripped the spear with both hands. There was no mistaking what he just said and what he was going to do next. He started maneuvering toward 978 with the agility of an acrobat and the look of a monkey. It wasn't as funny as it sounded, especially when he moved in closer. Dr. Carlton wouldn't take her eyes off of him for a second. She had her handgun ready and aimed directly at him.

While Dr. Carlton was watching Stickboy, 978 and Ryan would take notice of another strange looking character coming out of the woodwork. He stood at an average height with very short, thinning dark hair and a large build. Not quite as big as a sumo wrestler, but enough to be intimidating. He had a raging, almost possessed look in his eyes, along with puffy cheeks and big lips. 978 thought that Brute was a name that suited him, even though he didn't plan on mentioning it to Dr. Carlton or Ryan. None of these crazy looking characters were going to make formal introductions, as they were obviously more interested in hand to hand combat.

Several more of these unusual figures began to appear, with the most noticeable being two younger women who had similar builds and features. A closer look might make someone think they were sisters, maybe even twins. But 978, Dr. Carlton, and Ryan were not going to take the time to find out. One of them had their right eye partially sewn shut, with the same side of her face showing skin that was stretched out. It looked light plastic surgery gone awry. A fitting name would be Stitch. The other one had hair spray painted silver-colored and also looked like she had some kind of deformity on the right side of her face. An attempt to cover it up was obvious by the use of makeup to create black stripes. A perfect name would be Streak. For 978, Dr. Carlton, and Ryan, these would be the last two that they would get a really good look at before several more of these underground dwellers made their appearances known to them.

This was serious trouble that was completely unexpected. About a dozen more of these strange looking characters had come out to play, so to speak. 978, Dr. Carlton, and Ryan had the advantage because of all the weapons they carried. The problem was deciding how much firepower would be necessary to fight these creatures. All they could do was wait for one of them to make the first move, which didn't take long. Creep threw a torch directly at them, and it landed in front of 978. Stickboy threw his long spear at Ryan, who ducked as it flew overhead and stuck in the wall behind him.

"That does it for me!" shouted Ryan, aiming his gun directly at Stickboy. "No one is taking me down crucifixion style!" He began firing, barely missing the intended target. He'd never seen anybody move so fast, which suggested that this Stickboy character wasn't totally human.

Brute started moving slowly toward 978, Dr. Carlton, and Ryan. He wasn't carrying any weapons, none that could be seen anyway. Dr. Carlton did not want to just shoot this creature in cold blood, especially considering everything that happened to 978. Still, she was convinced that this Brute could easily crush all three of them in a matter of seconds. She fired several shots at part of the ceiling that was directly above him, causing large chunks of concrete to fall. What she hoped would happen did, a large chunk landed on the upper part of his back near the right shoulder, causing him to be completely disoriented. Moments later another chunk hit his head, causing him to fall to the floor. He went totally unconscious.

"He'll definitely feel that in the morning!" said 978, before he began to focus on the other attackers again.

978 felt ready to take on anything, especially after seeing Brute get knocked out cold. However, he was reminded right away that he didn't have eyes in the back of his head. Stickboy ambushed him from behind and suddenly had these long, stretched out arms and legs wrapped around his body. They both fell to the floor like wrestlers. 978 believed that Stickboy felt stronger than a Burmese python, making it nearly impossible to break free. Ryan wanted to shoot first and ask questions later, but both of them were moving so fast that it created too high of a risk of shooting 978. Luckily, Dr. Carlton did some quick thinking. She pulled Stickboy's spear out of the wall and slowly made her way over to the opponents as close as she could. For a moment the two of them stopped rolling around and Stickboy was on top of 978, attempting to strangle him to death. She stuck Stickboy with the spear in the lower back, and what happened next sounded almost impossible. The sick looking underground dweller let out a piercing, almost supernatural scream before releasing 978 and taking off like a bandit.

978 felt completely disoriented, and it took him a minute or two to stand up. He was amazed he hadn't gone deaf, and didn't think he had a chance of getting out of there alive. The two ladies best described as Stitch and Streak began their approach, looking like they were ready to devour him. He just stood there and watched the two of them move in for the kill, until he heard a voice from behind give him orders.

"Get down!" shouted Dr. Carlton, which got him to duck

down without hesitation. She had the flamethrower ready and pointed the thin wand directly at Stitch and Streak before they had a chance to attack 978. As the flames ignited the only other sounds heard were screaming. Stitch and Streak both fell to the floor and began rolling around, which eventually put out the flames. However, they were smart enough not to take off before round two. But Dr. Carlton was completely shocked over what seemed to be an instant recovery. It left her completely baffled.

"Can you believe this?" asked Dr. Carlton. "They all got away so quick except for the guy unconscious on the floor."

"I don't think any of them were totally human," said 978.

"Look at it this way," said Ryan. "You might have helped those two ladies improve their looks."

The three of them would have shared another laugh after Ryan's last comment, but were unable to do so after everything that just happened. They looked all around them and spotted Creep off in the distance, who just stood still and stared at them while making the same belching sound while breathing in and out. The rest of the underground dwellers in their presence weren't moving either. It was easy to spot the ones with physical deformities, while others wore white masks with blank facial features. No one knew what would happen next, but it was time to break the silence.

"Is that all you've got?!" shouted out Ryan, staring directly at Creep. "There may be more of you than there are of us, but look at what we've done so far! Who's next?!"

Creep slowly moved away from the dimly lit area and began to disappear. Ryan was about to open fire, but did not want to fire a shot in the dark. The rest of the underground dwellers started to back away, eventually vanishing as well.

"I guess they met their match," said Ryan.

"Do you think we've seen the last of them?" asked Dr. Carlton.

"For now, we have."

978 stood up straight and caught his breath again. He had seen enough for one night, but knew they still had a long way to go. He began to question how much more of this he could take.

"Let's get moving," said Ryan.

The three of them quickly got ready again. They were about to walk over to the edge of the platform to get back on the tracks, but a blackout occurred. They hesitated for a few moments, thinking the power would come back on, at least partially. Even having the place dimly lit made it easier to travel through the subway tunnels than being without any electricity.

Another couple of seconds went by, and 978 suddenly realized something very important. None of them remembered to put the goggles back on, and in the pitch black it would be more difficult to locate them. He honestly couldn't remember where he had put them. The longer the lights were out the more he would continue to panic and not be able to think straight. Not that he expected to in this situation, so he decided to speak his mind.

"I'm pretty sure about one thing," said 978.

"What's that?" asked Dr. Carlton.

"Whoever it is we're up against knows how to run the electricity down here!"

"Looks that way!" said Ryan.

"What should we do?" asked 978.

"Don't move. These folks will move in for the kill, and they know their way around here in the dark better than anybody! I'll open fire on them the closer they get to us. I'm sure if they think that were completely blind they won't worry about making a lot of noise, now both of you try to find your goggles as fast as you can!"

Before 978 or Dr. Carlton could respond a lot of rummaging and footsteps occurred, which were obviously being made by these strange creatures. Next they could hear a lot of high-pitched, sinister giggling and the belching sound that Creep made while he breathed, so they knew he was back in the picture. Moments later there would be another hint of a familiar character.

"NEW BLOOD!" a voice exclaimed in a hissing tone again.

It was none other than Stickboy, sounding just as energetic and hungry for human flesh as he did the first time around. Dr. Carlton may have been unable to see him, but she kept thinking about how she stuck a spear in his back and how loud unbelievably loud the scream was before he ran off. She wondered if these mutant-like creatures healed quickly, or maybe had a higher tolerance for pain. Perhaps a bit of both for all she knew. Her train of thought would be interrupted by a familiar voice.

"Don't move now!" demanded Ryan.

"What are you going to do?" asked Dr. Carlton.

"The only thing I can do!"

Ryan opened fire and showered the entire area with bullets except in the area where 978 and Dr. Carlton were standing. One of these characters had to get shot and killed while a few others more than likely got seriously wounded. Hopefully this archaic tactic would scare these creatures off for good.

It wouldn't be long before Ryan stopped firing. Some noise was being made by a few of these underground dwellers but it was hard to determine if any of them were injured or killed.

"You find the goggles yet?" asked Ryan.

"No," said 978.

"Find them quick!"

978 and Dr. Carlton heard Ryan's gun go off again before there was utter silence. They both knew what happened but they didn't want to believe it.

"Ryan?" called out Dr. Carlton.

There was no answer.

"They got him," said 978.

Seconds later the lights came back on. On the floor was

one of the dwellers, this one in particular wore a white mask with blank facial features. All 978 and Dr. Carlton had to do was look down to see plenty of blood flowing, indicating that death occurred because of several gunshot wounds in the chest. Other than that there was no one else in sight, but countless trails of blood which could lead them to wherever Ryan was taken.

"We've got to find him!" said Dr. Carlton.

"Do you think there's any chance he's still alive?" asked 978.

"We've got to try!"

"Is it even possible?"

"We'll track him down! With the equipment we have, I might be able to make miracles happen!"

At this moment, 978 had a little faith to say the least.

18 •••

The moment Ryan opened his eyes he felt a stinging sensation, forcing him to blink several times. There was some kind of powder all over his face, especially on the lips and the nostrils. It only took a few short seconds to figure out what it was: tranquilizer dust. In this day and age that stuff was easy to come by, not to mention the fact that it wasn't difficult to make. Even though he had no way of knowing for sure if these underground dwellers had enough sense or patience to cook up a batch of it on their own, it wasn't all that surprising that they would had some in their possession. The only other thing the old soldier kept pondering was getting ambushed from behind when the lights went out. He hadn't been hit very hard in the back or the head, which explained why he didn't feel a lot of pain. These crazy creatures must have thrown the tranquilizer dust right in his face just seconds after their attack.

Tranquilizer dust wasn't the most potent stuff out there, which is why the components needed to create it are readily easy to find. This meant Ryan hadn't been unconscious for very long, now he just had to figure out where he was. All he knew was that the place was pitch black, exactly how it was when he had been captured in Porter Square. Another thing he realized was that his body was in the upright position but his feet weren't touching the ground. His legs were spread apart, far enough to feel like he was stretching or in the middle of doing jumping jacks. Both hands were raised over his head, spread apart and tied up. He began to wonder if he was going to be crucified, or beaten and tortured to the point where he couldn't think straight anymore and become one of these mutant creatures. Maybe they would just leave him here alone in the dark to die slowly, quietly, and peacefully.

The next thing Ryan witnessed was some flickering lights. Then the room became so bright it blinded him. As soon as he began to regain his full vision he saw exactly what he had expected to see: a large number of the mutant creatures. Many of them were the same ones he fought against in Porter Square. Who knows where he had been taken. So many construction projects had been started down here to expand the subway system, all of which had been stopped completely several years ago due to lack of funds supposedly. The biggest disappointment it caused were the promises broken to the working class citizens, who were told this would create a larger number of job opportunities. Even the workers who were fortunate enough to be involved in this project were unable to finish what was started, and this was supposed to be the next Big Dig. At least that was how the media explained it.

Ryan had his eyes focused on the crazy creatures standing about twenty-five to thirty feet away. All of them displayed a wide-eyed stare. The creepiest part, however, was their high-pitched laughing and giggling. Ryan couldn't think of a word to define it. The only one that came to mind was otherworldly, and with everything that had happened so far he knew that was a distinct possibility. But he knew there was no chance of getting taken aboard a spaceship and being probed. They may have had some humanlike features, but that didn't mean you wanted to call them human. Ryan knew they could be anything or a lethal combination of everything. But the human factor never really sank in even if they could talk, which he was about to hear another sample of.

"NEW BLOOD!" announced Stickboy, again.

Despite being in such a dire situation and not having all of his strength back, Ryan had no patience for this.

"Can't you say anything else?!" asked Ryan, in a tone that was definitely angry. He actually started to feel more awake. "What's the matter? Can't get past your first words? You're like a grown man who can't get over his high school sweetheart!"

The response was more high-pitched laughing and giggling. Ryan figured it out pretty quickly. These folks simply didn't get it, much less care. They were more prone to the stereotypical cartoon-like behavior of cavemen. There was a better chance of someone like Stickboy obtaining the woman he desired by hitting her over the head, knocking her unconscious and taking her home. If things didn't work out he could simply have her for dinner.

Right now, however, Ryan wasn't convinced that he was about to be cooked up as a piece of meat. Not yet, anyway. He was tied up so they could toy with him, he was sure of that. Crucifixion was one theory that seemed possible, rituals like that weren't beyond their comprehension. He gave them a little credit, they obviously knew how to operate the electricity down there and use it to their advantage. That would explain why they were never found by any well-prepared search and rescue teams who were also armed and dangerous. Underground Dwellers may not be a bad name for them after all. They knew their way around every inch of these subway tunnels. It didn't matter if it was under bright lights or pitch black.

Ryan saw Stickboy produce a spear, typically what he always used for a weapon. Both ends were sharpened as usual. The only difference this time was that he lit one end on fire, and the flame would rise quickly. Ryan knew he probably had some flammable substance on it, which could have been anything from gasoline to insect repellant. Whatever it was, Stickboy was obviously going to "stick it" to the former soldier. Ryan knew what it meant to crash and burn, but for the first time ever would find out what it would be like to get stabbed and burned. This had to be a rare experience, especially occurring simultaneously with the same weapon.

"Burn...burn...BURN!!!" shouted Stickboy, aiming the burning spear at Ryan and laughing immediately afterwards, with the other Underground Dwellers joining in.

"So you can say something else?" asked Ryan, being sarcastic, figuring he had nothing to lose at this point.

That was enough to get Stickboy's attention. The expression on his face changed and he glared at Ryan, but only briefly He began laughing again and threw the spear, striking a few inches below Ryan's left arm with the tip sticking into the surface. It didn't stick very far in, so the long spear dangled down slightly. The flame on the tip of it continued to burn, but not very much, barely reaching the strap tying Ryan's arm in. Now the only option was to use as much strength as possible to break free.

Luckily, the straps tying Ryan down weren't constructed with strong material. But he knew it would take some time before he could break free. All he could do was push his left arm forward. If he moved it up and down these Underground Dwellers might take notice and become more aggressive, convincing them to tie him up tighter and continue using him as target practice. And it wouldn't be long before one of them hit him, more than likely causing him to slowly burn and bleed to death. Something he wasn't looking forward to.

However, it looked like the Underground Dwellers had other plans. Stickboy came forward to retrieve the spear, pulling it out and standing directly in front of Ryan, staring him right in the eye. For a moment he thought this creature was going to bite his head off. Instead Stickboy moved over to the right and the unthinkable happened: Ryan began to spin around.

At this point anything was possible. The former soldier knew he was now nothing more than a toll for random target practice. The stakes were high and he would get hurt. Eventually he'd be killed and he considered this to be the closest thing to a crucifixion. But in this situation he did not want to die over the sins committed by the Underground Dwellers.

Ryan started to think about how this scenario was like a life or death version of Wheel of Fortune, an extremely popular television game show that kept being revived over the past several decades.

The main difference this time was instead of winning big cash or prizes the big jackpot was a piece of him. These crazy folks would most likely cook up the flesh on his limbs later on and have a huge feast. Perhaps that was better than being eaten alive, but he didn't want either of those things to happen.

Ryan decided it was simply best to close his eyes. That way he wouldn't suffer from extreme dizziness or nausea. Then again, he wouldn't mind vomiting all over Stickboy. But that would have been a difficult task even if that nut stood right in front of him. He most likely would have thrown up all over himself if he continued spinning in circles.

All the former soldier could do now was keep his eyes closed and keep pushing his left arm forward. While keeping his state of mind in the present moment he was amazed that his entire body wasn't consumed by anxiety. This was a situation where anybody would have been justified to be panic-stricken. There couldn't be many people around that had been in the exact same predicament as Ryan.

It wasn't long before he felt vibrations, or pounding sensations as he would describe them, all around him. These Underground Dwellers had to be throwing dangerous weapons at their intended target, specifically Ryan, but he didn't want to open his eyes to find out what they were. Not yet.

He felt the strap slowly tearing off the more he pushed his arm forward. It wouldn't be much longer for him to break free. Then he heard footsteps on the right side. He briefly opened his eyes to see Stickboy walking away and eventually rejoin the rest of his people, if you wanted to call them that. Right now, however, Ryan wasn't concerned about labels. He wanted out, and he knew he had to do whatever was necessary to make that happen. Now it became much easier since Stickboy moved away from him, which meant there was enough time to reach for a weapon.

Ryan wasn't surprised when he found out that the Underground Dwellers didn't take the time to remove whatever weapons were still on him when they tied him up for target practice. There was something about them that was far too impulsive and impatient to perform such a logical task for their own protection and safety. But he didn't mind the fact that it made these circumstances a lot easier for him. It would only be a matter of seconds before his left arm would become free and he could take action, and these crazy folks stood far enough away for him to cause plenty of damage.

There was no point waiting for the so-called Wheel of Fortune to come to a complete stop. The moment Ryan's left arm became free he reached down for the first thing he could find, which turned out to be a mini-bomb. It was a bit odd, since he honestly couldn't remember packing one. Then again, he wasn't about to make any kind of attempt to recall exactly what he carried. These particular circumstances simply did not permit that. But he was concerned as to whether or not it was a live explosive or a dud, only one way to find out.

Ryan pressed the click button on the mini-bomb. He decided to roll it across the floor like a bowling ball, hoping it would travel a far enough distance and stop a few feet in front of the Underground Dwellers. He hoped this strategy might increase their curiosity and move closer to the weapon to take a closer look at it, which was a lot better than having them retaliate and throw God knows what at him.

He was right.

A few of these creatures, but not all of them, started to wander toward the mini-bomb. Seconds later, it went off, nearly blowing up in their faces. After that came a lot of screaming, then the entire group of Underground Dwellers took off. Ryan wasn't surprised to learn that these folks got startled very easily, despite this situation being rather extreme. Everything happened so fast that he hadn't noticed how long it had been since the Wheel of Fortune stopped moving. Of course he still felt rather dizzy from the experience. But who wouldn't?

Ryan was able to free himself quickly and easily from his odd hang-up. The primitive methods of these Underground Dwellers worked against them. But Ryan reached the conclusion that they would return in greater numbers, it was simply a matter of when. He also had a feeling that would be sooner instead of later, which made him decide it would be far more difficult to fight them off, despite their simple strategies, if they even understood the actual concept of strategies. Whatever the case might be, they sure knew how to find their way around the tunnels in the dark.

Ryan's dizziness slowly began to wear off, and his eyesight felt like it had been restored to almost perfect vision. It might have had something to do with the explosion. Then again, just about anyone would wake up considerably after an incident like that. The proof existed by simply watching the Underground Dwellers take off like thieves in the night, which was kind of what they were anyway. He started considering the fact that he still didn't sense any real shock throughout the entire ordeal, even if the explosion had heightened his sense of awareness. However, it was amazing that even seeing the burning flames a short distance away didn't cause a whole lot of concern for the old soldier. He was just grateful the fire hadn't spread very far much less create serious damage around him. The last thing he needed was to be cornered in a room thanks to a blaze he ultimately created, or have the ceiling start caving in with large chunks landing on his head knocking him unconscious, or even killing him.

Now Ryan had to pull himself together and concentrate on his number one priority: getting the hell out of there and finding 978 and Dr. Carlton. With any luck they were alright and searching for him, which meant it wouldn't take very long to find each other and continue their tumultuous journey through the subway tunnels. He also hoped that too much time hadn't passed for them to reach the Boston Common when they needed to. He would have understood if his partners had decided to move ahead without him. If his own death would benefit the lives of countless innocent civilians in the city, or better yet the entire country, that was okay by him. That's what being a good soldier was supposed to be. You might be able to program a replica with that mentality, or enforce that belief into a simple-minded clone for a short time, but nothing comes close to a human feeling that's in their heart and soul until the day they die.

Ryan determined that the width of the room he was in had to be close to thirty feet. The length was at least twice that or more, and the ceiling he just didn't make a conscious effort to figure out. It didn't really matter since the ceiling was solid with no ventilation shafts or major cracks. He remained grateful that it never caved in on him. Then again, the mini-bomb he aimed at the Underground Dwellers didn't cause a major disadvantage. The flames remaining from the explosion weren't burning high or spreading wide enough to prevent him from moving beyond the danger without being hurt.

Ryan pulled a gun out of his right holster. He was amazed that these creatures made no effort whatsoever to remove any weapons, despite their primitive mindset. Perhaps most of the people taken as hostages panicked easily, convincing them to think that humans weren't much of a challenge or a major threat. If that was the case he felt proud to prove them wrong.

The next decision came quickly and easily, Ryan moved toward the right side of the room so he could maneuver around the small flames that continued to burn. While doing so he took a moment to recall all the different weapons he had on him without performing an actual inspection. He now remembered that he was carrying a large number of explosive devices, instantly reminding him why the bottom half of his outfit felt baggy and slightly heavier. Yet he had to ask himself why he couldn't think about that the entire time he was tied up for target practice. Probably because the situation only allowed him to think fast and do whatever he could to get out of that predicament. Still, there was no recollection of packing that small mini-bomb he used. He decided to stop contemplating the matter and move forward. He was alive and free and that was what mattered most.

By the time he made his way around the small blaze he caused part of him wanted to take an extra couple of minutes to put the fire out completely, but time itself was crucial. These rooms and tunnels had been deserted for years, and the Underground Dwellers kept things up well enough that a small fire wouldn't cause much damage despite their destructive and chaotic methods.

Ryan took notice of the exit sign directly above the doorway he went through, probably more so than the obvious fact that the door itself had been torn of the hinges and placed on the floor a few feet in front of him. There was no way to determine how long ago that happened, not that it really mattered. Still, this was an entirely new experience for him, so it was only natural to be far more observant. He started to consider that maybe these creatures broke the door down to make it seem like it was open to the public, meaning those traveling through the tunnels who weren't Underground Dwellers. Human beings like 978, Dr. Carlton, and Ryan definitely fit into that category, with an excellent chance of having extra supplies. Not to mention the fact that these crazy mutants weren't referring to them as new blood for nothing, human flesh was obviously on the menu.

Ryan had to stop overanalyzing both the creatures' behavior as well as the predicament he was in. At this point in his life he didn't need anyone telling him he had post-traumatic stress disorder, and the present situation would only add to the already very long list of reasons why.

The lighting everywhere may have remained dim most of the time, but it was difficult not to take notice of the white walls and ceilings. Maybe if the people living on the surface regained control of these tunnels they could easily convert into a mental institution, which would be more than suitable for the Underground Dwellers. Perhaps the top brass at Peterson Prison could invest some money to expand the Psychiatric Unit down here, a practical purpose to say the least. Still, he wasn't about to share that thought with 978. Even if the guy was able to keep the guard job after this ordeal was over he saw it as highly unlikely that there would be any serious consideration whatsoever. Ryan knew he wouldn't do it himself, especially after the three of them encountered that monster-sized bat and had their run-in with the Underground Dwellers. He may have scared them off with that mini-bomb, but the conflict wasn't over yet.

Ryan started to realize that he didn't pay much attention to the description of most of the Underground Dwellers when they took him for a spin. The only exception being Stickboy, who took the honor of making it possible, this was probably because he was still suffering from the aftereffects of the tranquilizer dust along with the acquired dizziness of spinning in circles. At this time, however, it felt like all that had worn off. His recollection of which of those crazy folks were present started to increase significantly. With the exception of Stickboy, none of them looked anything like the ones he and his two constituents had battled at the Porter Square Station. Actually, that wasn't one hundred percent correct. There were two women, so to speak, that he could recall. The physical deformities, mainly in their facial structures, suited them for names like Stitch and Streak. Whether they would respond to it or not would remain a mystery, which was okay in Ryan's mind. He just hoped that he wouldn't have to lay his eyes on them again, but the longer he was down here the chances were better that he would. The only other creature whose description came to mind was Creep. A name like that also being appropriate at first glance, it was also the first of the Underground Dwellers he'd laid his eyes before getting ambushed. Unfortunately, this would now remain in his memory for the rest of his life more so than the first time he got laid. The latter may have not been that great, but she was far more attractive than Stitch or Streak could ever be.

As Ryan continued moving forward, part of him kept thinking more about the white walls surrounding him than trying to find a way out. Then again, most people who were stuck in a situation like this would have trouble concentrating on one task. There were so many other things going on down here that had to be factored in as well. The Underground Dwellers would definitely be at the top of the list. He couldn't even begin to imagine where they had taken off to, but there was no doubt in his mind that these crazy mutants would be back soon. Thankfully he still had most of his weapons, and now that he was free the chance of eliminating a large amount of their population increased significantly. Most people should be smart enough not to go exploring down in these deserted subway tunnels, especially if they're unarmed. However, no one deserved to be preyed upon by monsters that only appeared in their worst nightmares.

Another thing Ryan began to realize was that there weren't any reflective services down here. Then again, it was understandable why there would be. The Underground Dwellers didn't seem like the types that admired themselves in front of a mirror, much less comb their hair or shave or powder their noses. They definitely had no concerns about dental hygiene, and probably had no idea what that term meant. It was hard to imagine why anyone would actually take the time to teach them how to use a toothbrush. There was no incentive to become civilized if you ran your own world where it wasn't necessary.

As Ryan continued to march through these large white rooms he was amazed at the amount of space in each of them. Another thing he couldn't help notice was how much bigger they were compared to the room he was tied up in. He wasn't even going to attempt to estimate the length and width of them. He was just happy that he was able to see clearly enough without having to worry about any major obstacles getting in the way. Perhaps being surrounded by white walls wasn't a bad thing after all, especially if they weren't made of rubber and you weren't forced to wear a straightjacket and stay heavily medicated. That tranquilizer dust those Underground Dwellers used on him was more than enough for one night, or any other drug for that matter.

Each room Ryan passed through had a set of large old-fashioned swinging doors rarely seen in this day and age. Upon entering the next room he immediately took notice of a small door on the far right end. It was partially open with light shining out. He double-checked his gun and quickly rushed over and stood outside. At this point he was rather impatient but had no intentions of just waiting to find out if someone was in there. He kicked the door all the way open and aimed it inside. There was no one to be found, as there was nothing in there but a small toilet with a sink and mirror on the right. He found it hard to believe the Underground Dwellers would have enough sense to use the bathroom. Still, despite their outward appearances and bad hygiene, there was no smell of urine or feces detected.

That was about to change, but not drastically. Ryan had to take a leak, yet hadn't realized how badly until now. Good timing may have played a roll in this, but regardless of what the circumstances were he would have been more fine with making his mark right on the floor if he had to. The behavior and habits of a dog were more appealing to him at this point than any thoughts or actions coming from the Underground Dwellers.

It seemed to take an awful long time for Ryan to complete the necessary business. He had no idea how long he might have kept it held in. Maybe it was a good thing he hadn't thought about it until now. If he was spending a typical night at home drinking a couple of beers then a trip to the bathroom would have occurred quickly, and more regularly. He was thankful he hadn't drank at all these past few days, especially after everything that happened since 978 and Dr. Carlton showed up while he was watching her office with that replica chasing after them. He still couldn't believe how hard that thing punched him, and that was before finding out it wasn't human.

However, the one thought the old soldier kept coming back to was what his mother said. She didn't like to drink. It was nothing against the taste of alcohol itself, but having to continually make trips to the bathroom. In her mind that took a lot of the fun out of it. Not so much for Ryan. But he knew he could never argue that point, and right now it seemed to be taking longer compared to a regular night of kicking back and pounding a few.

Whatever, there was no need to be thinking about stuff like that in the present situation.

Operation: Relief had been accomplished, and now it was time to move forward. Ryan zipped himself up and stood in front of the sink to look in the mirror. Even with the dim lighting he could tell that his complexion was extremely pale, making him nervous and jittery. He suddenly felt hot and sweated like a bastard, or at least he thought so. His reflection in the mirror didn't indicate that, even after feeling a stinging sensation in his eyes. He closed them for a moment hoping that might help, which it did. He took one last look before turning around to leave. He started to open the door and all the lights went out. It wasn't all that surprising but he decided to wait a minute for the power to come back on. While doing so he made sure his gun was ready, which was easy because at this point in his life he could perform a weapons check blindfolded. He knew he couldn't be too careful considering what he was up against, not to mention the fact that it was still pitch black. Then again, it didn't take Ryan more than a few seconds to do a safety inspection of the gun he was holding.

What happened next was something no soldier wanted to be left in the dark over, be it literally or mentally. It was the sound of guns firing, and not his own. Not knowing anything about the structure of these underground facilities made it difficult to determine where it was occurring. He heard the twisted, supernatural screams which could only come from the Underground Dwellers. Ryan knew that 978 and Dr. Carlton were probably coming to rescue him, but he didn't want to get his hopes up too high. The walls were relatively thick in his estimation, and coupled with their size there was no way to know for sure how far away the massacre might be.

As soon as Ryan stepped out of the bathroom, he received some assistance by the way of the lights turning back on. Granted, they weren't shining any brighter than before, but something was better than nothing. He also took notice of the trash scattered all over the floor, which wasn't surprising as he never got the impression that these Underground Dwellers were well organized. Another thing that got him was that the white walls were completely bare. In a way it helped brighten the rooms quite a bit, considering how dim the lights were most of the time. But he thought he'd see some type of graffiti in his travels. According to reports from life that existed above the ground these corridors and tunnels had been deserted for years, of course nothing could be further from the truth. As he saw it the Underground Dwellers had more than made their mark, even if they weren't artistically inclined. To some they'd be horrifying. To others they'd be fascinating. No matter who crossed paths or simply studied these creatures they would have an impact, along with that overgrown bat or whatever it was.

Ryan decided to do a quick visual scan of the room before going forward. He heard a hissing sound and quickly noticed something moving behind a random pile of garbage. It was probably a lizard tail, black in color and most likely a snake. Still, he wasn't about to investigate, and after everything that happened he knew to expect the absolute worst. It wouldn't surprise him if the thing turned out to be an outgrowth of a mythological sea serpent, convincing him to eliminate it. It had nothing to do with the mentality of shooting first and asking questions later. At this point of the journey it was something he didn't want to find out about. He aimed and fired off three shots, ending all sounds and movement from the designated target.

Now the only thing to do was push forward. Ryan only had to walk a few feet before he had to kick some thick paper-like debris out of the way. A normal reaction, but for all he knew there could have been another wild animal hiding behind it like another snake, bat, monkeys from Jupiter, anything was possible. What caught his attention next was the sound of rummaging and moaning bordering on growling. It wasn't far away, and it was probably connected to the gunshots he heard fired along with the blackout which occurred just minutes ago. An ambush most likely, hopefully caused by 978 and Dr. Carlton to put a stop to those Underground Dwellers that set him up for target practice.

As he slowly peeked through the next door with a finger firmly placed on the trigger, the first thing he noticed was the sound level increasing to a higher level. There were a couple of bodies lying on the floor, as he opened the door and stepped inside he would set his eyes on the massive slaughter on the Underground Dwellers. Most of them were dead, but there were a select few just barely clinging to life suffering from gunshot wounds or severe burns. Then again, most people who had run-ins with these folks probably wouldn't see it as suffering. More like putting them out of their misery.

When Ryan was all the way inside the room he briefly scanned the rest of the carnage laid out all over the floor. But after a couple of seconds he looked up and set his eyes on something he thought was perfect. Dr. Carlton was several feet ahead of him standing up straight with a flamethrower wand in her right hand and a shotgun in her left. She even smiled a little bit after realizing it was Ryan who entered the room, making him almost forget everything he was surrounded by, which wasn't easy to do.

"Wendy," said Ryan. "I think you just made our trip back up a lot easier."

"Damn right," she responded, laughing slightly. "Never mess with a woman and her flamethrower."

"Where's your friend?"

Ryan's answer came very quickly when the lights got

as bright as they could be. He turned around and saw 978 at the other end of the room at the fuse box which obviously controlled the electricity. The white walls and ceiling probably contributed to feeling blinded for a minute, his two constituents could feel it as well. Granted, it was already late in the day when they entered the subway and they weren't down there trying to get suntanned. Then again, it wasn't exactly pleasant when their eyes adjusted moments later, only to see what was left of these Underground Dwellers that were either dead or almost dead. Luckily, there were only a select few of them in the latter category, made obvious by either slight movements or growling-like noises. Without saying a single word, Ryan and 978 would take care of that problem immediately. The two of them just pointed their guns and fired a few shots into the chest areas of the few remaining creatures displaying any signs of life. In a matter of seconds, that was no longer the case.

"Do you think anyone will miss them?" asked Dr. Carlton.

"Not likely," answered Ryan. "Their own kind maybe, I'm sure there's a lot more of them down here."

"They can always feast on their remains," said 978. "I wouldn't put it passed them to do that. They might find some of these to be a little overcooked, though."

"I doubt they'll complain," added Ryan.

"I'll bet if they were an endangered species," said Dr. Carlton. "No one would be sad to see them go."

"I don't care if there's only a few of them left," said 978. "It's whoever or whatever else that comes into contact with them that will become an endangered species."

"Even though I'm a doctor, that's a more logical conclusion!"

After another moment or two of pulling themselves together, so to speak, Ryan couldn't help but notice that Ryan remained over by the fuse box.

"What are you waiting far?" asked Ryan.

"You still got your goggles on you?" asked Dr. Carlton.

"Yeah," he answered, finding them seconds later.

"Put them on," she ordered.

"You got it," he said, then did so.

978 then put his pair of goggles on and turned the lever down on the fuse box to turn the electricity off completely, causing another blackout. Not for them, thanks to the fancy eyewear. Ryan already knew how helpful this would be, but still felt he should question their method of operation.

"You do know how to get out of here," said Ryan. "Don't you?"

"Of course," answered Dr. Carlton.

"How long will it take?" he asked.

"I don't know," she said. "I didn't time it when we were trying to get down here, shouldn't be too long, though."

"I'm surprised you haven't asked us how we found you," added 978.

"In a way," said Dr. Carlton. "He found us."

"That's true if you want to nitpick, we still got pretty close."

"Alright!" snapped Ryan. "There's no need to have a big debate over it, let's just get out of here!"

He was pretty sure how they found him, but he figured it could be discussed on their way back up. What he just went through was probably a much more interesting story, but he didn't have any real desire to relive the memories just yet. Then again, being crucified through target practice spin-cycle style was definitely one for the books.

Dr. Carlton was the first one ready to go. All she had to do was put her weapons, the flamethrower wand and gun back into their proper places. She then turned around and headed for the swinging doors behind her. Every room down here so far had these types of entrances. Ryan thought they should cut off the top half of one set and build a saloon. But would the Underground Dwellers be able to handle the effects of alcohol? There was definitely no chance of getting tourists down here, except those who like guns and were looking for some target practice. That would appeal to enthusiasts of any kind of weapon who learned about the existence of these creatures.

Ryan had to stop himself for a minute. He couldn't believe that thoughts like these were going through his head. The main priority, and what should be the top priority, was getting out of this awful place. He stood still for another couple of seconds to let 978 walk in front of him, then followed from behind. He had no issue with being the last in line, as he more than felt a need to watch his back. It wouldn't surprise him if a monster smashed through a wall, or came down from the ceiling. That incident with the human bat, or whatever it was, that alone was convincing enough that anything could happen.

It didn't take long to figure out how Dr. Carlton found her way in and out of here. She was using an old GPS hookup and accessed Ryan's home computer for directions. Naturally this place would not fit under the category of a normal roadmap. But there had been enough information posted online throughout the years regarding the construction down here. Basic blueprints could be downloaded and transferred to a GPS system, recreating them to be interpreted as road directions if requested. At this point he knew he could trust her judgment to get them back to where they needed to be. He was also convinced that 978 could be a trusted ally. The old soldier just went with the flow, and to an extent didn't even realize that. For a moment he wished he'd made a mental note earlier to keep track of how much time it took to get back up to the station, Porter Square specifically. Or maybe they were farther ahead than that. Not likely though. He knew he hadn't been unconscious for long, just due to the fact that the small dose of tranquilizer dust only had a limited effect on most people.

Ryan still couldn't get past the fact at how well kept the

white walls were down here. Naturally it created a strange dynamic. He could honestly see it as a selling point if he were a realtor. It made him think of saying it had been designed by Wall-Mart. That was pretty lame humor, regardless of being down in this place and held hostage. He would probably wind up getting himself sued just for joking like that to the press simply due to the fact that it sounded exactly like the actual store. Political correctness is right around the corner. Even if it didn't cause any serious trouble, there would be somebody that would bitch and moan just for the sake of it.

The three of them entered another room filled surrounded with white walls. This time, however, it was completely spotless from top to bottom. That wasn't a bad thing, except in this situation due to the bizarre nature of everything that happened so far. Ryan was on edge again, feeling paranoid that someone else was in the room besides himself, Dr. Carlton and 978. He turned his head around to look behind him and kept staring at the wall, thinking there might be someone else in the room. He immediately took out his shotgun, instinct being the only motivation. What happened next he thought was impossible. A human-shaped figure came out of the wall, and just as white in color. At least two more of them appeared, almost as if the wall was coming to life! There was only one thing that he could do. He opened fire. All of them disappeared completely.

Naturally, 978 and Dr. Carlton were shocked. Especially when they turned around only to see a few bullet holes on what used to be an immaculate white walls.

"What the hell is wrong with you?!" snapped 978.

"I saw something," said Ryan, quickly figuring out exactly what caused him to shoot bullets unnecessarily. "The tranquilizer dust is what caused it."

"Even with a small dose," said Dr. Carlton. "There is always the possibility of hallucinations before the drug wears off completely."

"Obviously," added 978.

"At least we identified the problem quickly," said Ryan. "Let's just forget about it and get out of here."

"Are you sure you'll be alright?" asked Dr. Carlton.

"It's as good as it will get! That's all I know!"

After that discussion, the three of them wouldn't share another word until they got back to Porter Square. It didn't take them very long, but Ryan forgot to time it. He wanted to believe that it only took them another minute, but the time flew most likely due to the fact that he was anxious to get out of there. Part of him also wanted to make a mental note of all the ground they covered before getting back to where they needed to be. But he also knew that Dr. Carlton had all the information downloaded into the GPS device, meaning he could analyze everything later on his own time.

978, Dr. Carlton, and Ryan arrived in Porter Square the second time. They marched over to the edge of the platform and jumped down on the tracks. In a matter of moments they entered the tunnel that would lead them directly to Harvard Square. Only a minute or two would pass before they laid their eyes on something set up on the tracks that would help things big time.

"Check it out!" said Ryan, with much enthusiasm.

"What's that?" asked 978.

"It's one of those automatic carts used for emergencies. I think our luck has changed for the better. If we get it running we'll get to the Boston Common a lot faster."

"Do you really think that's possible?"

"These things run on small amounts of regular gasoline. I'll try to get it running with the fuel stored in one of the flamethrowers."

"Whatever gets us there faster," said Dr. Carlton. "I'm all for it. I don't feel like lugging all this stuff the rest of the way there and back, especially after everything that's happened already."

Dr. Carlton took off her backpack and handed it to Ryan, who pulled the flamethrower out. He took out a flashlight so he could take a closer look at the gas gauge on the cart, which read empty. He took the cap off the small tank and found a funnel lying on the cart that he placed in it. After that he opened the fuel line on the flamethrower and held it over the funnel for about sixty seconds, which was all the time he needed since that filled up the tank. He gave the weapon back to Dr. Carlton and turned around to start the engine, which worked instantly. Ryan felt an unbelievable amount of satisfaction, but he wasn't about to start bragging. The three of them put all the stuff on the cart as fast as possible before climbing aboard. 978 and Dr. Carlton sat down where they could find room and let Ryan take control of the vehicle, the most logical thing to do since he knew how to get it running. It wouldn't be long before they reached the Boston Common.

••• 19

978 couldn't believe how quickly the time had passed. He knew they were getting close to the Boston Common. The line they were traveling on had been closed down for some time, but it was very easy to hear the other trains coming and going from the Park Street Station. The closer they got, the louder the voices could be heard from the crowds up ahead. The majority of these people would be attending the Governor's speech, but there were probably just as many of them heading home after a long day of work. Things got much easier for 978, Dr. Carlton, and Ryan right before arriving at their destination. The lights in the tunnel were fully functioning and shining bright, which was unusual since there was still a short but significant distance to the station.

Ryan stopped the cart. His eyes lit up with excitement

when he saw an old subway car parked on the tracks in front of them. He turned off the engine and hopped off the cart to take a closer look. 978 and Dr. Carlton followed just moments later.

"Awesome!" exclaimed Ryan. "I was hoping we'd find this!"

"What do you mean?" asked 978.

"When I did security back at Alewife with Gary this was kept there for a long time. After I left he told me it got moved down here. We need to get inside so we can leave some stuff here."

"A giant storage room, so what?"

"You don't get it! While I worked at Alewife I learned how to operate this. All I need to do is check a few things. We might not have to travel all the way back on this cart."

978 felt somewhat relieved. He might not have been completely exhausted, but hiking all the way into Porter Square and fighting with those Underground Dwellers was more than he had bargained for. Crossing the bridge over the Charles River was beyond nerve-wracking. Heights scared him the most, so being on the outside of that claustrophobic tunnel didn't help at all. The most unusual part about hiking across the bridge was the see-through glass cover that extended far above the tracks. It looked similar to the overpass he traveled through each night to start his shift at Peterson Prison. But what made it more bizarre was noticing the platforms built on both sides of the tracks, which extended out to the exact length of where the glass stopped. This made it impossible to fall, but 978 did not feel any safer. The only thing more unsettling to him was seeing the helicopter fly over head with a spotlight on. Luckily the three of them passed by undetected. The pilot was probably conducting a routine patrol of the area, along with some surveillance around the Boston Common later on. In no time at all Ryan managed to get a door open on the subway car, and he and Dr. Carlton immediately went inside to sit down

and unload all the stuff they were carrying. Ryan his two constituents alone checked out the operator's engine compartment.

"Do you think he'll get this thing to run?" asked 978.

"I have no idea," answered Dr. Carlton. "He never said anything about this before. I just hope we can make it back without getting caught."

978 started feeling uneasy again. He knew they had an excellent chance of surviving this ordeal, but Dr. Carlton and Ryan weren't going to spot replicas of themselves. That could either work to his advantage or do the exact opposite, and a case of mistaken identity can cause more trouble beyond anyone's imagination. Even though a replica is supposed to imitate the person they are modeled after, the most difficult think is trying to figure out what tasks it has been programmed to do.

"What time is it?" asked 978.

"Twenty after seven," answered Dr. Carlton.

It would only be a short while until show time, which was 8pm. Still, the Governor wouldn't necessarily take the stage at that exact moment. Now 978, Dr. Carlton, and Ryan needed to remove their protection suits and dress casual. There wouldn't be any problems getting into the Boston Common with their backpacks on, despite being very large in size. The original idea was to look like college students, but they had a much better chance passing as mountain climbers. With any luck, it might make them look like hillbillies and appear less suspicious.

978 and Dr. Carlton could hear Ryan tinkering with the control devices in the front compartment. The best sounds they heard were the engine starting and Ryan shouting out in victory before he shut off the engine again. The ride back was guaranteed, meaning they wouldn't have to pay for a ticket. Then again, Ryan wasn't sure if his status at Alewife was still in effect. Not that it would have done him any good down here,

and he didn't want anybody to be able to trace him or his two constituents wandering through these deserted subway tunnels. Not to mention what the specific purpose was for doing so. His excitement caused him to get up and rush out of the front compartment to talk to 978 and Dr. Carlton.

"Tonight we are going to have the ride of our lives!" boasted Ryan. "This time the train is free and non-stop!"

"You won't hear me complain," said Dr. Carlton.

"Me neither," added 978. "Let's just remember to take the cart off the tracks."

"That won't be difficult," said Ryan. "Just give me a hand and it should only take a minute."

978 and Ryan quickly exited the subway car and walked over to the cart, which was only about ten to fifteen feet down the tracks. They had already unloaded all the weapons and extra gear, giving them one less thing to do. Ryan made his way over to the right side of the cart and motioned with his hand to 978, indicating to follow him. The two of them placed their hands on the vehicle, pushed up and slowly moved forward. This caused it to tip over and land on its side, completely clear of the tracks. 978 was surprised the cart wasn't very heavy, assuming it had something to do with a certain type of technology when constructed. Nevertheless, the route was clear. Their ride back was now obstacle free. Unfortunately, upon returning both Ryan and 978 would be made aware of yet another obstacle that might cause some serious problems. Leave it to the good old soldier to think fast.

"Ryan?" asked Dr. Carlton. "How are we supposed to literally crawl out of the woodwork without looking suspicious?"

"That's easy," answered Ryan. "I know it's boarded up at the tunnel entrance of this particular subway line, but I have some old blueprints I kept after I stopped doing security at Alewife. There's a passage that leads to a maintenance room that stays locked on the inside. We will definitely be seen while entering, but it will be very crowded and we won't look as suspicious. I also know there isn't a security post up ahead, and anyone working undercover will be far more concerned with crowd control and the Governor himself!"

"My God, out of all three of us you definitely know how to plan everything right. You probably didn't need us to come and rescue you from those creatures back there. I'd go as far as to say you've been craving an adventure like this!"

"You've been my sister-in-law for a really long time, Wendy. Something tells me you ought to know!"

As far as Dr. Carlton was concerned, Ryan had that adventure-type of mindset all the time. Maybe that allowed it to be more fun for him, or perhaps he still had a lot of leftover energy after retiring from the Air Force. The semi-frequent trips to Rio were no longer satisfying him, and real conflicts were a lot different than exotic getaways. She remembered back when her sister Marie was still alive and they watched those old Indiana Jones movies together. It didn't matter what that archeologist guy was up against, whether it be a serious battle or a deadly trap, nothing else on earth could be more fascinating. The greatest thing was that those movies were still fun to watch despite being made so long ago. Not to mention that dealing with snakes or bugs now seemed a lot easier to go up against compared to that giant bat or the Underground Dwellers. But after thinking about that a trip to Rio began to sound a lot more appealing.

978 and Dr. Carlton followed Ryan down a corridor that was a little more than six feet wide, and it was blatantly obvious that they were traveling directly behind the wall of the deserted subway line. They could clearly hear trains arriving on the other tracks as well as the voices of the passengers. Luckily it wasn't too loud, which meant they didn't have to worry about massive crowds once they became visible. Within moments they reached the area where the

maintenance room was supposed to be, at least according to Ryan. There were some large holes in the thin wall, and shining a light inside proved that X marked the spot.

"This should only take a minute," said Ryan, backing up a little. He used his hands to tear through the rest of the thin, tattered wall. The clearing he made was big enough that it went from his head down to his stomach. He kicked out the bottom area with his right foot, then the middle part with his right knee, which destroyed it completely. When he marched into the maintenance room, 978 and Dr. Carlton immediately followed. They quickly discovered some stuff that would prove to be useful.

"It looks like we hit another jackpot!" boasted Ryan, setting his eyes on some hardhats, identification badges, and a set of keys.

"It will definitely look more convincing walking out of here if were dressed like actual maintenance workers," said 978, looking over Ryan's shoulder to take a quick peak at this supposedly great discovery. "The hardhats seem to match the backpacks."

"There are also some coveralls here," added Dr. Carlton. "Do you think we should wear them?"

"Just the hardhats and badges," said Ryan.

"That gives me an idea. Ryan, you can be Sully. Mark, you'll be Biff, and I'll be Steve!"

They all shared a quick laugh together.

It didn't take them very long to prepare for making an entrance, especially considering they had left the protection suits back in that subway car, which thankfully, was operational. There wasn't a lot of effort required to put hardhats and badges on, and Ryan quickly figured out which key unlocked the door. Now they only needed to worry about was how to act once they were out in public.

"What should we do when we walk out of here?" asked 978.

"Just act like we belong here," answered Ryan.

"Like regular workers," added Dr. Carlton.

"Gotcha," said 978.

"I know," said Ryan. "If anyone asks we'll just say that we're conducting a safety inspection."

"That sounds alright to me. I'll open the door to let you guys out first, then I'll shine my flashlight back inside when I come out. I'll lock up and we'll head over to the nearest train line and I'll shine my flashlight down there, too. Hopefully most of those people will simply assume it's nothing more than a routine inspection, making us look the most productive we've been all night."

"It's too bad we're not getting paid," said Dr. Carlton, in a light-hearted tone.

"If I can find a way to make that happen, I'll let you know."

978 was impressed his two constituents could consistently keep up a good sense of humor, especially at such crucial moments like this. He was also pleasantly surprised that Dr. Carlton had actually called him by his real name. He knew all along that she, as well as Ryan, saw him as more than just a number. But hearing the sound of another voice saying Mark was very reassuring. Hell, he would be fine if the both of them referred to him as Biff for the rest of the night.

It didn't take very long for Ryan to figure out which key could unlock the door. He only had to push the door open a few inches to realize it would take more effort.

"Time to pump some iron!" he boasted, leaning his upper body forward while pushing the door open with the palms of his hands. The result was exactly what he had expected and the bright lights of Park Street Station blinded him for a moment. Still, it was a lot better compared to those hallucinations that caused him to shoot at the white walls a little while ago.

As soon as Ryan stepped outside of the maintenance room, 978 and Dr. Carlton followed him. Some people who were waiting for their train to arrive gave them suspicious looks, but that quickly changed after seeing the hardhats and identification badges. They had no problem looking like they belonged there. Ryan made eye contact with 978 then looked over at the maintenance room door, indicating to shut it. 978 knew what he meant and did so without hesitation.

The three of them made their way over to the station platform. Everybody they passed by only glanced at them. 978 occasionally nodded at anyone who made eye contact, hopefully strengthening the assumption that they worked there. He started to wonder if he, along with Dr. Carlton and Ryan, displayed a sense of authority. Considering the fact that the three of them had either worked in law enforcement, the medical field, and the military, he definitely wanted to believe so.

"Let's find the bathrooms," said Ryan. "Whether their crowded or not, wait for a stall to open. We can get rid of the hardhats and badges and prepare ourselves as much as possible for when we go outside."

"Don't forget it's the last chance to relieve ourselves," said Dr. Carlton, being sarcastic.

"We'll meet back here in ten minutes."

978, Dr. Carlton, and Ryan found the restrooms quickly, which luckily weren't very crowded. They locked themselves into stalls to prepare as fast as possible. For 978, ten minutes felt like more than enough time, so Ryan made a good call on that one. However, he couldn't believe how many times he had changed in and out of clothes or uniforms over the past few hours. The last time he had to do this task frequently was when he worked at a Halloween theme park back in college. He remembered that period of his life fondly, but he used enough makeup and costumes there to last a lifetime. He didn't even want to start thinking about what Dr. Carlton was doing in the bathroom, or anyone else for that matter. He honestly didn't pay attention to which stall Ryan decided to occupy. That suited him fine, he never engaged in long conversations with other guys in public bathrooms.

The three of them made it back to their meeting spot with three minutes to spare. At this point they were ahead of the game. Now it was time to head up to ground zero.

••• 20

For the Zen Lunatic gang, it seemed possible that everything could go smoothly. The four of them, Zen, Johnson, Rod, and Sid arrived at the Boston Common at the exact time 978 had ordered them to. Zen was a little concerned about keeping up appearances, because he didn't want to attract the attention of police officers. He had no reason to worry. It turned out there weren't a whole lot of cops patrolling around on motorbikes. In fact, there were quite a few civilians in attendance who arrived on motorbikes, many who were still cruising around with loud engines still cranking. It would take a little while for things to settle down, which suited the gang fine. It made them look a lot less suspicious or dangerous, allowing Zen to think that tonight's event provided the perfect opportunity to get away with murder. If he wanted to go out on top, then being part of a conspiracy to stage an attempted assassination was plain ridiculous. Johnson was right. Why not take down the real monster in this situation? Why not get rid of 978 altogether?

Despite all these thoughts racing through his mind, Zen was a bit surprised that he didn't feel the need to constantly look over his shoulder. There was no point, really. Considering the predicament he was in, he couldn't get into much more trouble. No matter what he decided to do tonight, he'd get locked up in Peterson Prison's Psychiatric Unit for the rest of his life. But with 978 taken out of the picture, that place would feel more like a utopia. Perhaps he could tell the new inmates that the former guard was Lucifer in disguise. The possibilities were endless.

The onetime leader, recruiter, and manipulator of the outside world around the Boston area would never be able to fully shake the fact that 978 had freed him the night before. The other three guys keeping him company probably felt the same way. At least Johnson had made things clear, and planted a lot of good ideas in his head. The guy wasn't some hopeless and desperate follower. A strong mind existed within this individual that possessed a unique thought process. Whether they succeeded in the outside world or got sent back to Peterson Prison's Psychiatric Unit Zen wanted to have Johnson at the very least be second-in-command to whatever movement he created next. Credit would be given personally in one-on-one discussions, significantly decreasing the chance of an ally or the other disciples turning against him.

Zen kept going back to the fact that 978 never liked him, so that offered no reason for the guard to recruit him or the other inmates. Then again, he realized that 978 probably didn't want him or the other three guys present or any other prisoner for that matter to be able to make sense of the situation at all. He also used to think that most of the guards would be a little more laid back outside of work regardless of the circumstances. But in this case 978 proved to be far worse than he could have imagined. He actually respected the guy at one point. Someone who didn't believe every fancy story told, someone who was always on the level. With 978 you just cut through the crap and got straight to the point. He had to admit that it saved a lot of time for him to prey on other guards and inmates.

Unfortunately, Zen had always hoped that it was only behind the walls where he would see 978's worse side, or any other guard for that matter. Like him they were human, or were they? Perhaps if the 978 he and his gang had been dealing with was some kind of machine instead of a man that would explain things. Logic would be useful right now to make things easier, but there was no way to prove this theory. Maybe the poor guy just became angry with the system over the past decade. A lot of red tape and formalities came into effect with law enforcement, even Zen knew that. There were procedures that had to be followed down to the letter, especially in the prison system. He started wonder if all this stuff he heard about prison reformation would do any good

978: Man or Machine? Having these thoughts bounce back and forth in Zen's mind became more and more overwhelming. Why should he be contemplating the new technology or policies being brought in for prison reform? The answer was plain and simple: Peterson Prison's Psychiatric Unit was the place where he would most likely be until the day he died. The guards probably didn't have any say in how things were run, and the inmates were never given any choices whatsoever, especially if you were sentenced to the Psychiatric Unit. Zen gave up on the notion of rights long ago. However, he did recognize the outside world as a place that offered a particular feeling that jail couldn't, which was opportunity. No matter where you are on earth, the choices are limited, but there would always be many more of them on the outside. Democracy is something people can believe in, but the word itself might as well be forgotten when you're behind bars.

It didn't matter what action Zen or his followers took tonight, if any at all, they would earn a one-way ticket back to jail. He knew even if they dropped everything and turned themselves over to the authorities or the Governor, the situation would not improve. Not for himself which was most important. At this point there was no reason to kid himself or anyone else. Looking out for number one had always been his way. That was how the justice system viewed him, how the media portrayed him, and how the public perceived him. That would never change. Once you're labeled as a criminal it was almost impossible to shake that. His thought process may not be totally consumed with the mentality of either a narcissist or a sociopath, but those traits would always remain within his genetic makeup. Somehow this particular scenario, regardless of the final outcome, would cause him to look worse than ever. The so-called justice system would insist on making an example of him. His jail sentence would get increased significantly and the media would make it look like he got off easy.

Zen started thinking about what his options might be after going back to Peterson Prison. Being stuck back in the Psychiatric Unit wouldn't be too bad. If the whole gang got sent back there it was highly unlikely that they would get their old cells back, much less be neighbors again. The powers that be would make that the top priority, at least in the beginning. The simple motivation being to keep up appearances, especially if the mainstream media wanted updates. That would definitely be the case over the next several months, perhaps years, depending on tonight's outcome. With all the controversy escalating because of the changes in technology and policies regarding prison reform, the scrutiny would continue to increase. In Massachusetts alone that would be the case for a long time to come considering the fact that the new prison reform bills going into effect was designed with the hope that it would set the standard for all prison systems throughout the entire country. Not many people knew this, but Dr. Fletcher had hoped that the concept could be sold worldwide. South America was guaranteed, the Brazil factory was manufacturing everything designed for the LEO1 technology. Except for the clones which wasn't a big deal since their use was considered by everyone involved to be short-lived.

Zen continued to obsessively think about what happened to poor Hoyt. In a way that was more or less his main frame of reference with everything leading up to tonight's event. The ruthlessness of that incident was something he always knew was way beyond him. But that had to be true of almost everybody who possessed even the smallest amount of humanity within them. The current leader of the pack may require pretty thick skin, so it's not surprising that a guard with almost a decade of experience would be pretty tough as well. But no guard, whether it's 978 or anyone else, could be methodical or precise enough to just cut through a situation like they were an actual machete. In 978's case a far more appropriate comparison would be a bulldozer, or better yet a wrecking ball. All four of them probably felt wrecked after witnessing Hoyt's demise. But they weren't enthusiastic to have lengthy discussions regarding the matter. Even if they were back at Peterson Prison in the middle of a group therapy session none of them would volunteer to bring up that subject.

978. What that guard did to Hoyt was something nobody could claim to have seen before, the exception being Zen, Johnson, Rod, and Sid. Hoyt could also be included, but the poor soul was more of a victim than a witness, possibly used as a test subject to proof that their abilities go beyond a human's normal strength. Zen had honestly never heard of an average guy just picking someone up by the neck with one hand causing strangulation to the point where consciousness is almost gone. He started to wonder why 978 didn't keep choking Hoyt to death. Shooting the escaped prisoner may have been quicker but a lot messier, which left the remaining four escapees with a bit of cleaning up to do. It could have been a lot worse, but equally unpleasant. Right now he wanted to get the picture of Hoyt's blood leaking through the sheets out of his mind, so back to contemplating 978's strangulation technique.

Zen had to continue reminding himself that it wasn't the actual strangulation which killed Hoyt, but the whole point of picturing that scenario was to help him forget about the bullet wound to the head. The simple term cold-blooded murder wasn't strong enough to describe it. Then again, the blood part was accurate. However, a human's blood was always warm regardless if they're a saint or a serial killer. Perhaps scientists should test the blood temperature of different types of people to see if the degree levels are significantly higher or lower. Throughout history there had always been plenty of psychological evaluations done, so why not invest more time on the physical aspects. Zen didn't have much expertise in anatomy or physiology, and knew no one would take his suggestions seriously.

Zen got back to thinking about 978 strangling Hoyt, making him consider the fact that what he witnessed wasn't impossible. But it was far more likely that an adult could do something like that to an infant or a small child.

Zen realized something. The picture of Hoyt's body wrapped up in sheets with blood leaking through was much easier to cope with than the possibility of strangled children.

Then again, none of these mental pictures contained anything he wanted to cope with, much less be a part of for any reason.

Disruption to the current thought process was about to occur.

"Do you want to split up to those different designated areas like we planned?" asked Johnson.

"What?" responded 978, caught off guard. "Yeah we should."

"Okay."

"Man, this city is not what it used to be."

"What was that?"

"Nothing," he answered.

For Zen, that was exactly what he thought his future held.

Not a damn thing.

••• 21

Park Street Station felt like an absolute mob scene. Whether that was the case or not was an entirely different matter considering the fact that 978, Dr. Carlton, or Ryan had made any conscious attempt to estimate the size of the crowd they were surrounded by. For the most part they were still letting that feeling of relief flow through their thoughts in regards to the restrooms not being overcrowded, which was far more important due to the simple need for what lied ahead later that evening.

978 started thinking that an actual mob scene might be easier to deal with compared to what he and his two constituents were about to go up against. There was always a presence of those types in and around the Boston area which were made up of gangsters, bookies, protection services, or bounty hunters. The public in general knew that law enforcement was supposed to protect and to serve, but that didn't apply to every aspect of day to day living for people residing in certain neighborhoods. The home turf would always be safe, but you weren't if part of your weekly paycheck wasn't donated to the powers that be, who worked as the neighborhood's watchdogs. For some folks it wasn't a bad deal, when you considered the fact that many of them only had to pay as little as 5%. Most people found it worthwhile to keep quiet, especially since everyone had way more money deducted legitimately as taxes. If 99% of these people were forced to choose between paying high taxes or protection services out of their own pockets, most would choose the latter, even if they didn't like who was in charge of the operation. Another reason was that the police weren't going to do anything about it. In fact a lot of the guys who

ran these rackets worked in law enforcement, and the amount taken from most residents was too small. Most of the local residents gave up reporting anything to the police, the government, or even the local media. The situation simply didn't attract enough attention to complain about corruption, much less create any major controversy.

Bounty hunters were an entirely different matter. If you stayed in the game long enough and made the right transactions with the right people, you could do pretty well for yourself. Depending on how reliable your main sources were along with a steady clientele, most investments would result in excellent profits. Most guys who worked in the field that earned a reputation for getting the job done with no hassles could usually set up arrangements that worked best for them. No deals, no negotiations, the absolute best of the bounty hunters made transactions, with the guarantee that the investment was worthwhile. A bounty hunter's services were utilized by just about everyone in this day and age, and that included some of the most important people in the government. The ones who survived in the field long enough were practically immune to prosecution. Three years of service without any mistakes meant you were good. Five years meant you were at the top of your game. The President of the United States would consider you for employment. If the job was done correctly and on time, the benefits would be phenomenal. Of course the pay was excellent, but it didn't stop there. The first option available was to invest the money into a permanent retainer, which put you on Washington D.C.'s payroll. It becomes a regular monthly check. The amount would be substantially less, but fixed taxes and health insurance would remain in effect until the day you die. If you had any criminal history a full pardon would be granted and the records would be sealed worldwide. Only the top brass at the White House would be able to access to that information. Of all three of them, Dr. Carlton had the most knowledge regarding that career. Ryan knew a little bit just from being in the Air Force for so long. 978 wouldn't mind so much if he could get his replica to do the dirty work, and top it off by having the paycheck directly deposited into his account!

As soon as 978, Dr. Carlton, and Ryan were upstairs and outside of Park Street Station, they immediately started to think about what they needed to do. It would have been smarter if they'd conducted a brainstorming session before arriving at the Boston Common, but they had to focus more on actually making it there before deciding what to do next. After everything the three of them had survived so far, there was no reason to debate the fact that they were fortunate to have made it there in one piece. Hopefully their trip back would be a lot easier, and they wouldn't be captured by the Underground Dwellers or attacked by a human-sized bat.

"There's only one logical thing to do," said Ryan.

"What's that?" asked 978.

"We should get as close as possible to the stage, specifically the area where the Governor is supposed to deliver his speech. It may be getting crowded, but we should have enough time to maneuver around everyone without causing any trouble."

"We also need to keep our eyes peeled for Zen's gang," added Dr. Carlton.

"That should be our top priority," said 978.

"Maybe we'll make it there before they do," suggested Ryan.

"That would be nice."

"If there on bikes they'll be making plenty of noise."

"Knowing the way these guys are," said Dr. Carlton. "They'll probably stand out pretty easily."

"She's right," said 978. "I've been working in the Psychiatric Unit for quite some time now. All of them, especially their leader, have a bit of a flare for theatrics, just from what comes out of their mouths alone."

"Yeah, that Burton guy alone definitely knows how to talk the talk no matter how absurd the subject might be."

"Sounds like he at least keeps you awake," said Ryan, slightly amused. "Unlike some politicians when they're making speeches."

"Are you referring to a certain someone who's going to take the stage in a little while?" asked Dr. Carlton.

"Not necessarily," said Ryan. "But I'll bet it's more interesting to hear certain patients go on and on telling their stories, no matter how far-fetched they might be!"

"I could make a career out of it. All I need to do is write a few books and change the names and say their fictionalized accounts. But after the critics make their assessment and find out that I'm a doctor they'll be convinced that I need treatment."

"At least you lived to tell the tales!"

Naturally, after this little discussion, the first thing that caught 978's attention was the loud sound of motorbikes. They weren't completely surrounded by them, but there were definitely more than enough to be overwhelming and alarming. However, 978 needed to consider the fact that he rarely attended events such as these, and was never overly political to begin with. The closest he came to it was in the workplace with one simple word: formalities. Right now that was the last thing he wanted to think about, and he seriously doubted that his two constituents wanted to hear about it either. With Dr. Carlton practicing medicine and Ryan being ex-military they knew all about formalities, even if that word wasn't specifically used by any of their employers. The Governor would definitely know what he was talking about, especially in present times being teamed up with Fletcher with this whole prison reform policy. He wondered if the Governor would feel as strong about it if there was a chance of finding out that the end result was Will getting shot to death.

It didn't matter.

No matter how successful they were tonight, the worst of the worst would be covered up somehow. Even if Fletcher was dead and his operation went under certain incidents would be sugar-coated, Will's death would be ruled as an accident.

The first thing to catch 978's attention was the loud sound of the motorcycles. They might have not been everywhere, but there were more than enough to be alarming. Of course 978 had to consider the fact that he very rarely attended events like these, or maybe it had something to do with anticipating seeing the Zen Lunatic gang showing up on them. He also knew the city of Boston wasn't what it used to be. He started to recognize that when he was a teenager, which was twenty years ago. Then again, most people know you slow down quite a bit the older you get, and your younger days just naturally felt more innocent and appealing compared to what you dealt with later on in life as a responsible adult. Still, it might have been a good idea to have made more attempts to keep tabs on the current events more often. But it was almost impossible to know if you were going to get stuck in a dire situation like this. Regardless, it might have helped.

As the three of them inched their way through the crowd, they each wondered exactly how long it would take to get to the center stage. Ryan had the least amount of patience for this kind of thing despite a strong military background, perhaps due to getting older with a lack of interest in political matters. He had a small amount of admiration for civilians who were passionate about politics, but at this point in his life there was something more appealing about living in the moment than worrying about debating certain points of view with others, no matter how important the subject might be. 978 feelings were divided in regards to their predicament, partly by simply wanting to maneuver quickly through this crowd but at the same time dreading laying eyes on the mechanical reflection with the same guard number, but in no way could this abomination truly be Mark Allen Royce. Dr.

Carlton had the best idea as to what they were getting into, at least in comparison to Ryan and 978. She felt the most concern for the poor guard who must have had a million thoughts going through his head, and who could blame him?

978 started to think about the Massachusetts motorcycles helmet law and the fact that it no longer existed. That wasn't entirely true. It was no longer strictly enforced. A police officer could not pull over someone on a motorcycle for the specific violation being the operator not wearing a proper helmet, unless the person is under 18 or if the passenger being transported is a small child not dressed in the required outfit, with just one part being a helmet. The only time an operator will be instructed to wear proper headgear would be at the officer's discretion depending on the violation. 978 always felt that particular law should have remained strictly enforced but he'd had enough sense to know that in this situation it actually worked in his favor, especially considering the fact that he saw the faces of these escaped prisoners every night he was on duty. However, he knew better than to make his presence known to them right away. As far as they knew he was with 609 assisting the Governor with tonight's affairs, and he wanted them to keep believing that after he spotted them, or four out of five that he knew were fugitives, up near the front of the crowd on the right side of the stage sitting on motorcycles. The easiest one to recognize was Johnson who had the big dreadlocks, Zen was on the left side from 978's view, and the other two were best known by their first names Rod and Sid. There was a part of 978 that wanted to keep referring to them by their numbers, but he was sick of thinking that way, and the fact that they had been set up as well, in a way that made them equal at this point. The last thing to come to mind was the name of the last escapee he hadn't seen, that being Hoyt. He was a little concerned about what might have happened to the guy, and hoped his replica hadn't cause the poor guy any harm. But he knew to expect

almost every scenario that came to mind, and if something did happen to Hoyt, it was most likely the replica's doing. This meant the entire Zen Lunatic gang including the leader, were probably scared to death of him.

"There they are," said 978.

"Who?" asked Ryan, breaking his concentration, "The escaped prisoners?"

"Yeah, they call themselves the Zen Lunatic gang. It's the four guys parked next to each other on the right."

"Is the leader the guy with the dreadlocks?"

"No, it's the one on the left. He's the so-called Zen Lunatic. His real name is Jack Burton."

"Now that I've got a good look at them, it won't be difficult to remember."

"We'll remember everything about tonight whether we want to or not," added Dr. Carlton. "Wait, there's supposed to be five guys present in the Zen Lunatic gang."

"I know," said 978. "What do you think happened to him?"

"Happened? I have no idea."

"You know what I mean."

"Don't think like that, we have enough to worry about without considering the location of every fugitive!"

"How long now before the Governor makes his speech?" asked Ryan, trying to keep them focused.

"You just gave me a great idea!" stated Dr. Carlton, all excited.

"What do you mean?"

"I still have 609's contact number. As far as everyone knows, I'm still working with Fletcher. She would know the exact time!"

"Make the call!"

"Alright, but give me a minute to move away from you guys, I don't want the three of us spotted together."

Dr. Carlton started to slowly maneuver through the crowd until she reached a distance of approximately thirty feet from both 978 and Ryan, with enough people jammed between them making it impossible to have eye contact. The main thing going through her mind, however, was referring to 609 as she. At this point the good doctor should know better than to talk about the replicas like they were regular people. Of course these things were supposed to act like human beings to the best of their abilities, and to the point where they were actually convincing. Now it was time to make the call to 609, the replica. She hoped that the conversation would go quickly and smoothly. It was also important to keep in mind that all of the replicas remained connected through neural networking, which meant that 609 might be able to figure out what's going on very quickly.

Dr. Carlton dialed into Fletcher's network directory, something she didn't want to think about. That creep was already in charge of all the new policies behind prison reform, words she visualized in her mind at this point in small letters. It was amazing considering her background. She didn't even want to mention it to Ryan. The idea of her becoming anti-government would shock everyone who knew her, but most of those people had no clue what was going on in her world. However, it wouldn't be difficult for them to realize that the functions of replicas and clones had been programmed to serve the top brass of the inside world. The worst part being that even some of the so-called top brass would remain unaware of it.

Now she had to press the numbers 6-0-9. The phone rang, with a combination of nervousness and anticipation that could not be put into words. She just wanted to be able to hold herself together long enough to endure the brief conversation.

"609 speaking," said the replica.

"It's Carlton," said Dr. Carlton. "I need to know what time the Governor will be on stage."

"In exactly twelve minutes. 978 and I will be there with him.

Where is Mark Allen Royce?"

"I.......took care of him, he's dead. I shot him."

"Where are you?"

"On my way, I'll be there when it's over. About thirty minutes."

"That's affirmative."

609 immediately disconnected. Overall, the conversation went quick and smoothly, far better than Dr. Carlton could have hoped for. For a moment, she started thinking about the use of the word affirmative. It just sounded so tacky, even when it came from the mouth of a replica. Still, the worse part was the possibility of the replica knowing about her and 978, a.k.a. Mark Royce, escaping from the prison last night. She had to be cautious. It was nice to think of the guard as someone with a name, not just a number.

Dr. Carlton was able to make her way back to where 978 and Ryan were without any problems. It would have been a lot easier to communicate with transmitters. She wasn't about to take any chances, though. There was a high risk of their conversation being picked up by 609. All eyes were focused on her by 978 and Ryan, who were eagerly waiting for an update. The silence was instantly broken.

"Did you get through?" asked Ryan.

"Yeah," answered Dr. Carlton. "We have twelve minutes until the speech starts."

"Probably less," said 978. "If you included the time it took you to get back over here"

"Then I'd say we have approximately ten minutes."

978 had a point. Dr. Carlton also had to consider the time it took to get back to her two constituents, making her immediately realize she should have kept track of the time with her watch. That would have made it easier to know how long it would take both replicas and the Governor to appear on stage. A few extra minutes would be allowed for the Governor's daughter to come out. Now it was time to receive

more input from Ryan.

"Let's just wait and keep all eyes on the Zen Lunatic gang," he said.

"Good idea," she responded.

The three of them managed to get close to the Zen Lunatic and his followers. If they kept their eyes completely focused, it might be possible to read every facial expression. That wasn't so bad if you considered that fact that it was a better job suited for a replica. The problem was they had a lot of other things they needed to do besides that, forcing them to quickly decide who should keep track of what. Dr. Carlton took the responsibility of watching the stage, which made sense since she was the only one of them who'd had any association with the Governor, his daughter, or the replicas.

The first signs of life to the naked eye appeared on stage in the form of replicas 978 and 609. There was absolutely no response from the crowd, not that there should have been, even with the big stage lights now shining at full power. Most likely it was because they anticipated seeing the man of the hour. Civilians didn't have to think about formalities if they didn't work for the government or law enforcement, nor would they really need to since they had their own lives to live. Perhaps nobody cared much since this Governor was so personable. By some miracle this politician made everyone feel safer, or at least had the ability to help the residents of the state of Massachusetts feel optimistic. Whatever it was it worked, and nobody complained.

About a minute after what the media-labeled as over-glorified bodyguards took the stage, the announcement was made over the loudspeaker for the Governor to come out for his speech. It would be a few more minutes before his daughter would appear on stage. She was the replicas main target according to the original plan. Of course her father demanded she be the number one priority above all us regarding protection. What he didn't know was that both of them were surrounded by the worst danger possible even if plans hadn't been made for an attempted assassination. The interaction he'd had with 978 and 609 left him a bit cold, but there was no harm done, and as far as he knew these two guards had always worked the overnight shift, and probably would have liked to have rested more before tonight's speech. He had worked those same hours once during a college summer break many years ago, which made him recall how quickly he got back home and went to bed as soon as possible. The best part was relaxing in the middle to later evenings before going back again. He could easily understand if these two felt the same way.

As soon as the Governor stood in front of the podium, he had to lean down slightly to speak into the microphone. Ryan was the first one to notice he was empty-handed, which meant the speech would be short and sweet.

"There can't be much time left," said Ryan.

"You're right," said Dr. Carlton. "Fletcher made it clear that the Governor needed to keep everything brief and to the point. There is no way he would have allowed anyone else to take credit or have access to a lot of information. It didn't matter even if a semi-decent politician like this guy had his back."

"I know politics is something you never really cared for."

"That's true, which is partly why I'm not up there on Fletcher's behalf, even though I don't mind this particular Governor."

"Good."

••• 22

For the Zen Lunatic, a.k.a. Jack Burton, he was consumed with a massive amount of anticipation for what was supposed to be his biggest moment. Unfortunately, a large dose of anxiety had begun to slowly take over. Probably more so, considering the tension he felt throughout his entire body. He hadn't been able to shake that feeling, which started when 978 had helped him and his followers escape from the Psychiatric Unit of the Peterson Prison. In a way, it felt more like a direct order to leave or else there would be some serious consequences. The fear gradually increased by the time the guard brought them to that old warehouse where they had to wait for further instructions. The Zen Lunatic gang quickly got a taste of the type of punishment they would receive when 978 took the life out of Hoyt right before their eyes.

But Zen knew better. This wasn't the way things were supposed to happen. The guard who killed Hoyt could not have been 978, at least not the 978 he knew. Anyone employed by the prison system long enough could easily be affected psychologically for the worse no matter how well they had their act together, but not to the point where someone working as a civil servant enforcing the law would suddenly snap and free prisoners, then top things off by murdering one of them to teach the group a lesson. There are many people out there who work on the right side of the justice system who have it in for who they believe are criminals, sometimes to the point where it's an obsession, but very rarely will a situation arise where they'll take out their sworn enemy in cold blood. If an innocent civilian is in danger resulting from the wanted fugitive's actions then the risk increases significantly of more lives being lost, an officer will have to shoot to kill. Perhaps those measures will be called for equally if it's a matter of self-defense. Zen thought 978 crossed that line the moment Hoyt was taken out, and deserved equal punishment.

The one thing Zen did not want to openly admit was the distinct possibility of one of his followers feeling more confident and less scared about how things would turn out tonight. That follower was Johnson, of course. Zen was still in charge, for sure, but it was this man he had vowed to make an equal partner in what he expected to be a dead-end future whose plans were initially being followed. If there was no future, why not go out on a high note? He envisioned Johnson as someone special. Not just a valuable asset, but possibly a friend as well, only time would tell what the future held in store for either of them. He thought about everyone who followed him blindly over the years, and was able to continue doing that behind bars. Unfortunately, there was only so much he could do there, and he should have thought a lot more about the emotional psyche of certain inmates. He wasn't just serving a standard sentence in the Peterson Prison, the Zen Lunatic and his followers were doing time in the Psychiatric Unit!

Zen began to visualize what Johnson would be like as an equal partner. He was always aware of his unique ability to talk the talk, perhaps the best role for his potential partner would be that of an enforcer. Johnson had a look and an aura that could easily fill that part. Hopefully, it would remain unnecessary to act out as harshly as 978 had with Hoyt. Of course he needed to keep in mind that Johnson had always worked for him and not against him. The line was clearly drawn between the guard and the fellow inmate in the neighboring cell as to where they stood. That would have always remained true but that became even more so at this point, but most people would have made a decision rather quickly after everything these guys had witnessed and experienced in such a short amount of time. It didn't matter how vulnerable they were, even those so emotionally disturbed and serving decades in the Peterson Prison Psychiatric Unit who had no incentive to live by Zen's word, much less enjoy living out fantasies inside their heads.

Zen started to think a little more about the idea of Johnson being the ultimate Enforcer. Not just as a casual nickname, the capital E would definitely be included. Then again, he had to keep in mind how legitimate that title sounded. It might not appeal to Johnson all that much considering the fact that it sounded like a tough guy type representing the justice system. However, the idea of being the one that all the other inmates had to answer to very well could, even if it meant doing a lot of the dirty work that he as the Zen Lunatic did not want to do. But if this plan got put into motion in a prison-type of environment, then he needed to figure out beforehand if it would be beneficial to him in the long run. Being known as the Enforcer sounded serious, and could cause both inmates and guards to think that Johnson has authority over him. The Enforcer did sound more a lot more important than the Zen Lunatic, but it didn't sound bad to allow everyone to have the impression that Johnson had the run of things. If any fellow inmates caused trouble they would have to answer to the Enforcer, meaning he wouldn't need to find a way to shift the blame onto someone else. As long as he had the last word in no one else would need to know. The final decisions would stay between Burton and Johnson, or the Zen Lunatic and the Enforcer.

Right now it didn't matter if he had a brilliant idea or if he was simply fantasizing, Zen could feel his spirits lift somewhat despite the predicament he was in. Or to be fair one that he, Johnson, Rod, and Sid were in. At this point Johnson was unofficially second-in-command, and possibly in equal partner in the near future, but he had to consider Rod and Sid as well. Since he honestly wasn't sure if he had everything, or anything, under control, he couldn't think of himself as a leader. Johnson must have sensed that, especially after single-handedly reconstructing 978's original plan they were expected to carry out. To others it might have come off as a strong suggestion, but he needed guidance. And since none of them were safe he had to admit they were all in this together.

Team work was the name of the game, to a point anyway. In the past whoever worked for Zen carried out his orders until the very end. Proof of that would soon appear on the stage in front of him in the shape of a father and child, or the Governor and daughter if it's considered necessary to be politically correct. Those two were the entire reason for Zen being here, the worst part was that 978 must have been enjoying every minute of it. He started to wonder if he had inadvertently planted the seed for what eventually blossomed into Fletcher's concept of Prison Reform, which was expected to go into effect nationwide almost immediately after it got put into motion throughout the state of Massachusetts and the rest of New England. Getting the other five states in on the new wouldn't be difficult since most new ideas for law enforcement were usually embraced right away, and the name of the game meant that if every state took to it the rest of the country would actually believe then it must be worthwhile to have everywhere. But Zen knew in this day and age that a unanimous vote or decision shouldn't be made just because a simple idea is off to a good start. In was sad, he thought, we're more than halfway through the twenty-first century and the majority who rule still don't try to see past the surface of whatever they're for or against.

Zen started thinking about the fact that if he was taken alive that it wouldn't be a big deal. The death penalty wasn't in effect in the state of Massachusetts, and it hadn't been for a long time. It hadn't been on any voting ballot to bring back decades before he'd been born, and Fletcher's new policies surrounding his Prison Reform bill would most likely abolish it altogether. Of course there would still be many prisoners facing death before their time was up, be it naturally or otherwise. Inmates could still have their lives taken by guards and not be reported as such. That was always what could be done to make it look like the inmate's fault, especially if they were already serving a life sentence or had a diagnosis of psychological problems. Making those intended to spend the rest of their days in Peterson Prison's Psychiatric Unit very easy targets. What's more unusual is that every state backs legal assisted suicide for anyone who has a sentence ranging from forty years to life. Unfortunately the process behind it is worse than the final result with plenty of formalities to follow, the first of which is serving at least half of the ruled sentence, then having to file a request through the court which takes another two to five years. The motive behind this very long and arduous process is to help the prisoners lose interest and give up completely, encouraging a pro-life value on those who are locked up for most, if not all, their lives.

But what is life to someone who wakes up in the same place and can only conduct the same routine on every given day?

You can only live inside your head for so long before it runs out of space, forcing the remaining sanity and creativity within you to burst shattering like broken glass all over your thoughts, causing bleeding that nearly drowns any optimism or belief in changing for the better. The remaining scars never heal, and all hope is lost for a full recovery.

There's no turning back.

Could the self-proclaimed Zen Lunatic ever be content?

With everything going on around him he had a chance, because no matter what happens tonight, as long as he survived intact very little would change for the worse. All the justice system could do was put him back where he came from, that being an environment he'd been accustomed to whether he like it or not. It wasn't so bad when you knew what you were up against. Charles Manson felt the same way he did, despite having no desire to take things as far as that guy had. At least he wasn't lying to himself when he said he never intended to hurt or kill anyone. He wasn't exactly a modern day Robin Hood either, but he had a better chance of fitting that profile than Manson.

Zen had to admit to himself that it did seem somewhat noble to take out 978. He may have been continuously contemplating the fact that he never wanted to be involved in something like this, but the situation started with the guard breaking him and his gang out of jail and forcing them into a ruthless mission, with the first step taken killing Hoyt. The whole thing was backwards, considering most people were likely to believe it was something that he would want to do. Part of him wanted to maintain his principles, but he'd never come out of this a winner, not to the world at large anyway.

At least in his mind he'll be getting even, and if he got caught a balancing act will go into effect. He'll go back to jail again in Peterson Prison's Psychiatric Unit. Even Charles Manson didn't have it that easy. Truth be told, being placed into a psychiatric care facility in any prison these days is a picnic compared to a standard incarceration, no matter what the length of the sentence might be.

"Two minute warning," said Johnson. "It's best to keep track of every second."

"Yeah," responded Zen, still stuck in his contemplative thought process, but keeping all eyes on the stage.

"The guards take the stage first before the Governor comes out, right?"

"That's the standard procedure. Any politician who is prepared to make a speech in this country is required to have some kind of armed security come out beforehand. At the Peterson Prison, or any prison for that matter, it's called a formality. That particular phrase actually applies more to the guards than us."

"I forgot about that. You hear that term used by the guards quite a bit, actually. But since they're supposedly on the right side of the law, they'll always be considered formal, and dare I say, superior to any of us destined to be locked up for a long time. But I honestly do believe the guards are viewed by the bureaucrats and higher-ups as just one step above us, which doesn't say much."

"Do you think so?"

"Look what 978 did to Hoyt."

"I don't know, something was out of place there, he must have been drugged or hypnotized or something."

"We'll never know, and after tonight is over it's not going to matter, anyway."

"I hope you're right."

The brief conversation left the gang with approximately another minute until show time. Of course Johnson was the only one who knew for sure, which was perfectly fine. Zen just wanted to keep his eyes on the stage. He clearly pictured the Governor starting his speech at the podium. That was somewhat strange considering the primary target was 978, a decision made between him and Johnson hours ago, but felt like it had been years in the making. What was most surprising to him was having no desire whatsoever to take out the Governor, much less the daughter, who was largely responsible for receiving the sentence he got to Peterson Prison's Psychiatric Unit. However, he had to remind himself that after the trial ended they never had to see each other again. Her father's political career hadn't interested him much, either. Despite feeling he could easily blame them for everything leading up to this moment.

The real truth, however, was completely different. 978 was the one who had broken him and his gang out of prison. 978 came up with the original plan for tonight's speech, which was drastically altered thanks to Johnson. Zen only had a short period of time left to serve, with a guarantee of getting out. Any great opportunities the future may have held were gone because of that awful guard, someone he had to see regularly on the night shift. Someone who never bought in to anything he said, including light conversations. Then again, being known as the Zen Lunatic meant that there was very little small talk, and if he was lucky enough 978 would treat it as such on a good day.

A very good day, there was no such thing as a great day inside the Peterson Prison, in the Psychiatric Unit or any other part of that place.

"Any second now," said Johnson. "We should be seeing the first signs of life on that stage."

"That's right," said Rod, in a soft-spoken tone.

"One being our so-called leader 978 and another guard," added Sid, sounding sarcastic and humorous.

The latter two hadn't said much since the gang departed from the warehouse quite some time ago. Zen was a little surprised at how casual they sounded, along with the dark humor. The positive side, however, was at least they were up to date with how things were supposed to go. Then again, these guys had embraced every word that came out of his mouth for quite a long time now. Years to be exact, what else did they know? At this point Zen was able to breathe a sigh of relief knowing he didn't have to spell everything out to them. Of course he also should have considered the fact that he honestly had no idea how intelligent they might be. He'd always been more concerned with his followers listening to what he had to say, and carry out orders without asking questions. For all he knew Rod and Sid might have the same amount of potential he now saw in Johnson, but right now wasn't the best time to determine if that was the case. And when it came to power, he knew not to spread the wealth out to far. First things first, see how Johnson works out before more grandiose ideas come to mind, much less try to fulfill delusional desires to expand on unrealistic goals he is very unlikely to reach.

While Zen kept contemplating future endeavors his eyes stayed focused on the stage. Two figures appeared and marched out to the front, each occupying sides. 978 occupying the left which was the right side to the crowd and

609 the right which was the left side to the crowd, putting 978 at a closer range to the Zen Lunatic and his gang. He didn't give any thought as to whether or not that worked to his advantage. Most people would think that a closer target was an easier target, it sounded logical. But fear consumed him to the point where it was almost painful.

The light went on, or to be more accurate the lights on stage lit up as bright as possible. They were extremely dim beforehand, the further back someone was in the crowd made it nearly impossible to recognize who came out first. But nowadays most people knew security always appeared first at any political speech, it had been a standard procedure dating as far back as anyone could remember.

Something inside Zen kept telling him to shoot 978 now and get it over with. That would cause a massive panic, but not compared to the chaos and commotion that would occur when the Governor, or any politician for that matter, is on stage, especially smack dab in the middle of a speech. He knew he had to wait, because it had to look like the Governor was the main target. The first priority in any assassination attempt was to protect the politician at all costs, meaning whoever is conducting security is more concerned with that and far less likely to open fire out into the crowd, even after successfully spotting the sniper.

A loud and distinctively voice boomed all over the loudspeakers declaring that the Governor would take the stage. Zen knew what was being said word for word, but couldn't actually hear anything. Maybe because part of him would rather be anywhere else, even if it meant going back to the Peterson Prison's Psychiatric Unit. Only seconds later the Governor stood at the podium and began to bond with the crowd. Of course that was far from the truth, it's just that Zen, like moments before, still couldn't audibly process anything, almost as if he was in the middle of a really bad dream. The only thing he could hope for now was the loud sound of gunfire coming from a trigger pulled by his own finger would wake him up to the demise of 978.

In a matter of seconds, Zen got the gun ready, without any input from Johnson, or Rod and Sid.

He took aim, directly at 978's chest.

Here goes nothing, he thought to himself.

••• 23

"LADIES AND GENTLEMAN, THE MAN YOU'VE ALL BEEN WAITING FOR: GOVERNOR DINELLI!"

For a split second that announcement may have lightened the mood for those thousands of people in attendance, along with the millions of people watching television, a computer screen, or even the good old talk radio. It sounded like the public at large should have expected to see a game show host take the stage. Regardless, this particular scenario was a lot easier for Ryan, who didn't like being used as target practice for the Underground Dwellers who had their own unique version of Wheel of Fortune, the kind that was supposed to cost him his life.

It didn't take very long for the Governor to come out and walk over to the podium. Ryan, 978 and Dr. Carlton, were anticipating the precise moment the speech would begin. While waiting, 978 kept his eyes focused on the Zen Lunatic Gang. He didn't want any innocent people caught in the crossfire. It didn't matter to him if it was the Governor's daughter or some loudmouthed protester. He thought it was bit odd that no one else took notice of those guys on their motorbikes. But in most parts of the city, whether it was the Boston Common or Harvard Square, were much more run down than ever before. It wasn't so long ago when he and Will cruised around together and their only complaint would be the condition of the roads. How young they were, not giving any thought to the fact that in the state of Massachusetts poorly constructed roadways had been a historical tradition decades in the making.

978 really needed to read between the lines more. With so many urban areas becoming more and more run down, which supposedly contributed to Alewife's subway line being shut down. Of course little did anyone know about what just happened to him and his two constituents down in those tunnels earlier that evening, which made him think about the hype surrounding the new Prison Reform bill. What made the public so crazy about it? How many of these people who voted for this Governor had ties to anyone working in the prison system, much less had any friends or family doing time behind walls? He was willing to bet not very many. The demeanor and charm the Governor had could make any issue discussed seem important, which was probably why Fletcher gravitated toward this politician, and Zen's connection from earlier days created the best advantage possible. But 978 knew that Boston's citizens should be far more concerned with the immediate dangers surrounding them in the streets than what's happening in places they never venture into, and never will. He should know being a guard who stumbled onto the master plan, then got forced into playing the lead part in it whether he liked it or not!

"Thank you everyone," said the Governor. "First off I want to say how much I appreciate all of you coming out tonight. It is very well known what my intentions are regarding improvements in law enforcement. I will eventually cover all aspects involved. But the main topic tonight is prison reform, with all the credit going to Dr. Aaron Fletcher. Although he is unable to be here this evening....."

978 stayed focused on the Zen Lunatic gang. Surprisingly, Zen took a gun out of his jacket. It didn't make sense. There was still a significant period of time before the primary target

would be seen. Was there a change of plans? It didn't matter. The only thing to do was stop him dead in his tracks. 978 took a gun out then grabbed Ryan's shoulder.

"Look!" said 978.

"What's happening?" asked Ryan, looking directly at the Zen Lunatic. "It's too soon!"

Those were the last words being said before the Zen Lunatic opened fire. The target was the 978 replica, who took a bullet in the lower left side of the chest, only causing it to stumble back a few steps. At the same time, 609 would leap sideways and push the Governor down to the floor. Staying behind the podium would also provide a significant amount of protection because unbeknownst to the public it was constructed to be bulletproof, and only allowed to be used for the purpose of protecting politicians. Too bad it didn't apply to anyone else in any other profession. Still, if tonight's top priority was protection the job was definitely being done.

The replica of 978 regained any balance lost from being shot by taking several steps toward the front of the stage, right next to the podium the Governor was now hiding behind. As the replica stared out into the crowd, it was unfazed by all the chaos and screaming that was occurring. The look on the face could only be described as calculated and emotionless. Some civilians in the crowd may have seen anger in the eyes, but their perspective might change if they found out it was a replica. Two more shots were fired by the Zen Lunatic, this time hitting 978's replica in the middle part of the chest area. After a quick scan on the audience Zen was spotted. It took a gun out at shot him several times.

Johnson, Rod, and Sid saw their leader fall off his bike onto the ground. How the motorcycle didn't tip over with him was beyond anyone present. He was barely alive, and these guys were ready to finish what they started. Without consulting one another, they each took out their own weapons and aimed at the 978 replica. Several shots were fired, none of which hit their target. Unbeknownst to them, some replicas were programmed to anticipate bullets getting fired at them after being hit only a couple of times, specifically in this case three. It could quickly determine where the shooter was located and avoid getting shot continuously, that way it wouldn't subject itself to the possibility of receiving further damage.

With the Governor safe hiding behind the podium, 609 stood up and marched out to the front of the stage not too far away from her fellow replica. After taking out a gun and firing several shots at the Zen Lunatic gang, a bullet grazed Sid on the left shoulder before falling to the ground. Rod threw a small object onstage in front of 609's feet. One would assume at first glance it was a modern day grenade, now known as a mini-bomb. Confirmation came quickly when an explosion occurred and 609 went up in flames, who took more steps forward, perhaps unaware of how humans react after being burned. Someone quickly ran out with a fire extinguisher and sprayed the replica down before it fell of the stage and hit the ground below face first. A large portion of the skin burned, and the moment it turned over and looked up the damage done was more than obvious. The eyes were destroyed, and the glowing robotic visual sensors could easily be seen.

When the Governor crawled out from behind the podium he stayed on his hands and knees, hoping he wouldn't get shot. He was very concerned about what just happened to 609. When he crawled over to the edge of the stage and looked down he saw something beyond his comprehension. Just looking in its eyes and seeing the sockets glowing was frightening enough. The rest of the bodily injuries went beyond any normal description. He didn't see flesh and bones. Instead there was some kind of metal machinery operating beneath the open wounds. The liquid that began oozing out of the body was too thick to be blood. The scariest part was watching this thing attempt to get up and start moving again.

At this point he decided he had seen enough and wanted to get out of there. Someone had a lot of explaining to do.

With all the chaos occurring at the stage, 978, Dr. Carlton, and Ryan had their own battle to attend to. With guns drawn, the three of them moved in closer to the Zen Lunatic gang. By the time they got there, Rod and Sid had started the engines on the motorbikes and took off. Johnson was kneeling down talking to the dying Zen Lunatic.

"I will take over as the leader in your name!" he declared.

"I have a better idea," said Zen.

"How?" asked Johnson.

"Be yourself. Become the Enforcer."

Johnson now knew his calling, and his identity, then got on his motorbike and started the engine.

"Wait!" shouted 978.

It was too late. Johnson quickly rode off, most likely to catch up with Rod and Sid. 978 could open fire with an excellent chance of hitting Johnson in the back. But he knew not to risk the possibility of shooting innocent civilians. He kneeled down to talk to the Zen Lunatic, who was barely alive with large open chest wounds.

"I knew," said Zen. "Somehow I knew."

"Knew what?" asked 978.

"I knew....it couldn't be you.....who shot me...who killed Hoyt ....it had to be some kind of monster....an abomination."

Those were the last words the Zen Lunatic, born as Jack Burton, would ever speak. 978 checked for a pulse. The guy was dead. He turned around to face his replica, which stood still staring at him. He slowly got up and looked at this abomination straight in the eye.

"Who are you?" he asked.

The replica gave 978 an angry, piercing look, and still displayed every possible similarity the two of them shared. It quickly turned around and took off like a thief in the night, which made a lot of sense since it stole his identity.

"Let's get out of here," said Dr. Carlton.

978 and Ryan agreed, and neither of them had to utter a single word to indicate that. The three of them would have to make their way through the panicked crowd in order to get back to the Park Street Station, which wasn't difficult since most people willingly began evacuating the area. Every single type of emergency vehicle imaginable: police cars, ambulances, fire trucks, even a helicopter hovering over the stage shining a huge spotlight on the bloodshed that occurred only minutes ago would play major roles in the ease of their escape.

This suited them fine.

24 •••

Despite all the justifiable chaos and panic surrounding them, 978, Dr. Carlton, and Ryan managed to maneuver through the crowd without much of a struggle. It should have been a bit more surprising, especially considering it was the Boston Common with countless thousands of people in an uproar over what looked like an attempted assassination. Everything happened very quickly, but time is irrelevant when dangerous situations like these occur, and when a politician is the target anarchy ensues both with the public and the press.

The three of them soon arrived at the entrance of the Park Street Station. They ran downstairs and were able to determine that any problem with crowd control in this particular area would be minor. In fact, it wasn't even half as crowded compared to when they first arrived. At this point a lot of people feared for their lives and were not going to stand around and wait for a train to come, making it a lot easier to take advantage of the situation. Ryan was convinced they didn't need to worry about keeping up appearances. He made his way over to the unused tracks with 978 and Dr. Carlton behind him and went back through the maintenance door. Now wasn't the time to stop for anything or anybody. The most important issue was survival.

Within minutes, the three of them made it back to the subway car. All the stuff they left stored in it hadn't been touched, which was a good sign. As soon as they got inside, 978 and Dr. Carlton took off their backpacks and sat down on passenger seats close to the front of the vehicle. Ryan entered the operator's compartment. He immediately started the engine, but wasn't going to let it idle, even for a couple of minutes.

The moment the train began to move, they all breathed a sigh of relief. It would only be a short amount of time before arriving back at the Old Alewife building. Endless hiking down the tracks and run-ins with the mutant-like Underground Dwellers would not be on the agenda. Ryan was pretty sure all the tracks were intact even though he hadn't made a conscious effort to inspect them on the way in. Being able to use that cart starting at Porter Square without any problems was proof enough for him. He didn't want to think of any more reasons to worry, but quickly realized he needed to. The train continued to pick up speed, and nothing he tried changed that. The further they moved, the faster it went. With every station they passed it seemed to go up a notch.

While crossing the Charles River the train began shaking to the point where it felt like it could easily tip off the tracks and fall into the water below. Once inside the tunnel, lights kept flickering on and off. Dr. Carlton thought she would have a heart attack when they passed through the Porter Square Station again. She caught a glimpse of a figure on the platform that looked a lot like Stickboy. 978 decided to go up to the engine compartment to find out what was going on. He didn't have to say a word before receiving direct orders from Ryan.

"Both of you stay back there and grab on to something!" Ryan shouted.

Ryan could barely see a moving figure on the tracks in front of him. It had to be one of the Underground Dwellers. There was no way he could stop, not that he wanted to for one of those mutant creatures. But the closer he got he shut his eyes to avoid seeing any more carnage. If there was a noise from the impact, he barely heard it and was unable to determine if that's what it was. He would wait a few more seconds before opening his eyes again to make sure he wouldn't see anything.

While passing through Davis Square, Ryan tried as hard as he could to pull the emergency brake. He wished he had checked it beforehand, especially since he was convinced that this subway car was older than him. All he could now was used the strength of his entire body to pull the lever. It was about four feet high, which gave him the idea to kneel down and wrap both arms and his right leg around it. He started to lean back hoping it would work. The brake slightly moved, then instantly went back all the way. Next was a screeching noise louder than anything the three of them had ever heard. The vehicle came to a grinding halt, causing Ryan to be thrown forward and hitting the window. He fell back down to the floor and was completely disoriented. When he got up he realized he wasn't injured, despite the fact that the glass was shattered from top to bottom. He went back to the passenger area to find 978 and Dr. Carlton slowly getting up off the floor.

"Last stop," said Ryan, confirming their arrival at Old Alewife.

"No kidding," said Dr. Carlton.

"I guess we should gather up everything and go."

"Good idea," added 978. "It won't be long before your friend comes around to investigate."

"That's a good point, and we probably shouldn't try to

sneak out the way we came in for that reason alone."

The three of them concentrated on the task at hand and quickly got ready to go. Right when they were about to look for another way out Ryan inadvertently dropped a mini-bomb on the floor. It happened so fast he wasn't sure how he could make a mistake like that. The vibe changed between all of them right then and there.

"You!" shouted 978. "Out of all of us you were stupid enough to let that happen?! Those things can explode on impact! You know that better than any of us!"

"At least it didn't!" snapped Ryan.

"Stop!" demanded Dr. Carlton, the most cautious of all of them. "At least we got out of this in one piece. Let's not even think about whether or not were lucky that thing didn't go off. Why don't we take another minute to calm down and get out of this place?"

978 and Ryan didn't say another word. They just barely nodded to her. But before anything else could be said or done a familiar sound occurred. That being a loud and screeching one, and not the same sound the subway train made went it came to a grinding halt. This one was supernatural, and when they turned their heads and looked up their eyes set on something they tried to forget about. It was a monster-sized bat creature, and who knew if it was the same one they had encountered before?

The giant flying abomination flew down from the ceiling it had been perched on and hiding for God knows how long. The closer it got made 978 quickly lean over to grab the mini-bomb. The thing opened its mouth and let out another screeching sound.

"Open wide you bastard!" yelled 978, throwing the mini-bomb at the face of the creature, who caught it and bit down instantly.

The explosion that immediately occurred was unlike anything 978, Dr. Carlton, or Ryan had ever seen before. The head blowing to bits was unbelievable, and what was left of the creature would fall to the floor right in front of them. Blood and portions of this thing's head and brain splattered all over the place, especially on the three of them. If they weren't so shocked by all of this they probably would have gotten sick and thrown up on each other.

It was that disgusting.

It didn't matter, though. Ryan was thrilled.

"You should pitch for the Sox!" he said.

"I'm all for it!" said 978. "For one thing, they get paid more than all of us combined, and they only have to throw balls back and forth. When we get back we'll have to hit the showers, a lot more than any of them need to all season!"

The three of them made a little more small talk between them. The only interesting thing said was Dr. Carlton would gather a sample of the creature's exploding head to bring to a lab and look under a microscope or some such thing. With 978 and Ryan that went through one ear and out the other. All that was left to do now was get back to the truck and make it home safely, at least back to Ryan's home. 978 and Dr. Carlton had nowhere else to go.

25 •••

"TERROR SWEEPED THE BOSTON COMMON TONIGHT, OPEN GUNFIRE AND BOMB EXPLOSIONS TOOK PLACE DURING THE GOVERNOR'S SPEECH. THE AUTHORITIES BELIEVE IT WAS AN ATTEMPTED ASSASSINATION ON THE HIGHLY RESPECTED POLITICIAN'S LIFE DESPITE THE FACT THAT ALL THE GUNSHOTS WERE DIRECTLY FIRED AT THE GUARDS ON STAGE. WE HAVE RECEIVED WORD THAT ONE GUARD HAS BURNED TO DEATH. THE OTHER GUARD WAS SHOT AT LEAST THREE TIMES AT CLOSE RANGE.

AUTHORITIES HAVE NO EXPLANATION OF HIS CURRENT WHEREABOUTS BUT BELIEVE THEY WILL LOCATE HIM SOON. THE NAMES OF THE GUARDS ARE BEING WITHHELD PENDING NOTIFICATION OF THE FAMILIES. THIS IS JACOB ROBINSON, LIVE, ON THE 11 'O CLOCK NEWS."

Dr. Carlton picked up the remote and turned off the television. That was all she needed to here. It may have been reported that 978 was missing, but at least he was safe for now. Still, he would need to lay low for a few days. It was a good idea for all three of them to maintain a low profile. She heard the bathroom door open. 978 had indulged in a twenty minute hot shower, as Dr. Carlton had before him. Luckily, they were able to wash off the smell of the remains of the head of that bat-creature off of their bodies, but their clothes were another matter altogether. He made his way over to the couch and sat down next to her.

"Did you catch the news?" asked 978.

"Yeah," she answered. "They say you're missing in action, but not suspected of any criminal activity. The best part is that your name hasn't been released to the public yet. When I contacted 609 earlier I said I killed you. And since that replica is pretty much out of commission, there will only be a brief search for yours."

"Great. I'm presumed dead but my replica continues to live on."

"I've already talked to Ryan. We'll have you fly down to Rio and stay there for a while. You'll have plenty of time to investigate the LEO1 factory and learn as much as possible about the new line of replicas being built."

"Forget it! The minute I walk into Logan Airport everyone will recognize me instantly. By tomorrow morning my face, most likely my driver's license picture which I hate, will be plastered on every single news channel and every major paper in the country. We also can't forget those computerized identification cards scanned at all the airports. There's no way around it."

"You're wrong. First of all, you'll fly out of Manchester Airport in New Hampshire. Second, you'll be traveling as Ryan. You'll be able to slip through without being detected."

"Travel as Ryan?"

"Sure, we'll just dye your hair and beard, and it's easy to get a fake pair of glasses. You can use Ryan's Air Force identification cards, which are also good for discounts because of his veteran status. He very rarely takes flights out of Manchester, so no one knows him there. You won't look suspicious."

"I see. I can't believe how quickly you can plan things like this on such short notice."

Ryan felt tempted to turn the television back on and watch old reruns, but he really needed to get some shut eye. Dr. Carlton said she was going upstairs to sleep in a spare bedroom that Ryan had prepared for her. She gave him a hug before getting up, leaving him to stretch out on the couch. He turned off the lights by pushing a button on the televisions remote control. Within minutes, he was out like a light as well.

26 •••

Four days had passed. It was early in the afternoon. The weather was cool and the sky was gray, but not a drop of rain was in sight, definitely not a bad day to drive up to Manchester Airport. 978 and Dr. Carlton were maybe ten minutes from arriving, but he asked her to stop off by the side of the road for a moment. They got out of the car and he led her through a small wooded area then down a small hill to a river, not far from where a campground used to be that his father took him to when he was a small boy which like all beautiful places, got sold and had condominiums built over it.

For some reason the river had always been known as Kailyn's Creek, but he never found any records to verify that. As long as he could remember the story was that of a young couple driving to the nearest hospital expecting the birth of their first child, which they already knew was going to be a daughter. Their car broke down, perhaps in the same spot where he and Dr. Carlton had parked. On top of that they both forgot their cell phones. The water was about to break any moment so the husband brought her down the hill as quickly as he could to the river where they proceeded to have a natural childbirth, the old-fashioned way, and the name they gave their new baby girl was Kailyn. Over the course of many years of his childhood 978 went online and searched for any information he could find regarding that story, only to turn up absolutely nothing. It became a private hobby for him, whether he recovered old press articles or looked up birth records in the town halls or hospitals all over New England, occasionally he would do a search nationwide if a lead was strong enough, but that was rare.

978 hadn't said a word to Dr. Carlton about this, even though she was standing beside him. Now wasn't the best time, they had to get moving. They quickly glanced at one another then turned around and made their way back up the hill through the wooded area again. Neither of them had rushed back to the car, but it only took them a minute at the most. Dr. Carlton started the engine and pulled back out on the road. Last in thought, it felt like they arrived at Manchester Airport almost instantly. She pulled over to park for a minute, just a short distance from the main entrance. 978 had a suitcase and backpack which he retrieved from the backseat.

"Do you need anything else before I go?" asked Dr. Carlton.

"I think I'm all set," answered 978. "Just find out if my family is safe and let me know as soon as possible."

"I'll make sure they're alright. I'll see you soon, Mark. I'm sure of that."

They held each other for a moment before 978, or Mark from this point on, got out of the car. He shut the door and nodded to Dr. Carlton as she drove off. He turned around and headed towards the main entrance. When he arrived at the revolving doors he noticed his reflection in the glass. Dr. Carlton had done an excellent job changing his appearance. Stuff called skin substitute helped with the facial features a lot, making him look more like Ryan. But the most amazing part was that she didn't need to apply very much of it. He looked closely at Ryan's main Air Force identification card and knew he had nothing to worry about. The funniest part was when he realized that Ryan's middle name was Mark. He may not need to tell everyone in Rio to call him Ryan after all. He certainly wasn't going to go by 978 anymore. His life as a guard was over.

He was no longer a number.

He had a name.

It would take some getting used to.

"Waiting for inspiration I have surrounded myself with the inspired and am learning to start being rather than waiting."

- Sarah Bergeron

www.ingramcontent.com/pod-product-compliance
Lightning Source LLC
Chambersburg PA
CBHW020754250626
47155CB00003B/1067